Big Wild Summer

STEPHANIE J. SCOTT

Cover and image design: Melody Jeffries Design

Edits by MK Books Editing

ISBN ebook 978-1-954952-04-1

ISBN print 978-1-954952-05-8

Contents

Author's Note

♥

Each book in the Love on Summer Break series can be read on its own. Throughout the books, you'll find common characters and settings that take place during different summers.

Keep up with book release news and discounts and join my author newsletter! www.stephaniejscott.com

Chapter One

♥

I never imagined the first day at my dream summer job would involve waiting alone in a supply shack to meet the boy I'd crushed on since seventh grade.

I was truly living the dream.

Hired at the coolest summer job in the vicinity of Ginsburg, Michigan—Midwest Wild Adventure theme park, featuring adventure-themed rides and a pretty dope water park.

Best of all, what Midwest Wild Adventure had was KJ Keene.

My longest-running crush. My now within-reach crush, a recently graduated senior and lifeguard at the water park in Wild Adventure (what everyone called the park, or if you were on staff, just Wild. I was *so* excited to call it Wild).

Not only would I appease my parents by taking on responsibility with a summer job, I could finally make something happen with KJ before he left for college.

Day one on the job and already I had an opportunity for alone time with KJ. All I had to do was wait here in this supply shack and he'd meet me. My friend, Chelsea, from West Ginsburg High arranged everything. She'd even gotten me the job.

It sure was hot in this shed. I lifted my hair and fanned my neck with a stray piece of cardboard. Moments ago, I'd shaken my hair out from a ponytail. Maybe I should put it back up. I wanted to look summer casual for KJ when he arrived.

I'd been watching KJ for years. He was a classic hottie. Tall, dark hair, that olive skin which people mistook him for half a dozen ethnicities—Mexican, Puerto Rican, Spanish. He was biracial Honduran and white and since junior year had a hint of scruff along his jawline. Cute, full lips and a real knee-buckler as far as grins went. His hair naturally curled at the ends in the humidity, something I'd noticed as late spring crawled into the heat of summer.

KJ was the kind of guy who showed up to charity events and looked cool doing it. He would spend the summer shirtless at the wave pool saving children.

I fanned myself some more. Kind of hard to look cute sweating in a shed beside metal racks loaded with tools and boxes. Two folding chairs angled toward each other with an ancient portable stereo on the floor between them. I could sit but nerves kept me standing. A single bulb with a chain pull provided light.

I checked my watch. Any minute now he'd be here. Maybe he had trouble escaping the wave pool. This was my first real shift, but Chelsea promised to cover for me at the Little Adventurer Kid's Zone. She'd told me it was key to get time with KJ before the summer started rolling.

The door to the supply shack creaked open. By instinct, I leaped behind cover of a shelving rack positioned in the middle of the space. I smoothed my hair against my shoulders and my fresh-from-the-box staff T-shirt. I took a breath and stepped out.

A hulking figure stood in the doorway. I squinted as my eyes adjusted from the bright sunlight streaming in.

The person who entered had brown hair that limped against wide shoulders. Arms like cannons nearly burst through the sleeves of a Midwest Wild Adventure Crew T-shirt. A huge dude. Besides the fact he probably wasn't much older than me, he looked like the kind of guy who worked the door at a night club or appeared as back-up to the bad guys in a movie.

He scowled my direction. Definitely not the easy-going KJ smile.

"Oh hey," I said, edging the nervousness from my voice. "I'm, um, waiting for someone."

The guy sighed. "He's not coming."

My heart dropped to my stomach. "What? Where's KJ?"

The guy shrugged. If you could even call it that. It was more of a twitch in his massive shoulder while the rest of his body remained solid and unmoving like a commercial-grade refrigerator.

"I just wanted to talk to him," I added, the nervousness spilling out anyway. "I know him. We go to school together."

He seemed to be waiting for me to finish talking. "They're all here. Grab one of those boxes. It'll look like you came in here for a better reason."

Who was they and here for what?

The big guy opened the door wider and murmuring voices carried past him. Who was here?

I took a box, the nearest thing to me, and followed him out.

Everything next happened in painful slow motion.

Menacing laughter circled the air. Someone pointed their phone at me and snapped a picture. Applause rippled through the crowd.

"One wild virgin down!" a voice declared.

My jaw dropped. *Wild virgin?*

Okay, first there was nothing wrong with being a virgin. I was and was proud to say it. I had a whole speech about women's autonomy and patriarchal standards of womanhood and I wasn't afraid to use it. My parents were frequently afraid because I was blessed-slash-cursed with what they termed a naturally sassy mouth. It bought me trouble, and often.

I looked at the huge guy who'd walked out ahead of me. What exactly did they think had happened in this supply shed?

"Real funny," the guy deadpanned. "You really *got* us."

"What's that girl's name?" someone asked above the laughter.

"I think her name is Elena something," came a suggestion full of pre-packaged innocence.

That came from Chelsea, who absolutely knew my name. She even knew my last name, which coincidentally, matched the theme park. De Wilde. It was spelled with an E on the end due to my uber-Dutch heritage, but it sounded the same when spoken.

I gaped at the faces before me, all in Wild Adventure staff shirts. "What is this?" I asked Chelsea.

Chelsea grinned. "You win."

To my horror part two, someone stage left set a pink plastic crown on my head. I yanked at it, but the crown's tiny plastic comb teeth snagged against my hair. The crown was eating my head.

Finally, I tugged the crown free, bringing with it a snarly sample of my dark red hair. The crown featured a middle gemstone with a "V" marked in Sharpie.

Forget my jaw hanging open, my face dropped to the ground. I shot my gaze to the big guy. He just stood there, all large and definitely not in charge. "But we didn't *do* anything."

"Doesn't matter." Chelsea sashayed toward me like a fictional siren. A siren who lured other girls to be pranked, apparently. "You believed KJ would meet you there."

Okay, sure, I wanted some solo time with KJ, but it wasn't like I thought we'd *do* anything. I'd just wanted to finally tell him how I felt since Chelsea...*dangit.*

Chelsea had been feeding me lines how KJ would be perfect for me. For *weeks.*

I was so stupid. So stupidly trusting.

I should have known day one was too soon for KJ to finally stop seeing through me like a freshly Windexed pane of glass.

I'd been set up.

Spotting KJ in the crowd, my pale pre-summer cheeks flamed redder than the fire engine ride in the Little Adventurer Zone. There was no escape. Just eyes and barking, howling laughter.

KJ held a hand over his mouth. He stepped forward, leaning in like he intended to share a secret. "Every year, girls try to hook up with their crush. We see who's gullible enough to go to the Love Hut and wait for their Romeo. I guess that's you."

Oh no. Oh no way no.

"That's not—" I fumbled for words. "Why did you—"

Lie to me. I couldn't complete my thoughts out loud.

Chelsea smirked. "Now you know how it feels."

I had no clue what she was talking about. We were *friends*.

It was like I was being crushed, slowly. The weight of my own humiliation pressed down.

"What's going on?" a voice boomed across the fenced yard. That would be my new boss, Terry.

Terry stood with hands at his hips like a gym teacher fired up for a round of burpees. Not that he'd be doing burpees himself. Terry had a wiry frame and translucent white skin streaked with SPF infinity-strength. "You kids pranking the new blood again?" He shook his head with the wisdom of a seasoned twenty-three-year-old night shift park manager. He held out his hand. "Give me the crown."

I walked two shameful steps toward him. It was stupid to feel any shame when 1.) I hadn't done anything to feel ashamed of, and 2.) I'd been duped by staff who knew better.

I handed Terry the stupid plastic crown.

I cut a glare at Chelsea. Her honey-blonde topknot bobbed up and down as she made a production out of stifling a laugh.

Chatter floated through the group until Terry blew a whistle. He really did channel gym teacher vibes. "Moving on. Where is Elena De Wilde?"

I slowly raised my hand.

He shook his head slowly. "Really turning out an all-star performance your first day, huh? You were supposed to be shadowing your team lead in Lil' Paul Bunyan Square. Can you tell me why you weren't in Lil' Paul Bunyan Square and instead in the Love Hut?"

Well, when he said it that way it sounded really bad. "Do Chelsea and KJ have to answer next? They were involved with this whole Love Hut set-up."

"Oh no she didn't," someone said and snickered.

Terry flipped his sunglasses up onto his sandy-haired buzz cut. "You think this is a joke? You abandoned your post."

An *oooh* chorused through the crowd.

"Can anyone here repeat for Elena what the number one rule is working at Wild Adventure?" Terry asked.

"Never abandon your post," the staff answered at the same time.

"Unless?" Terry asked again.

"Unless you have coverage," the group finished.

Terry looked at me. "You, Elena. Did not secure coverage. If this had been a scenario where you hadn't been shadowing another staff, you'd have left a children's area void of supervision. Do you know what happens when children are left unsupervised?"

"But they weren't—"

Terry cut me off. "Can someone tell me what happens when children are left unsupervised?"

"Lawsuits," the group stated as one.

"Exactly. Lawsuits. Allegations. Bad press." Terry folded his arms. "We have probationary hiring for a reason. We don't want another Cayden Moore situation."

The group chatter dwindled to silence.

I looked around at frozen, somber faces. I thought quickly. Who was Cayden Moore?

Terry paced in front of me. "In case you don't recall, Cayden Moore was a child injured here last summer. A huge media blitz followed, declaring how our park was unsafe. *Not a place for families.* Thankfully, Cayden turned out okay—and the family was incredibly generous with their forgiveness. But we can't afford another hit to our reputation."

The heat of attention shifted from me to the guy next to me. The big guy.

I had so many questions.

The guy stared straight ahead, his eyes deadlocked on absolutely nothing. This guy's eyes pooled with black. Like a very dark lagoon.

A chill ran down my arms and it was still eighty degrees out here.

I was now fighting total social humiliation and a public reprimand from my new boss. I'd disappointed authority once or twice and survived—mouthy girls didn't get away scot-free every time. I knew what I had to do.

Grovel. I had to make this right.

"I'm so sorry," I said to Terry. "It won't happen again."

"You're right it won't happen again." He flipped a paper over on his clipboard.

Great. One day down and I was about to get the chop. My dream job lasted one whole day.

"I'm reassigning you," Terry stated. "You're moving to the old park. You'll be on go-karts with Jonah."

The crowd shifted, this time to look back at me. Their faces, a mixture of shock and pity. One sneer belonging to Chelsea. What was her *deal*? KJ at least had the decency to look a little guilty.

"Who's Jonah?" I asked Terry.

He pointed to the scary dude with the dark eyes. Who now stared daggers at me.

"How did your first day go?" Mom asked the next morning in the kitchen.

I sat slumped at the island extending from the kitchen into the breakfast nook. I would have slept in, but I was due back at Wild Adventure in an hour. First shift closing followed by an early shift today. Brutal.

I should quit while I was not ahead. What was the point of going back? Chelsea clearly had a past beef with me. KJ thought my crush on him was one big fat joke. And my boss called me out for breaking the most important rule before I'd technically even started.

The more I thought about it, the better idea it sounded to ditch day two. I'd left the park last night eager to stay ahead of the *wild virgin* chants following me to my car. All through the drive home and as I attempted to shower away my humiliation, I obsessed about what happened. How had I wronged Chelsea?

I couldn't go back.

Mom closed the fridge after pulling out a pre-made smoothie. She had on yoga clothes and her hair pulled back. Probably a flex-time morning before heading into her office later as a mortgage loan something-or-other. "Was that an answer? I thought I heard a grumble."

I groaned into my cereal. "I'm not sure it's going to work out."

Mom set down her smoothie. "Elena."

"Mom, you don't understand. The job...it's not what I thought."

"Working at a theme park isn't the same as going there with your friends. It's work. It's a job. We talked about this."

"I know, but I've already been reassigned. They called it the old park." I wasn't familiar with all the insider park terminology. "I'm supposed to work by the go-karts."

"I thought you were working at the kid's park. That's what you told us you were hired for."

"I know, but—"

"She probably blew it already." My younger brother, Eli, breezed by, making sure to shove the stool I was sitting on as he passed. Milk sloshed out of the bowl, across the counter, and into my lap.

"I did not *blow* it." I'd nearly blown it. Big difference. "There was a misunderstanding. Those jerks—"

"Please watch your mouth, Elena." Mom pressed her fingers against her forehead and moved them in small circles. "Employers aren't as forgiving as your family."

Eli snorted. "Told ya."

"It wasn't my fault...entirely." I didn't know where to begin.

"Go-karts sound dangerous," Mom said. "What will you be doing?"

"I have no idea. Maybe it's better if pick up some babysitting jobs. Or how about the golf range by the highway. Maybe they're hiring?"

Mom had her eyes closed now and was breathing in through her nose and out through her mouth. Finally, she opened her eyes. "You're going back. Apologize for whatever you did and make it right. Then ask for your position back with the children's zone. I don't want you working with those fast cars."

Calling a go-kart a car was a stretch, but whatever. "I *did* apologize," I said. "I don't have a choice where I work. Terry was pretty final with his decision."

I'd caught him after the closing meeting to ask if the reassignment was a solid switch, slipping in another apology for ditching my post to not make out with my lifelong crush.

He'd said, "I'm final with my decision."

Sounded final.

"I'll go back and tell them you and John won't let me work there," I said.

John was my stepdad who followed my mom's lead when it came to anything parenting related. His own two children were adults—his son in graduate school at Michigan State and his daughter a teacher in Ohio. Both of them hadn't exactly warmed easily to me and my brother. We were the "other woman's family," which was hardly fair because John was divorced from their mom before he dated our mom. And believe me, I knew the timeline. My own dad was not divorced before he'd chosen another family to be with. I lived with that knowledge every day.

Mom's deep breathing was now accompanied by stretching where she circled her arms out and above her head, then down to what she called her heart center.

She stopped the yoga moves and looked at me. "I want you to go to work and ask to do the job you were hired for. Be responsible, Elena. John and I won't be able to dig you out of trouble forever."

I sighed. "Fine. Just...don't tell him about this. I'll figure it out."

"Elena," Mom cautioned. "I won't keep secrets from my husband. We're a family now."

How could I forget? She kept reminding me. It wasn't that I didn't like John. I liked him. A lot. My mom was crazy about him and she'd been the happiest ever since they'd started dating a couple years ago. Our lives were easier now that we didn't worry about money every single second like when she was raising me and Eli on her own.

Anything that threatened our current situation I needed to stay on top of. Right now, that was me. If I couldn't hold down a job, if I was a constant mess, that put strain on Mom and John. Dad had no problem leaving us, so I couldn't chance maybe John might come to the same decision.

I finished my cereal and grabbed a bottle of SPF sunblock and a West Ginsburg High cap on my way out the door.

I tried hard not to be some kind of problem child. So, I ran my mouth occasionally. I stayed out of bigger trouble. At least I hadn't cost her and John serious money or court fees. My friend, Holli, had went through a whole thing last summer covering for her sister's drunk driving accident. Holli was one of the good kids trying to do right and botching it. Something I could totally sympathize with.

I took my keys from the tray by the door and went through the open garage to my car parked in the driveway.

Maybe I should have stuck with the cross-country team instead of quitting to work a summer job. Then I'd be with Holli and Christina and my other friends on the team. But I'd gotten bored with running. I was okay at it, but it wasn't my passion or anything, and the training was something else. Intense conditioning, long runs, and then meets in the fall.

I'd started daydreaming of quitting last season. I wanted to do something fun with my summer. Make new friends. Work somewhere cool. Wild Adventure was it.

Now, as I headed out to the highway for the quickest route to my new job, I dreaded my choice.

Chapter Two

♥

Mission one: get my kids' zone position back. (Beg if necessary.)

Mission two: Get close to KJ.

Back at Midwest Wild Adventure, my hand paused on the door handle of my car. How could I get close to KJ after what happened at the *Love Hut?* He'd *laughed* at me. Everyone had laughed. Every one of my new coworkers on shift yesterday.

Horror struck all over again.

Did I even want this job back? Maybe I should sabotage it. Then they'd *have* to fire me.

If only it were that easy. Mom made it clear as crystal I needed to get back to work.

With every ounce of courage I could muster, I pushed open my door and headed inside the park.

The door to the employee office shut hard behind me and rattled a framed aerial photo of the park hung inside the entry. Whoops.

"Who's slamming my door?" The voice coming from farther back in the office did not belong to Terry. He wouldn't be here until at least four from what I remembered. This voice was older. Deeper. More of an East Coast sound to it, like how people on TV spoke when they were from New York.

From an office with a gold-plated sign on the door reading *The Big Cheese,* a deeply tanned white man appeared. He had a long face and wrinkles that looked softened through the wash. His hair thinned at the top but he wore it swooped and to the side like a boy band singer. "Was that you slamming my door?"

It was main entrance, but whatever. "Uh, yes. Sorry about the door."

I approached with my hand out for a formal handshake. John, my stepdad, did the handshake thing when his business colleagues came to the house to drop off documents. Sometimes they talked about golf. All super boring, but I still paid attention, watching for useful information. "I'm Elena De Wilde. I work here."

"De Wilde, eh?" His face perked. "Well, isn't that wild. De Wilde in de-wild." He chuckled. Slow at first, then louder, longer.

This was about to get old fast. But seeing he came out of an office reading *The Big Cheese*, I laughed like he'd said the funniest thing I'd heard all week. "That's hilarious. You're the first to point that out. I didn't even notice it myself."

He pat his gut, which was fairly trim for an older guy. "I'm a bit of a wordsmith, myself." He finally noticed my hand thrust toward him and shook it. "I'm Uncle Frankie. *The* Uncle Frankie."

I blinked and smiled. No idea. "Wow, so great to meet you."

"Likewise." He looked past me to the vacant front desk. Beyond that, a hall led to where our personal lockers, staff bathrooms, a break room, and a kitchenette existed. I'd gotten the tour yesterday. "You need something, Miss De Wilde? I may own the place, but usually Jennifer up front takes care of the day-to-day."

The owner, the cheese. "Yes, actually, I do need something. Yesterday there was a misunderstanding. I was reassigned from the kids' zone to go-karts and—"

Uncle Frankie winced. "Ooh, ouch. You must have screwed up, kid. Go-karts?"

What was with the go-kart hate? "Er, yeah. I mean, clearly the misunderstanding was a...misunderstanding. If you get me."

He nodded, seeming to think on this. "As long as you didn't abandon your post, it should be workable. You didn't abandon your post, did you?"

I cycled through responses. "Well, see, I had someone covering—"

"During a planned shift break?"

Not exactly.

He shook his head. "Ah, see. That's the number one rule. You can't ditch a post. Ever. See a cute boy and go running off? Nope. A pretty girl like you, you'll catch some eyes. Never leave your post without—"

"Finding coverage," I finished. I hated how he had me pegged already. I *had* run off to see a cute boy. Embarrassing. "Technically, I was still job shadowing my team lead."

He made a clicking sound with his teeth. "Hoo boy, a first day ditch? No wonder you got reassigned. That's a sin around here. Of the cardinal variety."

I didn't know whether he meant birds or popes. "So, there's no chance to undo the reassignment?"

"We don't do take backs at Wild. Another rule. No take backs."

I nodded as if this made sense. "Well, it was great meeting you. I'm sure Jennifer will have my reassignment paperwork then?"

Uncle Frankie's eye twitched. "Paperwork? This isn't the IRS, Miss De Wilde. Hitch a ride on the tram to the old park. We've got the big fella and the James Dean lookin' guy running karts. They'll find something for you to do." He made a shooing motion with his hands.

With Jennifer a no-show at the desk, I didn't even have a last-ditch option to beg for my old (but new) job. I could leave the park altogether. Go get a smoothie with vitamin B boost, see a movie, and call it a day. Only, Mom and John would be furious. They told me I needed to stick with this.

Outside the office, I checked the park map on a bright blue kiosk looking for where to find the tram. I'd come here every summer, but usually I stuck to the water park or a quick round of the "dry" rides. I'd always been warned away from the old park. It was run-down with old rides no one cared about anymore.

A body crashed into me from the side.

"Oops." The voice sounded anything but apologetic.

Chelsea. "Hey. Why did you do that? What's wrong with you?"

She whirled around, her curls bouncing around her round-cheeked face. She had the look of someone sweet, but the bite in her tone ruined the effect. "You can dish it but you can't take it?"

"Dish what?"

She scoffed. "Stop playing dumb. You know what you did to me."

I did not know what I did to her. I was curious, though. "At school?" I guessed.

"Yes," she said with exasperation. "In Drama."

She waited.

Drama. We'd both auditioned for the school play. I'd gotten a part in the production with a small supporting role. She had not. Chelsea was, sad to say, terrible at acting. And at singing. Also, a bad dancer. Her two left feet warred with each other while everyone else moved three steps ahead.

I would never tell her she was terrible at those things. Not to her face. Had I said something without thinking and someone leaked?

I'd learned the hard way too many times about talking behind people's backs. So much so, I made a point not to do it. Instead, I said what I needed right to their face. So much easier.

Maybe I *had* told her she was terrible.

Regardless, I wasn't down for humiliating anyone in front of a crowd. I wasn't like, *vindictive*, just a little messy with my opinions sometimes.

Chelsea grunted in frustration. "Whatever. Anyway, now you know what it feels like. And now you get to join the rejects like I did. Go have fun with the grease monkeys."

She spun on her heel.

She'd had to join rejects? When and who? I really did not know Chelsea the way I'd thought.

"Can you tell me how to get there?" I called after her.

She stopped and turned back. "*What*?"

"I don't know how to get to the where the monkeys are."

Her dirty look turned filthy. "They're not *actual* monkeys. I'm talking about the gearheads who run the go karts."

"Right. Can you show me?"

She stomped back. "You want me to *show* you how to get there?"

"Look, until yesterday, we were friends. I don't know anybody here besides you and KJ and you both seem to think I'm a joke." I braced myself for the truth, because why not. "My parents won't let me quit and Uncle Frankie said no dice to getting the kid zone back."

Her voice lowered. "You talked to Uncle Frankie?"

"Yeah. Just now. In the office."

She straightened and her chin pushed back into her neck. "No one just *talks* to Uncle Frankie. He's the owner. You shouldn't have even been in that part of the building."

"Well, it's not like anyone was around to tell me otherwise. You got me this job and then first thing, you embarrass me. Now I'm stuck here. So, are you going to show me how to find the monkey karts or what?"

Her started to speak and then stopped. An internal debate seemed to be happening she didn't let me in on. "Fine."

I small sense of relief filled me. "Okay then. Thanks."

"You're welcome."

We stared at each other.

"Follow me." Chelsea headed the direction I would have picked last.

Riding in an open-air tram beside a known enemy made for a rather uncomfortable second day on the job. Still, Chelsea delivered me as promised across the park, beyond Adventure Falls Water World to the racetrack.

The automated tram shuttered to a stop with a computerized voice announcing to exit with caution.

"So maybe you can introduce me to my new coworkers," I said to Chelsea.

Only silence followed as the tram started up. I twisted to see the back of Chelsea's curls as the tram motored away. With Chelsea on it.

All right. On my own.

I shaded my eyes as the sun's increasing heat bore down. Seriously, I could leave and no one would notice.

Except my parents would notice when I didn't go to work. Or if I faked it and loitered all day at the movies or the mall or something, they'd for sure notice when I never had any money from the job I supposedly worked.

That was the deal. If I didn't have school team sports, I needed to get a job. My mom had this hang-up about it. She'd worked at sixteen, and she needed to see me suffer the same torture or she wouldn't be satisfied.

I followed the paved path under an archway noting the Go Zone. When I was younger, Mom warned this section of the park was for *older kids*. She'd made it sound scary and boring at the same time.

A growling buzz sounded. On the track, one lone kart sped past. I walked closer to the tire barrier bordering the course. Now that I had a view of the winding track, I watched the solo racer fade into the distance. After a few seconds, the driver appeared again, still far off, but visible. The kart zipped through the turns with ease.

These things looked pretty fast. And kind of cool.

I stood at a point where the track horseshoed and doubled back on the other side. The driver disappeared, my view blocked by a structure where empty karts waited off the track.

Suddenly, the kart appeared and headed straight toward me. A helmet obscured the driver's face.

The driver should be turning by now. No, really. Why wasn't it turning?

That kart was gunning for me.

I jumped back from the tires.

At the last minute, the kart turned sharply. The back end swung out and clipped the tires, jerking two tires into the space I'd just occupied.

A laugh disappeared into the fumes. I coughed from the exhaust and stumbled farther back.

I checked my watch. The park had officially opened for business, but the Go Zone was a ghost town. It might as well have been haunted.

A skinny kid in a Wild Adventure Crew T-shirt jogged toward us. He had bronzed skin and dark hair flipped up in the front using a styling product.

"Are you James Dean?" I asked, thinking of who Uncle Frankie said worked here.

A mouth full of braces smiled at me. "Heh, I wish. I'm Nando. Miles Fernando is my full name, but everyone calls me Nando. Good to meet you, Elena."

"You know who I am?"

"Uh, *yeah*. From yesterday's closing meeting."

My eyes fell shut for a moment. "Right. Sorry about that."

His energy level must have been high since he couldn't seem to stand still. "Don't be sorry. Those guys are jerks. All of the new parkies think they're better than us."

"New parkies?"

"The kids who work the other side of the park. Over here, we're the Midfits. Like Midwest misfits? Get it? Come on. Let me show you around."

He turned and walked backward, chatting as he moved ahead. "By the way, James Dean is an iconic actor who died like, forever ago."

I felt myself blush. "Yeah. I knew that." Sounded familiar, at least.

We ended up beneath a long structure in varying hues of brown and orange. A roof extended above a section of road connected to the outer track. Rows of go-karts were parked beneath it in the shade.

Nando brought us to a counter at the back wall, lined with rows of stacked helmets, with a door labeled Staff beside it. I wouldn't be surprised if there was shag carpet in there like the basement of the rental house Mom, Eli and I lived in before she met my stepdad.

In the distance, a garage with its door open revealed more karts.

"This is Go Zone HQ—a.k.a. the Pit," Nando said. "Where the *action* lives."

He said this with genuine excitement. Then again, he barely looked old enough for legal employment, so maybe being allowed out of the house without an adult was excitement enough.

"During the day, we spike sometimes, but night is where things pick up," he went on. "You know, it's pretty cool to have a girl out here. Uh, assuming. I mean, I shouldn't assume to know your pronouns."

He looked at me, waiting.

"I'm a she and a her," I answered. "Why did you think I wouldn't show up today?"

He let his head slump to the side. Said nothing.

I nodded. "Fair enough. So, what will I be doing around here?"

"Nothing. Send her back."

The voice came from behind me, low and gruff. I turned as a hulking figure lumbered past. Crew T-shirt, shaggy hair somewhere between brown and dark blond, and jeans more grease than denim. A helmet tucked under his arm.

The scary guy from the meeting. And did he say *send me back?*

"Hey." I stepped toward him as he headed for the open garage. "I said hey!"

The guy stopped but didn't turn. "We don't need your kind here."

"My *kind?*" I looked at Nando for confirmation this guy was off his rocker. Off-roading off his rocker more like it. "You were the one racing the track just now, weren't you? You jammed those tires at me."

I thought I saw movement, like the faintest puff of a laugh. "Maybe you're too flinchy to be down here."

I'd show him flinchy.

Okay, I probably would not show him flinchy. This guy looked capable of tossing me over his shoulder Neanderthal-style to fling me into the bog. That's right. There was an honest-to-goodness bog back by the garage. Orange plastic caution fencing hunched along the grass around it, probably having once stood upright.

"I'm not leaving," I stated.

"I don't care," the guy responded.

Rude. I looked again at Nando. How did such a thoughtful kid work with such a judgmental dude?

Nando shrugged at my unasked question. "Jonah's just Jonah."

And I was expected to watch what I said around this guy? "I was sent by Uncle Frankie himself." Sort of. "I came here to work and I'm not going back." I folded my arms and waited.

The big guy turned. His hair parted enough to see his eyes. Those dark murky eyes. Only today in the sunlight, they didn't seem so menacing. His face didn't come across nearly as shadowed. Beyond his scowl, something else lingered there. Thoughtful. Menacing? Maybe just sizing me up.

Who cared, though, if he was such a prickly prickler that no one could get close enough to tell.

"Put her on helmets," the guy, Jonah, said to Nando, not me.

"Are you who I'm supposed to report to?" I asked Jonah. "Because if you won't talk to me directly, this isn't going to work."

"Fine by me," Jonah said.

A sigh came from my right. From Nando. "Elena, look. Jonah isn't the greatest people person. No offense, Jonah." He held a hand up to the guy twice his size and weight. "We could use the extra help. She can be one of us."

A low grumble sounded from Jonah. "It's not open season to be one of us."

With that, he moved on to the garage.

Nando looked at me. "He's not so bad once you get to know him."

I watched Jonah disappear into the garage. "The rest of the staff are terrified of him. I saw the looks they gave him last night. You shouldn't apologize for him. He was rude on his own and doesn't deserve people covering for him."

Nando moved into my line of sight. "*You don't know Jonah.* He deserves way more respect than what people give him." His words came out impassioned. Fierce even. Soaking wet, this kid was maybe an even hundo on the scale, but right now he was as menacing as the guy he defended.

I held my hands up in mock surrender. "Okay. Got it."

Nando tilted his head for me to follow him. From behind the counter by the helmets, he unearthed a lanyard. "Here's your crew pit tag. I'll go over the basics before the crowds pick up."

This day was strange, but what else could I do but go with it? "Sure. Fine." As long as I didn't get fired and also got paid, I could work with this.

"Elena?"

"Yeah, Nando."

"I liked how you dished it back to Terry. You asked if KJ would get heat for what he did. And you questioned Jonah when most people won't even talk to him. I respect that."

"My mom calls it being mouthy."

He returned a pleasant smile. "It works on you."

I smiled and it kind of hurt, like it had been a while. "Thanks. I'm trying to stick this out." My throat grew tight and my lip trembled. Worst timing ever. I took a breath. "I thought he liked me. KJ, I mean." I twisted the lanyard, inspecting the park logo on the shiny plastic. "He always seemed so nice. So...well-rounded. That sounds dumb I guess."

I liked KJ because he seemed above playing typical cool guy games. He acted friendly with people and I found it appealing. How unstoppable a couple we could have been, befriending everyone, just being laid back.

Now, I didn't know what to think. And that hit hardest. I sighed. "I can't believe I fell for it."

"Those kids do that prank every summer." Nando's face clouded.

"Did they do it to you?"

"*Obviously* I'm not going to fall for someone telling me to meet in a shack called the *Love Hut*."

"So, they got you."

He sighed. "Totally. Her name was Madison. I thought she was my soulmate."

"When did this happen? Were you here last summer?" He looked thirteen.

"I'm sixteen *thank-you-very-much*," he said, somehow reading my thoughts. "My doctor says I'm a late bloomer. I should hit a growth spurt any day now."

I leaned back against the counter. The smell of gasoline and tires clogged my nose. I would reek when I got home.

"I didn't like being tricked either," I told him. "I thought Chelsea was my friend. We've spent weeks hanging out at school. Anyway, sorry that happened to you. I promise I'll never intentionally humiliate you for a cheap laugh." I held out my fist.

His fist met with mine for a bump. "Thanks. Appreciate it."

Something metal knocked nearby. I turned to see the edge of a large shoulder and stringy brown hair retreat behind the building.

Chapter Three

♥

While my first shift at the Go Zone got off to a bumpy start, by my second day, I was ready to try again with a better attitude.

I was also fully ready to ignore Jonah should our paths cross. Hopefully, we wouldn't have to work together much since he believed I didn't belong on his side of the park.

"Elena, my lady," Nando called to me after I shut my car door.

"Hey." I joined him to walk in for another opening park shift. "This is way closer than taking that weird retro tram."

Thanks to Nando, I now knew the "old" park had a whole separate employee entrance and parking area.

"No problem. Figures the new parkies wouldn't tell you."

Nando walked with a swagger I usually saw in older and—no offense to him—cooler guys. Maybe I needed to adjust my version of cool.

Once at the Go Zone, I followed Nando to the staff break room through the employee door by the helmet storage. Fake wood paneled one wall, and orange and olive green hues made up the kitchenette area. Legitimately old from the looks of the chipped paint and worn counters and not a retro throwback style.

Nando leaned against a yesteryear vending machine. He pounded a fist against the glass and a plastic wrapped bundle descended. "Cool, huh?"

I suppressed a smirk. "Yeah. It's…real cool."

He grabbed the treat. "We take what we can get out here. Anyway. Let's see who's on shift today." He walked to a wall-mounted memo board with a handwritten schedule tacked on with push pins. "It's Saturday, so everybody's here to rotate in."

Hopefully, everybody except Jonah.

The door opened and two guys entered. Neither Jonah, so that was a win.

One of the guys walked past me and hit a fist against the vending machine. Nothing came out so he added change and pressed a button. He swore under his breath as the item tumbled down. Taking out the loot, he held it up. "I wanted Combos. Dry pretzels? No thanks."

Nando snatched the pretzels. "Dad, this is Elena."

I froze. Did he say *dad*? The guy in front of me was Black and older than me, but probably not by much. Nando, Mexican-American and sixteen by his own admission. The math for dad to kid did not add up. Then again, I was from a blended family myself, so maybe this was a step-parent situation. Possibly an adopted father—

"They just call me Dad," the guy said. "My real name is Mark. It's because I wore a polo and khakis to work.

Once." He shot a look at Nando and headed out the way he came.

The second new guy, white with shaggy brown hair and pointed shoulders, stood in front of the memo board rocking to music in his headphones.

Nando stepped next to him. "Audio. This is Elena."

"Hey...Audio," I said to the guy who continued existing to his own soundtrack.

"Everyone's got nicknames around here," Nando explained. "They usually happen with time. Come on. Let's see if Blender is here."

"Hey, Elena," Audio said as I followed Nando out.

I turned back. He was still reading a notice tacked to the board and didn't appear to have moved. He'd said my name, though. I wasn't imagining it.

Outside, we crossed the gravel path to the garage set back from the track.

"We call those doors *bays*," Nando said, pointing to the four garage doors. The farthest door from us stood open.

Inside, a guy with black hair squatted in front of a tire. His hair was shaved on the sides and spiked on top into an almost mohawk. I got the impression he didn't bother enough to do the daily styling, so the hair fell across his forehead and spiked softly in the middle.

The guy stood. If the concept of cool could become sentient with real working legs and a face and body, it would be this guy in front of me. He had a solid built body that wasn't bulky, a white T-shirt that looked lived in but not worn, and the hair game definitely worked for him.

I snapped my fingers. "I got it—James Dean!" Like, a 2.0 Latino edition of the actor I now recognized. And I'd bet my first paycheck he side-gigged in a band.

A literal garage band. I snickered to myself.

"This is Blender," Nando said. "Blender, this is Elena."

Blender gave me the barest of chin nods. "I'd shake your hand, but you don't look like you'd want to get greasy."

Not sure if insult or honesty. I mean, I didn't *want* to get greasy. But I worked at a go kart track. Chances were me and grease would do hard time together.

"Hey," I said instead. I desperately wanted to ask if he played guitar.

"Blender's our main mechanic. Certified even." Nando nodded toward a framed certificate on the wall. The certificate itself had the Midwest Wild Adventure logo in the corner.

Blender shook his head with a slight grin. "That certificate is a joke. I couldn't get another job with it or anything, but I've been working on cars since I was a kid. Just so you know, the only other person who should be changing tires is Jonah. It's a liability thing."

"Sure. No tire changing. Got it." A thought struck. "Jonah doesn't have a nickname?"

Nando and Blender exchanged glances.

Blender shook his head. "Nah. Jonah's his own thing."

He certainly was.

Children's voices carried from outside. Nando clapped his hands together. "Time to get moving."

I followed him out and took my station behind the counter by the helmets. Nando took point at the *Are You As Tall As Paul?* sign—that would be, tall as famed lumberjack Paul Bunyan, the park's inconsistent mascot. The branding seemed kind of irregular now that I'd had to learn all the different areas of the park.

"Maybe next year, buddy," Nando told a kid who didn't clear the required height to drive the kart.

"Come on, man! I'm just under!" The boy kicked Paul Bunyan's boots at the base of the sign as his friends ran ahead through the turnstile.

Mark, er Dad, corralled the riders toward me for helmets. A frenzy followed with everyone grabbing different sizes. My parents had freaked about the park not being safe, but here I was, *administering* safety. Maybe I'd make them proud after all.

Mark—I couldn't handle calling him Dad, it was too weird—directed the riders into the pit by the karts. He ran through the safety precautions. As the riders entered their karts, he pointed out the difference between the brake and gas pedals.

An angry voice caught my attention. The too-short kid was yelling at Nando. I started toward them when a tall figure emerged from the other side of the building. Jonah.

With his six-foot height and solid build, he advanced like a lumberjack with intent to jack up some lumber. "Hey," Jonah's low voice boomed.

The kid stared at Jonah.

Then the weirdest thing happened. Jonah crouched. Now he faced the boy at eye level.

I couldn't hear what he said, but the boy shook his head in agreement and circled back out of line. Jonah stood and disappeared. A moment later, he returned and handed the kid a green flag. He told the kid something else.

Stoplights mounted at the sides of the pit switched on.

"Drivers! Start your engines!" Mark bellowed.

The engines revved and roared. A sound effect beeped in time with Mark counting down. *Three, two, one—*

At the same time the stoplights flicked from red to green, the kid with the flag yelled, "Go!" and waved his flag back and forth. The karts took off and raced from beneath the covered staging area and onto the track entrance.

Jonah and the kid high-fived.

I blinked and Jonah had the flag again and walked off.

By the afternoon, I'd swapped helmet disinfecting with Nando to manage lines and check the height restrictions. A surprising number of kids tried to cheat the *Are You as Tall As Paul?* sign. Paul did not get enough respect.

Taking my break in the staff room, I delighted in the idea of a few minutes to myself. I was normally a social person, but the constant reminding of the need to be as tall as Paul really drained a gal.

The door swung open, ending my precious alone time.

Jonah walked in, his silhouette blocking the light from the door. He stopped when he saw me. And stared.

I snapped my attention to my peanut butter and honey sandwich from home. I'd wanted chips to go with it, but the vending machine spit out beef jerky instead. I slid the jerky to the opposite side of the table.

Jonah trudged past me to the vending machine. I couldn't see him from the position I sat, but heard the now-familiar pound against the glass and a crinkly thump that followed.

A bag of Combos landed in front of me.

I whirled around. "What is this?"

Jonah said nothing. He pulled out a bag from the small refrigerator in the corner by the sink. Then he sat down directly across from me.

It wasn't like there were many options for seating. The small round table by the fridge had boxes piled on top of it. Someone's jacket covered the seat at the end of the table. The same jacket sitting there since my first shift.

Still. *Right* in front of me.

Jonah's height was impressive even sitting down. He took up nearly two spots with those lumberjack arms leaning against the table and his lunch spread out in front of him. Funny, with a cleaned-up haircut, he could be a live action Paul Bunyan himself.

Were the Combos some sort of peace offering? Was this a test? Maybe I should save the Combos for Mark since he'd wanted them.

Jonah unwrapped his own sandwich. A good looking one with layers of lettuce, cheese, and deli meat. Special sauces slid out of the thick roll used for bread. I didn't see any wrappings from a sub place, so maybe it was homemade. My own smooshed bread lunch wasn't cutting it.

We both ate our food. I didn't dare touch the Combos.

I should probably say something. If he'd wanted to be by himself, he could have chosen to eat outside. Or sat farther down the table and put on headphones or something.

Finally, the silence became too much. "Do you like working here?" I asked.

I thought I heard a grunt. Did grunt mean yes in Jonah-speak? Or was he chewing?

Since he seemed focused on his food, I peeked up to get a better look at him. Jonah's height and broad body were intimidating, but for working around the exhaust and heat, he didn't look nearly as sweaty as I felt. Even his hair, though it hung in his face, looked clean. He might even use conditioner.

"They'll let you back, you know."

Jonah? Speaking to me? "Oh, really? Who?"

"Your friends on the other side of the park."

"*Friends* is a loose interpretation."

He took a bite and finished chewing. Point to Jonah for not talking with his mouth full like so many guys I knew. "You want to go back."

He said it like a statement.

"I don't know," I answered as if it had been a question. "If my judgment is so bad I'd fall for such a lame prank, then I have no business going back there or even being near him—them." I cleared my throat. "Never mind. I'm fine here. I don't need them or anybody."

Jonah didn't say anything further.

"I mean, they humiliated me," I went on. "Chelsea has some weird grudge against me and she won't tell me why. She turned KJ against me. I'm not crawling back to them. I refuse. I won't do it."

I stared at the unopened Combos.

"I didn't poison them." He wadded up his sandwich wrapping and stood from the table. "Just figured you didn't want the jerky. Only Blender eats the beef jerky."

I pressed my lips together. Slowly, I took the package of Combos and delicately opened the bag. As Jonah left the break room, I scarfed them down.

Later back outside, I found Audio doing line management bopping to music in his headphones.

"I could use you on garbage," Nando called to me.

I pushed my hair behind my shoulder. "Excuse me?"

"Those bins are overflowing. Here. I'll show you." Nando tossed me a pair of gloves.

He flipped open the top of a garbage bin and hefted the huge bag up and out. He handed it to me. I smelled mustard instantly. The food on this side of the park was mainly of the handheld variety—hot dogs, fries, pitas with mystery meat.

I cinched the bag and followed Nando around the building through a locked gate with a giant dumpster. The mustard scent back here created a nearly visible low fog curling around us.

Glamorous, this job was not.

"So, Jonah," I started to Nando. "He's not much of a talker, is he?"

"He's been through a lot. Like I said, most people are afraid of him so they don't talk to him. Besides us Midfits on this side of the park, I mean. When it comes to the all-staff meetings, he stays to himself."

Twice today, I'd witnessed Jonah doing nice things for others. One of those others included yours truly. "What has he been through? Does it have to do with the kid Terry mentioned?"

Nando shut the gate and the dumpster behind us. "It's a sensitive topic, but yeah, it's about that kid. Last summer."

Folks who minded their business would leave it at that. I was not those folks. "What happened?"

Nando gestured for me to follow him to the helmets. I took his lead and wiped down the recently returned helmets with cleaning solution and sorted them back on the racks.

"You know the Log Jam ride?"

I scrunched my nose. "The log boat that's sort of like a roller coaster, but it's in a fake river?"

"Yeah. It malfunctioned at the starting gate and a kid fell in the water. He got stuck on something but the boats kept moving—I'll leave it at that. The worker who was supposed to be watching out wasn't anywhere. Jonah, he saw the whole thing and ran over to shut down the ride. Jonah got the kid out."

Horrifying. "Wow."

"The parents took legal action against the park. It was bad. Many, many thousands of dollars bad."

I could only imagine. I set three more cleaned helmets on the racks for the next group of riders.

"Jonah was a goner, but Cayden—that's the kid's name—his parents told Uncle Frankie how Jonah saved their boy and to promise not to fire him."

"Wait. I don't understand. Why would Jonah get fired if he saved Cayden?"

Nando lowered his voice. "I don't know how well you know Uncle Frankie..."

"If that's a question, the answer is I don't. I've talked to him once."

"Well, he hates bad press. He doesn't care whose fault it was. If you were there and you're named in a lawsuit, you're out."

"That seems unfair."

Nando shrugged. "All to say, Jonah is stuck here and still has his job."

This connected a few dots for me, but not all of them. "If he's so miserable, why doesn't he quit?"

Nando tilted his head in thought. "I don't know if he's miserable. He doesn't like to get into it with people, you know? Not a fan of drama. Also, not a fan of pretty much anyone but us Midfits. He'd rather stay away from the rest of the park."

Jonah told me my "friends" would take me back. He'd told me to go back to my kind the first time we'd spoken.

Jonah didn't want me here. To him, I represented the people he didn't like. "Hold up. You said someone hadn't been where they were supposed to be when Cayden got hurt. What's the deal with that? Did Uncle Frankie fire them? Does Jonah feel guilty about getting a staff member fired?"

Nando shook his head. "I've told you too much already. That's all I know and Jonah won't tell the rest. He's never told anyone."

Chapter Four

♥

As time dragged on during my shift, I thought about Jonah's situation as I made garbage rounds with a set of clean sacks. It made no sense whatsoever for Jonah to be exiled for someone else's negligent behavior. Why not out them? Why didn't he care? Surely, he cared. He could crush them! Physically!

That got me thinking about the prank. I was in exile because of someone else too. Well, and my blurty-blurterton self hadn't exactly helped.

Chelsea had some past beef with me. I'd need to figure out why. Had she been the mastermind, or a mere participant, suggesting they set me up? Nando said new parkies did Love Hut pranks every year.

That hadn't been KJ's fault. Maybe he'd been swept up in the prank and hadn't thought of it in a malicious way. From everything I knew about KJ, he wasn't a malicious kind of guy.

I thought back to what I'd imagined this summer would be. Working near KJ and taking slushie breaks together. Just getting to know him outside of school.

"Elena!" Nando shouted at me. "We're going to need a mop and the biohazard bucket. A kid blew chunks in a kart."

My eyes fell shut. This was my life now.

Face it, Elena. You'll never have KJ. You're too much a loud mouth. Too much a try-hard. You belong in the sticks with the biohazard bucket.

If I was anything, I was stubborn. Even if that all were true, I still believed a fighting chance existed in there somewhere for me and KJ. I needed to get Chelsea out of the way. It wasn't revenge so much as payback. Wait, that sounded bad. Not payback so much as comeuppance. Karma? That was a bit gentler.

Sometimes karma needed a little nudge.

Jonah and I ended our shifts at the same time, both gathering in the break room to clock out and collect our things.

I'd been thinking all afternoon we had more in common than he probably realized. Okay, more than *I'd* realized. We'd both been ostracized by the staff on the other side of the park. Him for way bigger reasons than me, but for him they were a long time brewing. We could be of use to each other. I wasn't sure exactly how, but if we got to talking, we could figure something out.

I took my time in approaching Jonah now that he stood still in the break room. First, for a big guy, he was kind of a hard one to catch. He was always doing something. I hadn't wanted to pester him earlier while he worked with Blender on the karts. Safety first and all that. I thought I'd seen him free and alone at one point, but sweat had gotten into my eyes and I mistook him for a tree trunk.

"Hey, Jonah!" I bounced over as he grabbed a backpack from the short row of wall-mounted hooks by the door. "Can I walk with you?"

He grunted.

I would take that as a *sure*. A reluctant yes, but not a no.

Outside, he held the gate open for me to walk through into the employee parking lot.

"So, Nando and I were talking and he said—"

"Nando talks a lot. Maybe too much."

Oh. "Everybody likes Nando. Who doesn't like Nando?"

"Didn't say I didn't like the kid. Just runs his mouth too much."

I saw that as a credit to Nando. He ran his mouth without running into trouble, unlike me.

I needed a different tactic.

"Hey, so I meant to tell you I'm sorry about what happened at the...hut." I found it hard to say this to Jonah for some reason. "It was super embarrassing and I'm sorry you were dragged into it."

Jonah stopped walking. I nearly ran into him since I trailed behind his long strides. He stared at me. "You're apologizing? To me?"

I tried to view him as a gentle Paul Bunyan, not Paul the Ripper—close cousin to Jack, obviously. "Um, yes?" I figured he'd appreciate an apology.

He grimaced. "We're a joke to them."

He'd said *we're* as in *we*. We, he and I. "Exactly. I know I'm new and don't know the ropes. You do and they still got you."

His gaze turned to cold steel. "They didn't *get* me." The words came out in a near growl. Then quieter, "No one gets me."

He started walking again.

Why had I assumed we had anything in common?

"I know this is a long time going on for you," I said as I attempted to catch up. "For me, it's fresh. I'm all hot and bothered. I was thinking maybe we could be hot and bothered together."

He slowed and turned a fraction toward me.

Yikes, what had I just said? "That came out wrong. I only meant we've both been wronged and I'm fired up just thinking about it. You came into the shack. They set up you too. Aren't you mad?"

He stopped in front of a nice-looking SUV. An older model, but it looked well cared for even if on the basic side. "They're not worth getting mad over."

"That doesn't make sense. Humiliating you—or attempting to—and humiliating others, seems worth getting mad about. Even if it's not for yourself, they're trying to trick people for their own amusement. The whole wild virgin thing is so rooted in systemic patriarchy, it's a real wonder they consider themselves worth listening to."

He shook his head, as if talking himself out of something. "I went in there to warn you. I wasn't set up."

Oh. Well. I...didn't know what to say to that. "I don't know what to say to that. Thank you, I guess. I hadn't seen it that way."

He grumbled again, something to the effect of, "No one usually does."

I could still save this. "I appreciate you looking out for me."

"It wasn't a special favor." He turned from me and opened his driver's side door to get in.

I caught the top of the door. "Hold on. I think maybe we can be useful to each other."

I'd like to say he raised an interested brow or had a perk in his eyes, but Jonah defied those types of facial expressions. If anything, his glower deepened.

Forging ahead. "Um, I would like to respectfully request your assistance to get them back. If you'd be interested in joining me."

"I would not." He pulled the door closed. I yanked my fingers from the door frame in time before losing precious digits.

"But they used you," I said through his closed window, hoping he could hear. Not a problem I typically had since I knew how to demand attention with volume. "I know there's more to the story with Cayden Moore."

Ha! *There.* Delivered like an investigative reporter. A career I'd once considered but lost interest in after watching hours of YouTube bloopers of news reporters. Too many opportunities for viral shame.

As I'd hoped, his window powered down. I began another plea when Jonah cut me off.

"Don't ever say his name. You weren't there. You don't know."

The window rolled up and Jonah drove off, leaving me standing in the parking lot, literally in his dust.

Chapter Five

♥

I was on trash duty taking care of barrels along the paved path from the Go Zone to an old sit-down restaurant called Final Lap, positioned overlooking the track. This and the pita stand were it for eating options, yet park guests seemed to throw out tons of food wrappings.

Bracing for mustard gas when I opened the next bin, I lifted the trash bag up and out. I looked up and froze. Chelsea stood in the distance by Final Lap. She didn't have on her Wild Adventure staff tee but a tank top and shorts with platform wedge sandals. Cute sandals.

Something wet hit my ankle. Trash flowed out a side tear in the bag. Right across my foot.

I muffled a shriek, holding the bag away from my body. I glanced to Chelsea—whew, she hadn't spotted me. A girl I recognized from the water park named Kaitlyn chatted with her. Both appeared off-duty based on their clothes. Two guys joined them, coming from an entry point to the park by the restaurant. As if anyone came all the way out to Wild Adventure to eat at Final Lap.

Chelsea looked up. *Eep!*

I turned fast and jammed the trash back into the barrel. Pungent mustard and ketchup fumes struck in two-punch combos. I gagged and shoved the bag harder, the bulky plastic warring with the shape I demanded it fit back into. I needed to make a break for it. I had no cover out here. Only blazing sun.

Leave the trash and go!

"Is that you, Elena?" Chelsea called. "Are you *running away?*"

She and Kaitlyn laughed. It was like they were projecting their voices to be heard this far.

I could run or I could face them. I mean, I'd confronted Chelsea already and she wouldn't give me a straight answer about why she'd set me up. It wasn't as if she truly had the upper hand.

I pivoted toward them and put my hands to my hips. Then I remembered my dirty trash gloves. I straightened my arms and hovered them at my sides.

This was apparently all quite amusing to Chelsea and Kaitlyn.

Chelsea strut toward me in those very cute sandals. "Trash duty on the reject side of the park? You must have messed up bad."

"Or I'm keeping the park clean, which is what I'm paid to do." Ha! There. I was a totally responsible park employee. Take that.

Chelsea's upturned nose and stink face told me she did not in fact take that. Or she smelled those overheated condiments. "You fit in here more than I expected."

"Totally," echoed Kaitlyn.

Rude. So rude.

I could be rude back, but the trash juice running down my leg distracted me from crafting a good insult.

"Come on," a guy behind them said. "It's hot and I'm hungry."

"I don't know why you're so miffed at me," I told Chelsea. "This is getting old. Girl fights are so basic."

She scoffed. "Don't talk to me like that. This is *not* over."

She and Kaitlyn circled back to the restaurant. Another person jogged toward the door to join them. "Wait up!"

KJ Keene. He took long graceful strides. He also wasn't dressed in his park staff shirt but a plain black fitted T-shirt and casual long slouchy shorts. Like a page out of a summer catalog. Chelsea hung back, letting KJ get the door for her.

That should be me.

Chelsea shot a look my way and grinned. My blood simmered.

"Stare much?" a voice said behind me.

Nando handed me an empty trash bag.

A pang hit me. I was the trash girl. Literally. I held trash with trash-juice coated rubber gloves. And my summer crush just disappeared to eat overpriced burgers and seasoned fries with my nemesis.

I had an honest-to-goodness nemesis. And the truth was, I'd lost my shot at KJ when I fell for that stupid prank and ran my mouth in front of everyone after it happened. I couldn't blame anyone but myself.

·♥·♥·♥·♥·♥·

Later as the afternoon slid into evening, the crowd dynamic at the Go Zone shifted. Instead of families with kids, the lines filled with teenagers and older folks solo of children.

Apparently, our side had a special partial park wristband that cost a fraction of what the rest of the park cost, and a night park pass for the few hours open after six p.m.

This was when Blender would emerge from the garage in cleaned up clothes. He'd just exist near the kart loading zone and women would flock to him. I'd never seen anything like it and I'd observed a lot of popular guys out of habit.

My experience with Blender so far gave me an older brother vibe. He was a good-looking dude for sure, but I had no idea how old the guy was. He could be twenty. He could be thirty. He could be immortal.

Me and Nando, now off of line management since no children needed to be reminded of their height shortcomings, stood around awkwardly until something needed to be done. It was like that sometimes. A million things happening all at once or absolutely nothing.

Watching Jonah work was kind of a marvel in itself. The guy seemingly moved from place to place with lightning speed despite his hulking frame. He was on top of everything as it happened.

I was cleaning up the helmets when Blender appeared.

"I haven't seen you drive yet. You want a break?"

"Drive the karts? Oh, no-siree. Nope. I'm good."

He tilted his head. "Hold up. Have you ever driven a go-kart?"

I shook my head. "Not really my thing I guess."

"Okay, well that's changing." He held his hand out for me.

A small crowd of adoring girls and older women watched as Blender hand-escorted me to the loading zone. And delivered me right in front of Jonah.

Blender pat me on the back. "J, get this girl set up. She's a first-timer."

I appreciated he didn't use the V-word. Again, not because of shame, but because it made virginity more of a stigma. First-timer had a more precise, less loaded meaning to it.

If Jonah bothered to look annoyed, I was sure he would have right then. "I'm busy."

Blender laughed easily. "Give it up, dude. We're fine. And we can't have Elena working the pit if she's never even driven a kart."

"It's fine, really—" I started, but Blender handed me a helmet.

"That one, there." He pointed to a kart parked farther back in a row of karts currently out of circulation.

"I'm not falling for some trick," I told him. "Fool me once, shame on...is it shame on me? Because what happened with that love shack was not my fault."

Blender gripped my shoulder in a steady squeeze. He got right in my line of sight. "We don't trick each other around here. We're like family on this end of the park." His eyes held an intensity that freaked me out. Different than Jonah, but equally as serious. "You hear me? We save a few karts aside for staff if we need to go out. These are the good ones."

He let go and melted back into his cool crowd lingering behind us.

Which left me facing Jonah. "Sorry."

"Don't apologize." He turned and walked toward the kart. "Let me show you how it works."

Two karts sat side by side. Jonah stood by one and instructed me how to get in. I'd seen park guests do this all day every shift since I'd started. Not exactly rocket science.

Still, the worn pleather felt foreign against my back.

He turned the engine on. Jonah had his hand on the back of my seat and leaned in, explaining the gas and stop pedals. He didn't talk to me like I was stupid or anything, but he did explain everything even though I'd heard him say the same exact routine to park guests before every new ride and the countdown to go.

"You good or is this too much?" he asked.

I whipped my head toward him. Had he actually just asked me that? Gone was the grumble and gruff attitude.

"I'm fine. I can drive a car. It shouldn't be hard." I swallowed back my ego. "It's a little scary."

"That's why we do helmets now. Too many lawsuits."

Yikes.

Jonah climbed into the other car beside me and revved the engine. Then he pulled his own helmet on. "Ready? I'll count down."

"Is this a race?" My heart revved its own engine inside me.

"Obviously."

Sheesh!

"Three, two, one, Go!"

And then we were off.

I hit the gas hard. Jonah was clearly letting me off easy since he was no longer side-by-side with me, and let me merge onto the track ahead. Okay, maybe not. Jonah zipped up beside me in his own kart once on the main track. No other racers were on this stretch as they should be headed back to the loading area by now.

I slowed a little at the first curve. The track moved across a bridge and then around a series of smaller curves. I turned the wheel and jerked to one side. This steering was loose. I needed to keep easy pressure on those turns. Handling the wheel with more ease, I finessed the next curves like a pro.

Jonah burst forward on a stretch of straight road, blowing exhaust in my face. I coughed and sputtered. Gross, and no. I had to catch up!

Craning my neck to see around him, I spied the next sharp turn. I eased on the gas and tried to not go too hard on the steering wheel, and when I met the curve, hit the gas harder and turned.

My tires screeched. I hung on tight and steered into the turn like Mom taught me to steer into a skid on icy roads to balance out any fishtailing. I bet this looked pretty cool.

I zipped around the bend and nearly caught up to Jonah. His head turned, looking back at me.

That's when I gunned it and came parallel to his kart.

I waved. This was super fun.

His head turned back forward and he drifted his kart closer to my space, thinking I'd back off.

Did I seem like the kind of gal who backed off? Jonah didn't know me.

I did not back off.

Jonah was forced back to his side. Another big turn was coming up that would take us back toward HQ. I slowed, hugging the inside barrier and putting more force on the wheel this time for a sharper turn. Then gunned it to cross in front of Jonah.

Only he was too quick. "Dangit!" I yelled into the wind.

Jonah still had the jump on me. Okay, so he'd put in at least a full season and even worked repairing the karts. Of course he would be better at this than me.

But I hated losing. I really hated it.

Not being a sore loser was one of those things I'd had to work on my whole life. When I played board games and my brother clearly cheated or whined that I wouldn't let him off easy, I had to remind myself to lose gracefully. Maybe sucking at losing was why I quit the cross-country team. Not because I was bored with it, but because I wasn't as good as the other runners like Christina and Holli. They were always finaling with competitive scores at meets. I was grateful to not finish last.

And once I *had* finished last. Which made me pretty dang mad.

I couldn't let Jonah win without a fight.

I pushed my thoughts aside and focused on the back of his bumper like I did when I distance ran and picked off other runners. Gain a few feet, push, and pass. Only I couldn't make the kart go faster. And another turn was coming up.

Jonah cut across, taking the turn close—right in my path! I was forced to back off.

Or was I?

I hit the gas and jerked the wheel to take the outside edge. I focused straight ahead, to the next turn that zagged us from the previous zig back toward the finish.

Jonah was just ahead of me on my left now. That's when I saw it. A lone shoe sitting defenseless on the track. Right in front of Jonah.

He'd have to move into my space or risk running over the shoe. These karts were low to the ground, so it wouldn't pass under. I could drift to let him swerve...or not.

My heart drilled through my chest. *Decide now!*

I barreled straight ahead.

Jonah tried to swerve but the tire barrier bounced him back. The shoe went flying.

Cheers sounded from the pit. I sailed past the finish.

Jonah was right beside me. Had I won, or a tie?

I'd actually be cool with a tie.

Pressing the brakes, I took the slow curve back to the starting line until I reached a stop. My heart was having a dance party. I slid off the helmet and got out of the kart on shaky legs.

Jonah still sat in his idling kart.

Blender ran to us. "That was dope! J man, she really had you there."

Jonah finally stood and removed his helmet. He turned to me. "You said you'd never driven a go kart."

I was breathing kind of hard. "I hadn't."

Blender pat me on the back. "Natural talent. Nice work. Consider yourself initiated. No one's ever come so close to beating Jonah first try."

Jonah did not look thrilled by this news. Meanwhile, I greatly enjoyed not sucking at something. I pumped a fist in the air. "Yeah!"

Nando jogged to us. "That was gripping. Are you okay, Elena?"

I ran a hand through my hair only my hand got stuck. My face hurt from the wind. "Yeah, I'm fantastic."

Jonah, barely looking at me, said, "Nice job." Then he walked off.

That was probably all the praise I'd get out of him.

Nando squinted toward the track. "Hey, is that my shoe out there?"

Chapter Six

♥

It was another night closing the park and this time we had a staff meeting with Terry on the other side of Wild Adventure.

"Do they ever have meetings on our side?" I asked Nando.

He opened the back gate for me. "Never."

We headed to our cars to drive to the opposite side of the park. At least then we wouldn't have to come all the way back to leave for the night. Nando didn't have a car and relied on family to get here, so he rode to the meeting with me.

I followed Blender who drove a pointy car I'd learned was a Pontiac Firebird from the early 1990s. Bumble-bee yellow with a black racing stripe and shiny chrome rims. He called it a muscle car, which I thought was hilarious. Laughing at his muscle car was the first time I saw Blender slightly lose his cool. *Slightly.*

For my punishment in making fun of his bumble bee, I'd endured a lecture on the history of muscle cars. Believe me, I'd run out of laughs by the time he finished.

I parked two spaces from him—no way would I risk dinging his door with my basic sedan. Together, Blender, Nando, Audio, Mark-slash-Dad and I walked in through the new park employee entrance.

Jonah had the day off. All day, I'd noticed his absence. Funny, I hadn't realized how much he kept things running until he wasn't around. He never made a show of anything, but quietly set us up so we didn't have to think too hard when the lines stretched. He was the one who secured the helmet area using a pull-down gate that locked over the counter. When I'd tried shut the gate myself, I bruised my hand.

We filed through to the back courtyard behind the staff offices. I tried not to panic at the sight of the shack set back by the fence.

"Don't sweat it," Blender said as we congregated in a spot nearest the exit. "We've got your back."

To be honest, I felt cooler than ever walking in with these guys. A lot of that was Blender, but Audio and Mark were pretty cool once they started talking. I'd gotten each of them to say three whole sentences to me so far and they were all nice sentences.

Snickers sounded when I came into view of the other park staff. I was probably over-thinking. No one cared that much about me. Out of sight, out of mind, right?

I watched Chelsea and a girl I'd never seen stare me down. So they *were* caring about me.

But why, though?

Beside me, Blender pulled out a pocket tool and snicked open the knife.

The girls gasped.

Blender casually picked at a piece of grime under his thumbnail with the knife, then smoothly closed the tool and slid it into his pocket.

Beyond them, KJ stood with a group of guys. Tall, tanned, and laughing as they spoke. A flutter moved in my chest. That wide easy grin turned my knees to pudding.

Just then, he looked up and noticed me. He flashed a more subtle smile. I glanced either way. Unless he was checking out Blender, KJ was smiling at me.

KJ visibly laughed to himself. He pointed and mouthed, "You."

I could die. Right now. Instant death. KJ Keene was *silently communicating* with me.

I tossed what I hoped was a causal wave his way. Heat surged through me.

KJ was a good guy. I'd mistakenly lumped him in with Chelsea and the prank. The more I watched him and the way he carried himself, how he interacted with the others, he'd been manipulated too. Chelsea and the others with their dumb games. That was so beneath KJ.

"Move it, shrimp," a rude voice said as Nando knocked into me.

A guy with sporty sunglasses and a twine and shell choker-style necklace pushed past us.

"No thanks, I'm allergic," Nando responded.

The guy stopped and turned. He had a dead look in his eyes. "Huh?"

Nando stood at his full height. "You called me shrimp. I'm allergic. Keep it moving." He shooed the guy away. "*Anyway*," Nando said to Blender, as if they'd been deep in conversation before interrupted.

The guy continued to gawk. I laughed. Nando barely seemed fazed by the insult.

Or maybe he'd built up an armor over time. I'd also assumed Nando was younger than his age. I glared at the guy who'd called Nando a shrimp. "Get lost."

Only the guy had already walked off to his own group. Dry rides. I'd remember that.

"Hello, Wild crew," Terry said as he walked out from the offices with his clipboard and a fresh sunburn. "Let's make this quick since it's late."

He reviewed discount days coming up for the Independence Day weekend. Updates about two food stations, *yada yada yada*. Just about everything he talked about had to do with this side of the park. "Except Go Zone," was a frequent modifier. We really were our own thing.

"Now, here's where I have a special announcement," Terry said. "A new initiative to liven things up around here."

I noticed most people were talking among themselves or openly scrolling on their phones. Everyone but the Midfits.

Terry noticed the lack of attention too. He cleared his throat. "Phones down. Eyes up here." He made a motion where he pointed two fingers out and back toward him.

The group eventually quieted.

Terry continued with a tight smile. "It's been a hot summer so far and the water park is getting throttled. We've got two log jams. The wave pool and the actual Log Jam. Meanwhile, other zones are under-utilized. People are complaining about the lines. We've got food shortages at the wave pool stand and their lines clog the line for the bathroom. Too much time to wait for pool cleaning."

Nando made an *eek* face. He leaned toward me. "Pool cleaning during park hours means there was an accident. *If you know what I mean.*"

Ew. I did.

"This is where you all come in, my trusted Wild crew." Terry beamed with the wattage of the Go Zone night-time flood lights. It was kind of neat to see the track lit up at night. "We need to even out park flow and direct traffic to our under-used zones. To make this interesting, there will be a contest. With prize money."

Now Terry had everyone's attention. Until people began talking over him.

"How much?"

"How do I win?"

"Do I have to share the money? I don't want to share if I have to share with Craig."

"Hey!"

That last one must have come from Craig.

The excitement seemed to thrill Terry since he let the chatter ride.

"How do we play if we work the wave pool?" KJ asked.

Terry raised a hand. "Great question. You can direct guests to other park zones during peak hours. We'll track numbers using our usual park metrics and the cash out numbers at the food stands and merch booths around the park. Show some love to older rides."

The dry ride staff made some noise. "That's right!"

"Adventure Zone rules!"

They were the so-called neglected rides?

If the new side of the park had neglected older parts, how would us Midfits stand a chance at grabbing any prize money?

"Does this incentive include the old park?" a voice asked from behind us.

I turned to see Jonah.

"When'd he get here?" I asked Nando. Amazing how a guy so large could slip in unnoticed. "He didn't even work today."

"Jonah doesn't miss a staff meeting."

Seemed weird to be so invested when he'd almost been fired for saving a kid's life, but what did I know?

Terry's beaming smile flickered like a bulb ready to short. "Of course. Every zone is included per park regulations. I'll post the official rules in the staff office."

"In both park offices?" Jonah asked.

Terry's smile frosted over. "Of course."

A grunt sounded behind me which I assumed was Jonah's concluding remark.

Nando nodded toward Terry and kept his voice low to me. "That's why Jonah comes to the staff meetings even when he's off work. On watch for shenanigans."

Very interesting dynamic. Terry definitely feared Jonah. I suspected it had more to do with the incident at the park last year than Jonah's size or intimidating presence.

The meeting now dismissed, none of the Midfits made a break for it like the others, who clung together in cliques while exiting to the parking lot. Instead, Blender and Jonah led the rest of us inside to the staff building. Jonah stopped in front of a bulletin board with posted announcements.

Wild Park Zone Incentive! a blue flyer shouted along the top.

Jonah tore it from the board.

"Hey!" I said. "Terry told us we'd get a copy for our side."

Jonah gave me a pitying look. "He did say that, didn't he."

He handed the flyer to Blender. "Take care, guys."

Jonah was always doing that—walking off before a conversation was finished.

I followed after him, out the staff building and through the exit into the parking lot. "Hey. Jonah." I struggled to catch up. "What's going on with you and Terry?"

"Nothing."

"Then why does he look freaked out every time you talk?" I winced. That definitely came out wrong. "Not because of you, but like, because he's afraid of what you will say or something."

Jonah continued to walk.

I kept up with his pace. "You never want to talk about stuff. But you're here on a night you didn't even work."

He stopped. "Does that bother you?"

"I'm curious. You could have had Blender report back. You trust him, don't you?"

"I'm the one who watches out for us. That's not on Blender. It's important to me."

He was almost actually looking at me now instead of looking past me. What he said felt important. That he'd said it to me felt especially notable.

"Thanks," I said. "For answering me, I mean. I know I'm annoying. I just want to do a good job and I'm trying to understand these..." I moved my hands around. "Workplace dynamics. This is by far the strangest job I've ever had. And I did a lot of babysitting for kids whose parents were in couples therapy."

Jonah tittered—that is to say if Jonah was capable of tittering. He shook with some internal reaction. "You're not annoying," he said. "You're..."

I hung on to each word. "What?"

"Different."

I was *different*? Than who? I got the sense he didn't mean it as an insult. And I hoped he didn't mean something basic like *different from the other girls*. I liked my lip gloss and cute shoes and I also liked working the pit at the Go Zone. That didn't make me different, it made me not a stereotype.

While I went through that mini-lecture in my head, I decided what he said was a compliment. "Well, thank you."

Jonah looked at me. I could tell because I could see his eyes now that a breeze swept back his hair. His eyes didn't seem so much like a lagoon as dark pools with hurt and other complexities behind them. His features softened, like he'd relaxed from hardening his expression and allowed a piece of his real self to show through.

Just then, an "Oooh-*oooh*" voice came from deeper in the parking lot. "Look at them together!"

A group of Wild staff loitered beside a nearby car. Chelsea's unmistakable face stood out among the others. KJ was there too. KJ...who'd I momentarily forgotten.

"Elena's moved on from you, KJ!" Chelsea's voice carried crisp and clear. "She's with the worstie of the beasties!"

"The what of the what?" I lurched toward them, when a strong hand held me back at the arm.

"Don't bother." Jonah spoke low. "They're not worth it."

"She called you a worstie and a beastie. I don't know what either of those mean."

"They call me a beast," he explained. "And they think I'm the worst of us."

I stared at him dumbfounded. I'd really found a whole lot of dumb in this conversation. "Have they *seen* the late night hotties Blender pulls in? It gives the lifeguards a run for their money on a weekday. Maybe not a Saturday but—" I shook sense into myself and also shook away from Jonah. "Never mind. You know what?" I called to the group. "You all are *mean!*"

A beat of silence passed before a reaction came. That reaction was laughter. Outright laughter.

Also, the laughter was mean. Point proven.

Okay, so it wasn't much of a burn. But I spoke truth. Name calling should have been left back on the elementary school playground. And not even left there, because how unfair to those kids to leave something so awful for them to deal with. I'd done my fair share of ganging up on unsuspecting new kids, but I'd learned my lesson with time. It hurt to be on the wrong side of teasing. I wasn't about to stoop low like that now that I knew better.

Blender and the others joined us.

"You getting heat from them?" Blender edged forward with a disaffected but also highly affected look on his face.

"Yes—" I said at the same time Jonah said, "It's fine."

Beside me, bass from Audio's headphones pounded. Wordlessly, he took out his phone, held up the camera, zoomed in on the loiterers, and snapped a pic. He slipped the phone back into his pocket. He turned and did an elaborate handshake with Blender, then next Mark, followed by a fist bump to Nando and Jonah. He looked at me and tipped his chin up. Then, he walked off to an ancient station wagon.

Okay then.

"These jokers are always trying to start stuff," Blender said. "Ignore them."

"They called you guys beasties."

Blender laughed. "I've been called worse. Look, I'm going to take off. Let me walk you to your rides."

With Nando and Mark following, we moved as a group to where we'd parked. More comments sounded out of earshot. If I'd wanted to hear them, I would have listened harder.

I turned and walked backward, facing the remaining Midfits. "You know, we can beat them."

"Elena," Nando said gently. "We don't like to engage in violence."

"Not physically, I mean at that zone competition. We'll rock that contest and win the prize money."

Blender ran a hand along the scruff on his chin. "We bring in an okay crowd at night, but I don't see us winning."

"We can," I said, even more convinced now. "We need someone on tram duty and an inside guy at Final Lap. We need someone on social media working the park hashtags and we need a stash of those night pass bracelets."

They stared at me.

"It could work. We can do this."

Nando stared at the ground. Blender looked thoughtful and still really cool. Mark and Jonah, less convinced.

"Okay, it's late," I said. "I'll have a packet of information for you all tomorrow."

More stares.

Blender held his fist up for a bump. "Stay safe, Elena. We'll talk world domination tomorrow. Nando, you need a ride?"

The two drifted toward Blender's yellow muscle car.

I blinked. Mark had already left apparently, leaving only Jonah.

"You don't have to do this," he said.

"I don't want to see them win."

"They always do. It's best to get used to it."

I could practically see the filmstrip of past experiences play out on his face. Never winning. Being thought of as a loser. The person to be feared or ignored.

Jonah would probably storm off if I reacted too sympathetically—he didn't strike me as a guy into being pitied. But I'd seen how he cared for our side of the park. How he talked to kids like they were real people, not just another guest whining about lines and the heat. How he kept everything running and made sure to include all of us on what mattered.

He cared about this job. Enough to show up on a night he didn't need to work.

Deep down, I believed he cared enough to win. I only needed to convince him.

Chapter Seven

♥

If there was any proof I didn't deserve a healthy functional relationship with a hot summer crush, it was my loud mouth getting me in trouble. Again.

I'd arrived at the park early for my next shift and stopped by the main employee building. I didn't *need* to, but Jonah's point about watching for shenanigans made me curious. First, a trip to the bulletin board with staff information. Second, a sweep of the employee room to listen for chatter.

To be covert, I wore a hat.

The bulletin board displayed a new blue flyer to replace the one Jonah had taken. An extended list of rules for the game appeared beside it. The wave pool and Log Jam staff couldn't advocate for their zones since the whole point was to shift traffic away from those areas during peak times. They could assist another zone.

If we were to gain more park guests from the highly trafficked areas, then it was key for us to build trust with those staff. Get a few of the water park staff to funnel guests to the Go Zone.

My connection was KJ. KJ, who'd made silent communication with me last night at the all-staff meeting. KJ who I had an in with.

Unfortunately, Chelsea also worked at the wave pool. A complication.

I did my sweep of the break room and ran into exactly those two people.

"Hi!" I said altogether too brightly. My hat disguise was a lost cause—it was my high school cross country cap, the only non-winter hat I could find in my rush to get going this morning. We all went to school together, so who was I fooling? "How's it *going*?" My voice, still too perky.

KJ returned a smile. "Hey, Elena. You know, I figured I'd see you more this summer. How is everything ...there?"

I set aside the fact he couldn't even name the side of the park where I worked. Or maybe I was reading into his words. "It's great. I nearly beat Jonah my first kart ride."

Chelsea's face scrunched into a sour pout. "I can't believe he was *touching* you last night. Did you two make out in the Love Hut? Because—" She made a gagging sound.

Okay, rude. Very rude. I was determined to not sink to her level at the bottom of a drain. "I'd like to wish you both well on your endeavors with the contest. Friendly competition is good for the whole park. You know, that whole rising tide lifts all boats thing."

"Um, you don't even work in the water park, so I don't know what boats you're talking about." Chelsea made an exaggerated *can you believe her?* face to KJ.

"It's an expression," he told her. "It means the work done for the good of a few can help the good of many."

Her face fell. "Oh. Whatever." She looked back at me. "You aren't actually thinking more people will come to your reject zone, are you?" She must have noticed my hopeful expression because she plowed ahead, making her voice go fake syrupy-sweet. "Aw. You did. You thought you might not suck for once."

KJ winced. "Hey, Chels. No reason to get down on them when they're already—" He stopped himself. "I mean, things are never so great there, so..."

I waited. I wanted to hear the rest.

Chelsea rolled her eyes. "They're a bunch of gross grease-head losers who don't care about Wild like we do, Kay'j."

She actually shortened KJ to just the sounds those two letters made—*cage*.

Ugh. Like sand in a paper cut to my ears.

My jaw clenched. I inched closer. "Oh, we care. We care a lot. And we're going for that prize money. And we're going to win."

Her mouth hinged open like a mailbox. "You're trying to *win*? You are so delusional. Elena, I'd love to see you fail, but even this is too far."

Other staff buzzed in the background, either turning quickly to pretend they weren't listening or openly watching us. My declaration that the Go Zone planned to win was out there for anyone to hear.

KJ looked back and forth between us. "What's with you two? I thought you were friends."

Chelsea huffed and turned to him, huddling close and talking low. "I *told* you. Remember?"

KJ held his hands in front of him. "Look, I'm staying out of whatever's going on here. Elena—good to see you. Take care, okay?"

With one last lingering look—had his look lingered? He seemed to linger a moment—he moved past us and left the break room. I couldn't help the sigh at seeing KJ. In person, he was so tall and gorgeous and perfect.

Chelsea shook her head, looking at me. "Pathetic."

She was the last person I wanted to catch me gawking. "Still not going to tell me why you've got a bug up your butt?"

She made a horrified face. Good. I hoped she was imagining the visual.

Her expression settled. "If you don't know, then you're a worse person than I thought."

She spun on her heel and headed for the staff bathroom.

Back at the Go Zone, I started with Nando on my plan for Operation Zone Wars (abbreviated OZW). Nando made himself the ideal sounding board for just about anything, plus I could take him in a fight if I had to.

Kidding—I would never.

"I'm not sure the guys will be sold on this," Nando admitted after I showed him my notebook with a solid nine point plan. Sure, there were coffee stains on the lined pages, but I'd found the notebook, and the overturned disposable coffee cup, in the backseat of my car. Beggars usually didn't get to choose.

I did my best not to notice the slow park traffic today. A reminder how uphill this whole zone battle would be.

"You're friendly, Nando. We'll use that. You know the Final Lap servers, and the kitchen crew all know you by name."

Nando folded his arms and rested back against a wall by the helmet rack. "I don't ask them for things. That's why they're nice to me. I treat them like normal people."

And that was the reason we'd recently come into a steady supply of hot soft pretzels and curly fry baskets directly to our break room.

"If they already like us, they'll want to direct guests here. The park has promotions in place already at Final Lap with those cheaper wrist bands for our side of the park. It's not like we're coming up with something new for them to do. What do you think they'd want from us in exchange for pushing those passes?"

Nando considered my question. "Exclusive track time."

"Great idea. We can do that. Terry never comes out this way. He wouldn't know if we kept the track open another thirty minutes past closing on a slow night."

He shrugged, obviously not convinced.

"What else can we offer?"

Nando scanned the area. "Blender."

"What about Blender?"

"Just like, hang out time with him. People think he's cool."

"He is cool." That got me thinking. "What if he did a free clinic on fixing up the karts? Something exclusive."

"I was thinking more like the ladies who hang around him."

I glanced toward the garage where grinding sounds blasted out. "We can't put Blender on a dating app. That would be—" Genius. "Unethical. We need Blender's buy-in to get any head start on this."

Jonah appeared, first as a long shadow across us and then as a body attached to that shadow. "Are you still recruiting for your popularity contest?" he asked in a dry tone.

I considered this a personal victory—Jonah speaking to me unprompted. And about something I wanted his input on anyway. "Operation Zone Wars—OZW—and yes. I am. It's not about popularity, it's about getting back at those jerks who think we're lowlifes."

"So, revenge is your fuel."

I'd stuck my foot in my own trap. "Don't you want to show them up for once?"

Jonah glowered. "I don't want to spend time thinking of them, so no."

"Okay then, think of it is as giving the Go Zone the glory it deserves." I slid my notebook across the counter facing toward him. "I did some research on Wild Adventure. The go karts are original to the park and used to be the main attraction. What's now our employee lot used to have bumper cars, a motorized boat remote control thing, and a Ferris wheel. This was way before our time."

Jonah looked bored. "I know about the old park days. My folks used to come here."

Nando pushed off from the wall. "My parents did too. Once the Ferris wheel tilted and someone slid out of their basket. They were dangling from twenty stories up!"

"It wasn't that high," Jonah told him. "And those things happened at different times. The wheel did tip, but no one was on it at the time. The basket incident was different."

So Jonah knew his stuff.

"Someone definitely dangled out," Nando said. "My mom said it's the reason she went back to church."

"So the park took out the old Ferris wheel," I went on. "When they bought the land on the other side and added new rides, they relocated the bumper cars, took out the boat thingy and made the Log Jam ride. Later, they built the water park. Then they paved the old section of the park."

It made me sad for some reason, imagining bulldozers crushing amusement rides and erasing its existence with asphalt.

"You know what else my parents told me?" Nando said. "My dad said there used to be festivals out here. Concerts set up in the parking lot. People would come for the music and then they'd drive the karts and do the Midway. That's what they used to call the part with the prize booths and cotton candy."

Blender joined us. "You all talking about the old park?"

Nando nodded. Jonah grunted.

"This place used to be lit back in the day," Blender said. "A few old school punk bands played the Wild parking lot. The stories are legendary."

Blender scanned my list, but his expression remained the same. "I'm going to take off. I only came in to finish a couple things. I've got a show tonight."

I saw myself reflected in Blender's mirror shades. "A show?"

"Car show. The muscle cars you think are so funny." He gave us each a chin nod and left for the employee exit.

"The bumble bee is in car shows?" I asked Nando.

"It really is a cool car." He shook his head, probably still in disbelief I'd laughed at the muscle car thing. "He's saving up for another car he can restore. Blender's got this whole other life making connections with classic car dealers and stuff. A lot of cool rides come through his uncle's body shop."

"I wonder why he doesn't work there," I mumbled, which I thought had been to myself, but when had I ever been quiet?

"Because he cares about this place too." Commentary courtesy of Jonah standing by. "And they let him do what he wants. Some of us don't want that to change."

I didn't miss the bitter edge in his tone. So, it wasn't only not wanting to deal with the popular kids. The Go Zone had its own thing going and he didn't want that fractured.

"Let me get this straight. You *want* this side of the park vacant?" I knew this would press him to agitation and didn't care. "That seems selfish. And seems off your brand of caring and watching out for us."

His gaze sharpened. "You don't know what you're talking about."

I didn't know if I'd pressed him too far or if saying *us* and including myself in that bit bothered him.

A group of park guests streamed off the tram and headed our way.

"Want to race again?" I asked Jonah. "We can fill in some of these karts with the other riders."

Sometimes Jonah and the guys rode with the guests to watch for hazards blocking the track.

He leveled a look at me. "No."

"Afraid you'll lose?"

Beside me, Nando made a sucking sound with his teeth. "I wouldn't, Elena."

Jonah moved past me to take a helmet. "You're on."

Yes! I took my own helmet. "If I win, you have to help me with OZW."

He had the gall to sneer. "Sure. You'll lose."

"Guys?" Nando said. "Maybe lay off the competition for a minute while I get these guests started."

I left the counter and headed toward a kart, following close at Jonah's heels. "You didn't say what you wanted if you win."

He slipped into the same kart he'd ridden in the day we'd raced. Blue with a yellow number 12 on the door. I got into the kart beside it. Lucky 13.

Good thing I wasn't superstitious.

Jonah revved his engine. "If I win, I'll get you back to the other side of the park. Where you belong."

Chapter Eight

♥

This time racing Jonah, I knew what to expect. I'd driven a kart a dozen more times, mainly at closing when guests trickled out. The times I drove with guests, usually Nando and I would hang back and drive once the riders hit the first curve. We looked for trouble on the course. Of course, we did some zipping around and passing maneuvers to keep it fun.

Now that I had more familiarity with the course, I could perfect my technique.

Though, Jonah could drive this track in his sleep.

Nando reviewed the safety instructions and prepared the parks guests for the ride, then counted down. My foot itched to hit the gas, but I waited, like Jonah. When the riders emptied out of the covered portion of the pit and merged onto the track, I squinted to watch for when they hit the first turn.

"Three, two, one—" Jonah said beside me. "Go!"

We both blasted off and stayed neck and neck until the merge. I cut to the inside track to gain the advantage.

All through the first leg of the course, we each angled to pass each other. Ahead, a rider trailed far behind the others.

"Ease up," Jonah called out to me.

I was super tempted to keep going, but safety ruled as the priority and we were on the clock. I eased up on the gas and stayed a good distance behind. The driver ahead slowed some more.

Jonah motioned with his hand that he would drive ahead and for me to hang back. He drove parallel to the park guest and waved at them. "You okay? Need any help?"

I couldn't hear the response, but saw Jonah return a thumbs up to me. It was probably a kid, since some of the riders looked young even if they cleared Paul Bunyan's height chart. At the next curve, I viewed the kart from a different angle. Short rider with slight shoulders. A kid.

Jonah continued driving side-by-side with the kid.

Meanwhile, my adrenaline for the race waned. I relaxed. I kind of loved being out in the kart. Now that our race was on pause, it gave me space to think.

We finished the first lap and I veered off to the pit, letting Jonah drive the remaining laps with his kid buddy.

"Uh-oh." Nando waited with a look of dread when I approached. "He didn't run you off the road, did he?"

I told him about the slow driving kid. "Sorry I left you here to deal with everyone." The line for the karts had grown. We'd have to split the next group.

"It's okay." Nando watched me. "I'll help you with the zone war if you want. I have some ideas."

"All right!" I signaled for a high-five. We were all about high-fives or fist bumps, but so far, I wasn't in on the special hand combinations.

I took helmet preparation again for when the riders were set to switch out. Funneling drivers in and out and our routine safety checks kept us busy for the next twenty minutes.

After the next racers were off, Jonah found me at the helmet counter.

"You listened to me," he said.

I tilted my head. "You know the track better than anyone."

"I thought you'd drive ahead to beat me."

I pushed back the offended feeling snaking up. "Not when there's a kid involved. These karts are kind of scary the first time. I'm seventeen and I was freaked."

"You didn't act freaked."

"I play a good game when I want."

He didn't say anything to that. He looked thoughtful.

"Besides, I already know you don't think I belong here," I told him. "Message received loud and clear. I'm not going to let your opinion get in the way of doing my job and keeping park guests safe."

Jonah's face clouded. "I didn't mean—I just thought, if you want to get back to the other side with your friends, I could help you. That's what I meant." He had that softened look again when the hardness fell away.

"I have a few ideas to get some of the wave pool staff on our side." One of the staff. On my side particularly, and obviously a bit selfishly, but it was also for the challenge. "What were you thinking you'd do to get me there?"

He seemed a little unsure, like he might have said something and then hung back on it. "I talk to Uncle Frankie sometimes. I could ask him to put you back there."

"Eh, that's probably a dead end with Uncle Frankie." I tapped my newly-shortened fingernails against the counter. It was too much a pain to keep up a manicure out here. "I sort of talked to him my second day and asked him myself. He said I'd blown it. Summarizing of course."

"Huh" was all Jonah said.

"Like I said, spending some time with the new parkies will lay a base for the operation. I get it if you don't want to be involved. I'm looking for any reasons to be over there while I'm on the clock. That way I can network more and target the right staff."

He studied the counter and my tapping fingers. I stopped tapping. "You want to hang out with new parkies all so you can convince them to send park guests here? That's what you want?"

"It's one point of many in my OZW plan, but yes."

"They can't stand us. If you wanted to go back to work with them, sure. They aren't going to help us."

"KJ might."

Jonah grimaced.

"I know KJ!" I couldn't keep the hyper from coming out. "We both go to West Ginsburg. I've been to a ton of his games. Some of my friends and his hang out. My former friend...Chelsea," I struggled to say her name. "Anyway, I saw him earlier and he said he expected to see me more this summer. He said he'd see me around. That's an in. I need time with KJ to form that bond."

Jonah muttered.

"What?"

He shook his head. "Nothing. Figures it would be KJ."

I didn't like that tone. "Some of his friends might be jerks, but KJ is a good guy. He has a lot of friends at school without being stuck up."

Jonah folded his arms. "People aren't always what they seem."

Well, of course they weren't. That's why you had to get to know them. It was why I'd wanted to spend this summer getting closer to KJ.

"I have a plan," I reminded him. "I already know KJ, and we have a good chance of nudging him to our side. We get more guests and more park cred. That's like street cred but it's focused here at Wild. And ultimately, prize money. I just need to not screw things up. I'm not the best at keeping my trap shut as you've probably noticed." I laughed a little too loud at my own criticism. "Not blurting out whatever I think is something I have to be aware of, like, all the time."

It happened today already. More than once if I counted my second laughing spasm after I asked if Blender called the belts on his car delts like deltoid muscles. Sometimes I was hilarious...to myself.

Jonah clenched his fists, then flattened them against the counter. "You shouldn't change who you are to be around someone. Sometimes the things you say are...needed."

This was the nicest thing Jonah had ever said to me.

Based on his mildly stricken expression, Jonah appeared mortified to have said it.

He cleared his throat, returning to his usual scowl. "Where's that list?"

I fumbled for the notebook on the shelf below the counter. "Here."

He scanned it. "Give me some time. I'll get back to you."

Scowl or not, I counted that as a win for Jonah edging to my side. Things were looking up.

"Want a job do to?" Jonah asked me an hour later. I was almost out of here but bored to tears now that park traffic slowed.

"Sure. What's up?"

"We're out of these disinfectant wipes. There's a stash in the water park."

The water park. "Is this a mission?"

"Go do the thing you said you'd do." He set an empty container of the wipes in front of me.

Now we were cooking. I had a mission.

"The fastest way is past Final Lap up that path. We have a golf cart, but I'm not sure taking it is a good idea."

"What's wrong with the golf cart?"

"Nothing. You know how to drive one?"

I scoffed audibly. "Can I drive a *golf cart*? I drove here. In an *actual* car." And nearly beat Jonah in a go kart race my first time. "How hard could it be?"

Jonah's expression morphed as if contemplating. "I meant since you're going alone, you might not want to drive a vehicle you're not familiar with. It's a pain driving so slow through the crowds."

"Oh." Well, then. "I'll walk. Thanks."

With that, I took off. Crossing the park felt like a slice of freedom, no longer chained down in the pit. Okay, nobody chained me and I didn't hate it. But when I'd imagined working at Wild Adventure, I'd assumed I'd see more of the park. Then again, I hadn't expected to be an outcast in the outer rim.

Okay, stay positive. I needed wave pool staff on my side to show the rest of the park that our side mattered.

I wound my way across the wide concrete path, past a collection of tree sculptures in animal shapes. Bushes trimmed to look like bears and, from the tall, long shape of one, possibly a giraffe. Only, the bushes were half dead, giving off a zombie vibe.

The entrance to the water park loomed ahead where staff checked wristbands for appropriate access. I flashed my employee badge at the guy stationed by the gate and held up my empty box. "Hi. Do you know where these are stored?"

The guy, white with a splotchy tan and mirrored shades, shrugged. "I guess maybe the supply shed by the wave pool?" He turned away to check wristbands for a family. They had full park access based on the color of their bands.

Beyond the gate, the wave pool stretched in neon blue with a lifeguard posted in a tall chair above it. More staff patrolled the area. A familiar one with dark hair and dreamy eyes.

I passed through the gate, feeling rather important with my staff badge and a reason to see KJ. Way more so than a park guest in water shoes and wet clothes. I had a mission.

KJ saw me approach and his face brightened. "Elena!"

My heart soared. "Hey. I'm here for some supplies."

"Sure you are." He winked.

Dear heaven above, how would I survive this? I begged myself to stay cool and collected. This was not easy in ninety-degree heat staring at a shirtless heat source.

Had I mentioned KJ was shirtless?

"I just got done up there." KJ gestured to the lifeguard stand. He grabbed a shirt from a small booth along the fence marked Staff. He pulled the Wild Adventure shirt down over his head. "It's good to see you."

I could not describe what I was feeling. I wanted to say words, but words did not come out. Speechless? Was this what being speechless felt like?

I tried to laugh and halfway managed. My breath made noises, so that was a start.

"So, they let you out, huh?" KJ asked in an easy way, implying he either understood I was having a hard time speaking or else he was completely oblivious.

"Yeah. Yup. I'm out," I said. "I've been trying to find reasons to break out."

He tapped the empty disinfectant box I carried. "Good one. Most of these are in the big storage unit back at HQ, but you were smart to remember we have a stash. Let me show you."

I followed him to a small building beyond the pool under cover of real and fake brush. The real bushes had scraggly branches and the fake were light up palm trees.

KJ opened the locked door with a key from a ring clipped to his belt loop. He ducked inside and I stepped behind him, hovering in the doorway. He handed me two boxes. In the cool dark room, a tight fit for more than one person, it reminded me of the dreaded Love Hut.

"Thanks for these," I said. "You know, a good way to cool off is to take the karts for a spin. Wind in your face, fresh air in your hair and all that. You could tell the guests they can dry off at the Go Zone. Then they can order food from Final Lap."

He grinned, but it faded almost as quickly. "You sound like you've been talking to Terry. I wouldn't put too much time into his ideas. If the wave pool is packed, so what? It means we're doing good business. You saw it out there. We're not even busy today."

I had seen. There were more people jammed in the wave pool and filling beach chairs than the Go Zone brought in on our best nights.

KJ leaned an arm against a metal shelf, looking all gorgeous. "So, Chelsea said you have a crush on me."

I froze, my smile static in place. My vision iced over.

He laughed softly. "Sorry if I put you on the spot. I think it's sweet. When it happened, I didn't realize the Love Hut set-up was about me. If I'd known, I wouldn't have laughed like that."

I gripped the boxes I held. "But didn't you see my face? My very humiliated and shocked face?" Seems that would have been signal enough not to laugh.

KJ winced. "Ouch. I deserved that. My bad."

My mouth tasted sour. So now he knew I'd been crushing him and he knew I'd been humiliated.

His expression softened. "Don't stress about it, okay?"

Easy for him to say. He looked like he didn't stress about anything.

I decided to be honest since we were laying things out. "It's just...I've admired you for a long time. Maybe the longest out of anyone—but it's not like, an obsession or anything. I am fully capable of not crushing on you. I can stop the crush at any time and I can be totally okay with that."

"Aw, why would you stop crushing?" KJ pretended to pout. "I just found out."

I needed a box fan directly to the face. I stepped out of the room to give myself space.

KJ exited the storeroom to follow. When he turned to lock the door, he leaned past me, his shoulder angled close to my body. I'd never been this near to KJ without other people around.

He finished with the door and stood in front of me. "We should hang out later. A bunch of us are going to a party at Craig's."

"Craig..." The guy who someone didn't want to share prize money with. "Does he work at the wave pool?"

"He's at the Log Jam."

Nice. We needed support both places. But never mind about that—KJ WANTED TO HANG OUT WITH ME. "I'd love to."

"Here." KJ slipped a Sharpie from his shorts pocket. Adorable—he was prepared!—and wrote a number on the side of the disinfectant box. "Text me later. I'll tell you when and where."

I left the wave pool walking on water.

"It worked!" I burst into the pit, running full throttle to Jonah at the same time a batch of riders took off for their first lap. I showed him the box. "KJ's number! I got his phone number."

Jonah didn't look up. "Color me surprised."

He wasn't exactly a colorful guy to begin with, but whatever. "This is good news. Not only did I get invited out tonight, but it's a party at Craig's. Craig of the Log Jam. We need an in with the wave pool and the Log Jam for our plan to work. This is perfect."

"If you say so." He walked toward the point where the starting track merged with the outer loop. He kicked a tire in the barrier back into place.

I followed after him. "It's part of our plan—"

"Your plan."

I took a breath. "My plan, yes. I know you're doubtful, but I think it could be good. Even long term. Not just the money, but improving relations between the parks."

He made a noise somewhat like a grunt but also like how I'd sounded when trying to speak to KJ earlier where the words wouldn't come out. I waited for Jonah to tell me some more how my idea was dumb or to tell me to go away. Only he didn't.

"So, this party." I braced myself for my next words. "I was thinking maybe you could come with me tonight."

He laughed but not in a way that sounded like he thought I was funny. "To their party? No. Way."

I figured he'd say no, but he didn't realize the genius of the idea. "Then you could see they're real people. KJ is at least. And they can see that about you instead of being afraid of you."

Jonah shoved his hands into his cargo shorts pockets. "I like that they're afraid of me. They keep their distance."

I couldn't imagine he truly felt that way. I was a capital E extrovert according to the personality test I'd taken for a career coaching session in health class. I liked people. Even when they didn't all like me, I needed to be around them.

I watched as Jonah tracked the riders making the turn at the farthest visible point. He seemed pretty content observing. Maybe he didn't care about being around people.

For me, I watched people too. I liked to find out a fact about someone and bring it up around them later. Like a common interest or a way to show someone I pay attention to what they're into. But it was kind of exhausting sometimes. Because I liked being friends with a lot of different people, it meant keeping up with a lot of information.

Stupid extroverted tendencies making me all dependent and tired.

The drivers raced past us finishing their first lap.

"I don't know nearly as much about Wild Adventure as you," I told Jonah. "I think there's a lot I could learn. It'd be nice to have support at that party. I still feel new around here."

"So ask Nando."

"Nando has a curfew. Also, his mom forbids him from going to high school parties."

He turned a fraction toward me. "Forbids?"

"Yeah, she's super strict. You know, it's part of the whole church attendance thing why he can't work Wednesday nights or Sunday mornings."

"I didn't know that."

I waved off his comment. "I'm sure you did. Nando's always complaining about the rules his parents put on him. His cousin working at Final Lap is the only reason he got this job."

Jonah glowered. "Seems like you know plenty. You don't need me."

I knocked my heel against a tire on the barrier. "I know about *this* place. I don't know about the park or about everyone else. Look, I'm going to this party for us. I need moral support."

"You keep saying us, but it's for you. This was your idea."

"Right, but it's *for* us. You, the guys. I want us to have a fair shot at this prize and a fair shot at, you know, being accepted."

He looked at me now. "You want those things. We don't."

I looked back at him. His eyes glinted and the hard line of his jaw softened. I didn't believe him.

He might not have wanted to be accepted in the same way as me, or maybe even by the same people, but I believed he wanted acceptance. And respect.

I wandered back toward the pit. I'd worked the afternoon but I wasn't scheduled to close, so I could leave in the next twenty minutes. I had big decisions to make. Hair and make-up for starters. Who I could convince to come with me tonight so I wouldn't have to go the party by myself. Christina or Holli or maybe my old cross-country friends. I hadn't done any socializing since starting this job and was due for some fun.

I sent off a round of texts to cross-country friends. Then to KJ. My finger hovered above the Send key.

Sent.

This could be the first of many texts.

After clocking out in the break room, I headed back up front to let Mark and Nando know I planned to leave. Both of them were farther down the track tending to an off-roaded kart.

Jonah appeared in front of me again. "Did you find someone to go with you?"

"I'm waiting on some non-Wild Adventure friends to text back."

He made an *mmhmm* sound. "Good luck." And he walked off.

Chapter Nine

♥

I ended up going to the party solo.

Holli texted from the beach town where her grand-parents and her boyfriend lived, so she wasn't around. Turned out Christina was on vacation with her family up north. I didn't even know what my own friends were up to now that working at Wild Adventure consumed my time.

For as much a people person as I was, I still hesitated to walk into the party alone.

In a better world than this, I'd have been fine since I knew KJ and Chelsea. With Chelsea now in her own hostile zone, I only had KJ. The rest were nameless faces I'd seen at staff meetings. I didn't even know who Craig was or anything other than he jammed or unjammed logs at the park.

But I'd been invited to this party and not only did I have work to do for Operation Zone War, I also wanted to have fun. My parents OK'ed a curfew of twelve a.m. (yes!) after admitting they were impressed by my work ethic. I'd officially earned my first paycheck.

The address KJ texted me belonged to a house outside of Ginsburg proper in a nearby township where the roads had number or single letter names. I slowed as the house address came into view on the mailbox by the road. I parked in the long driveway behind a car with a Ginsburg East sticker on the back window.

And didn't get out of the car.

This was stupid. I'd walked into a brand-new job by myself. *Yeah, with knowing Chelsea and KJ.*

I wished I knew whether KJ planned to drive or ride with someone so I could watch for him.

And Chelsea. I hadn't even asked if she'd be here. What if I walked in and she was the only person there? Maybe Craig had a big family and these other cars belonged to them?

Woman up, Elena. I put my hand on the door handle and pushed it open. I channeled good energy and positivity on the way up the driveway. The garage door stood open, revealing a few empty chairs. I walked past them to a door in the garage leading to the house.

Inside, a few people gathered around a kitchen island. One guy looked familiar from the park. He didn't tell me to leave and he wasn't yelling about wild virgins, so that was a good sign.

I gave them a small wave. "Hey."

The red-headed guy I'd waved at came toward me. Light freckles dotted his fair skin and he wore an unbuttoned Hawaiian print shirt with a Wild Adventure T-shirt under it. Not a staff shirt, but one from the park retail shops. "Hi, I'm Craig. You're KJ's friend, right? Thanks for coming."

Wasn't this all I'd ever wanted? To be associated with KJ? I couldn't believe this was happening. "Yeah. Is he here?"

"Not yet. Come on. Do you know anyone?" He nodded toward the group standing near us.

I shook my head no.

Craig introduced me to everyone in the kitchen and a few others hanging out on a screened-in porch off the open sliding door from the dining room. None of them worked at Wild Adventure, so, a plus to me, I started with a clean slate.

I opened the bag of chips I'd brought—my mom taught me to bring food anywhere I'd been invited. Just then, KJ walked in through the kitchen. A ray of sunshine beamed in behind him.

Not really, but in my mind, yes.

"Elena." He moved toward me with an arm outstretched. He didn't go in for a hug, but rested his hand on my shoulder which I was completely fine with.

KJ looked at me with his own soft brown eyes. "I'm glad you came. *Crush*."

I might pass out on the spot. Either from swooning or sheer embarrassment, toss of the dice.

No, I could do this. I could speak real words in KJ's presence. "Yeah. Um, good to see you."

Music from the back porch grew louder. A familiar song I liked, which helped me relax.

A group entered from the front door. Faces I recognized from Wild Adventure. I watched as they approached. A white girl with blond hair wearing an oversized baseball jersey made eye contact.

"You're the girl who—"

"Won the Wild Virgin crown. Yup, that's me." Might as well beat her to it.

"That had to be *so* embarrassing for you."

"Sure was." Might as well not deny it.

"And the guy who came out of the Love Hut before you?" The guy beside her, Black with close-cropped hair and wearing a Ginsberg East football team T-shirt, shook his head. "He's one scary dude. What's his name? Jasper?"

"Jonah," I corrected. "He's tall, but he's kind of a softie when it comes to kids."

KJ laughed. "Elena, you're being generous. He's not like some, I don't know, *toddler* whisperer."

His friends joined him in laughing. "Toddler whisperer," the girl choked out. "Sounds super sketchy."

"He's not...like that." My own words faded as another figure entered the front living room.

Jonah himself.

I blinked at the sight in front of me. Jonah? Here at the party? The very party he said no way he'd come to?

"What's *he* doing here?" the girl in the baseball jersey whispered, loudly, to the guy beside her.

KJ returned a hand to my shoulder. I couldn't escape the feeling it seemed a protective gesture.

Craig moved past us toward the door. "Jonah. Hey, man, I didn't know you were coming."

Jonah nodded once and his gaze found mine. It shifted to the hand at my shoulder.

"I'm glad you came," I said brightly. "I invited Jonah, Craig. I guess he already knew where you lived."

Craig held up a fist for Jonah to bump and *Jonah did.* To my own shock.

"Oh, Jonah and I go way back," Craig said. "Before Wild Adventure times. We don't see each other so much these days."

Jonah again had no response. I heard a faint grumble, though who knew what that grumble meant.

So, if Jonah knew Craig already, then he never needed my invitation. Actually, it was mildly irritating he already knew Craig. Craig of Log Jam made up a key point in my plan. Jonah even *read* the plan and said nothing of having an in with him already.

But he was here now, and for whatever reason, it felt like support.

KJ slid his hand to the center of my back. I blinked, snapping to reality. Was my back sweaty? I suddenly felt quite warm. I moved forward, adding a few more inches of space between us. A nervous laugh escaped.

Jonah made his way farther inside, nearing us by default. The air between KJ and Jonah grew as thick as humidity by the lake. Only we were inside with air conditioning. Also, the humidity was actually tension.

"Jonah, good to see you," KJ said with his easy-going style.

Jonah merely stared at him.

I laughed nervously. "Um, so, Jonah, there's some good beef jerky here, not that junk that falls out of our vending machine."

Jonah now stared at me.

Okay, weird transition to beef jerky. "So you know Craig," I said instead. "That's cool. Do you live way out in the sticks like he does?"

"Hey," Craig said with forced offense. "We're only ten minutes from the town line."

"I'm in town," Jonah answered.

"Elena," KJ said, leaning in. "Did you meet Adrienne? She's on the back porch. She runs cross-country for East. Maybe you know her."

Ah, KJ remembered I ran cross-country. Well, used to. That was thoughtful. He gestured with his chin toward the back porch and for me to follow.

I turned to Jonah. "Come with us. I'm terrible at meeting new people. You know me." I changed my voice so it came out low and kind of dopey. "Always runnin' my mouth."

Was that a grin from Jonah?

He settled a scowl on KJ. "I'm fine."

Yikes. Well, he *had* told me he wasn't a KJ fan.

I tried my best not to be concerned with Jonah as KJ and I made the rounds talking to different people and digging into snack food. Jonah wasn't my responsibility. Even though I'd invited him, he knew Craig already.

But I couldn't help myself scouting for Jonah's location every time I moved through the house. He and Craig talked for a while. Then a girl joined them and I saw a rare sight—Jonah laughing.

The smile changed his face. His hair still shaded his features. making it difficult to see the full change, but when he laughed, it was like the smile pushed back his shadows.

The girl said something to him and he laughed again.

I found myself glaring. What made her so funny? I could be funny. I could be real dang funny.

"What's the deal with you and Jonah?" KJ asked, seeming to note where I looked from our spot on the creaky patio furniture on the enclosed back porch.

I'd nearly forgotten KJ's arm hung out behind me across the top of the wicker couch. Nearly. "Deal? There's no deal. We work together."

"I work with Jonah too, but I'm not constantly checking what he's doing."

Busted. "You're on the other side of the park. You know it's not the same thing. If it was, no one would have made such a big deal about me getting sent there as a jail sentence."

KJ shifted and I caught the sharp scent of his cologne. The smell reminded me of what someone would wear in a private home library while smoking a pipe and sifting through important documents. Like, old rich guy cologne. Weird. "I meant to talk to you about that. I can ask Uncle Frankie to get you out of there. He likes me."

Funny, Jonah had said the same. Now I had two inside guys offering to get me out.

This should have been what I wanted. Again, I found myself resisting. "I don't know. I finally feel like I know what I'm doing in the pit."

"The *pit*?" KJ grimaced. "Elena, you can't be serious. You shouldn't be down there with them. It's not safe."

My heart kicked up a notch, and not from swooning at KJ's cheek dimple—which was in fact, both cute and hot. "We follow all of the safety guidelines."

For a bunch of teenagers and however old Blender was, we ran a tight pit. How likely was it that a seat belt would completely detach after a few laps around the course? But the guys never skipped the belt checks. We checked off safety lists in the morning and at close. Even though nobody monitored our lists. I'd yet to see Terry on our side or Uncle Frankie.

KJ leveled a look at me. "I don't mean safety guidelines for the rides. I mean them. The guys. Do you feel okay out there?"

I couldn't believe he was asking this. "Nando is ninety pounds soaking wet. Audio exists in his own world, and Dad—Mark—keeps to himself. Blender, he's like an older brother."

"And Jonah?" KJ asked. "You left him out."

I picked at my fingernail. How to sum up Jonah? "I'm trying to get him to talk more, but he's so...secretive. No, not secretive. More like highly introverted but also protective. Of himself and of other people. He's a tough one to crack."

KJ inched closer as I spoke, which sent my collar steaming. I tugged at my slouchy shirt layered over a fitted camisole. Way too many layers right now.

"Is that what he is?" KJ asked. "A fascination? You want to crack the mystery of Jonah?" His smile sparkled when it said it, like he was stoked to uncover a mystery himself.

"I think so. He's definitely interesting. I'm not scared of him, if that's what you were asking. I feel totally safe working with him."

KJ's expression hardened. "He's not a gentle guy, Elena. No matter what act he's putting on around kids."

Agitation set in. "Why do you think it's an act? Jonah doesn't care what people think of him." Another glance through the open patio door into the house to where Jonah sat, I noted how he gave Craig his full attention as Craig spoke.

"He doesn't care about much besides himself."

That didn't feel true, and KJ's shifting vibe sent me scooching away from him. The wicker seat squeaked in response. "I see him care every day. Maybe he doesn't care about the same things you do."

KJ flinched. "You're defensive of him. What has he told you about me?"

"About you? Nothing." Only that he didn't like him, but I had no idea why. "Look, you two clearly have something going on. Maybe you should work that out."

"Like you and Chelsea worked things out?"

Ouch. "I don't know why Chelsea is mad at me. She flipped the second I started working at Wild Adventure. She set me up for the Love Hut with Jonah. Is that why you think there's something between us?"

KJ leaned back, putting more space between us. "I thought you liked me."

I stumbled for a response. KJ sounded almost bruised that I might not like him. That I might like…Jonah? Which was ridiculous. I mean, I liked Jonah, but not like *that*. Not like I liked KJ.

I needed to re-focus. The plan. Operation Zone War. Yes. I needed KJ as an ally. I could start with mending the weirdness between them. "I think it would be a good idea to make amends with Jonah. You're a graduate now. You can put all this behind you." I fluttered a hand in the air.

KJ's gaze lowered to mine. "I don't want to leave everything behind."

I was definitely sweating now. That space in between my boobs that wasn't exactly cleavage unless I wore a push up bra? That space felt quite toasty.

I stood. "I think I need water. Ice water."

KJ stood with me. "I'll get it. There are bottles in the garage."

I breathed a sigh of relief after he left. I needed a chance to catch my breath. A two years ago version of me would faint on the spot if she could see KJ with his arm around the back of our shared seating. At a party with coworkers from the coolest place I could imagine spending my summer.

Glancing toward Jonah, pressure hit my gut. He now sat by himself. A whole house filled with people—people he knew—and he was out there by himself.

Not your problem, Elena.

Maybe Jonah wasn't my problem, but he didn't have to be alone.

I crossed through the dining room area to the living room and sat on an upholstered ottoman near the couch. A TV across from him turned to what looked like a video game being played by someone on TV.

"What are you watching?" I asked.

"It's a documentary about game development."

I watched a few minutes of the show when KJ found me and handed me water. "I wondered where you went. Watching TV?" His tone suggested this was a dumb thing to do.

Jonah didn't react.

"This is really interesting," I said to KJ. "So far it's talking about how game developers—"

"Did you hear what happened at the tower slide?" KJ sat on the ottoman next to me, nearly edging me off the side. "This kid tried to go back up the tube slide…"

I couldn't shake the sensation of being flattened by a steamroller. The rest of what he said faded as my attention flitted between him and the documentary, where a woman with rainbow-dyed hair stood onstage at a trade show demonstrating a new game.

KJ, now finished with his hilarious-to-him water park story, leaned closer. "Are you ready to get back to the party?"

My ears grew hot. "I think the whole house is the party. Even here."

KJ shrugged with one shoulder like he often did. "Sure. Cool." He glanced to Jonah, then me. "I'll be out back." He took off.

Had I just dissed KJ Keene?

"I thought you liked him," Jonah said.

I gasped. "I do!"

He made the slightest sound of amusement.

"You looked pathetic so I thought I'd throw you a bone." I winced at my own comment. "I don't mean you're a dog. You don't need me throwing anything at you. I wondered what you were up to is all. This gaming doc you're watching seems interesting."

Jonah, who'd been watching the screen, shifted his focus to me. "Do you play video games?"

"I used to. Now I just play games on my phone."

"Those count." Jonah sat forward with his elbows on his knees. "People sometimes assume gaming is violent shooters or kids' stuff. My aunt is a game developer at a company in Seattle. She's made it a career."

I found I held my breath watching Jonah shift into someone I'd never seen before. His voice came out less gruff. He had a more relaxed look when he wasn't busy steeling himself against everyone.

I pulled out my phone and swiped to where the gaming apps lived on my home screen. I faced the screen to him. "These are what I play."

Jonah looked at my phone. He pointed to a puzzle game with a dragon theme. "I know that dev. That's short for developer. I'm on an online forum with them."

"Really? That's cool. I never thought about the people behind making the games." I looked back at the TV. The rainbow-haired woman returned on the screen, sitting beside two other people from her development team. "That's not your aunt on TV, is it?"

Jonah offered a small smile. "No. The woman on TV is pretty well-known in the gaming world. My aunt thinks of her as an idol."

My question probably came across as super naive, but so far Jonah didn't act as if it was.

"There's a web forum I go where we talk game design," Jonah told me. "We challenge each other to make short mini games. Then we play-test them. You learn a lot, fast."

"You make games?" I asked.

"Try to. I don't know. It probably sounds dumb."

"Um, no." I slid off the ottoman to move to the couch beside him. "Making a video game from nothing isn't dumb. It's...interesting and creative. I never would have guessed that about you." I cringed. "I mean, I don't know much about you other than what you do at Wild Adventure."

Jonah returned to grunting as a response, his attention back on the TV.

Ugh. He was so exasperating. Here we were having a conversation and he shut down right in the middle. How was I supposed to—

"It's what I want to do," he said in a quiet voice. "Video game development."

So we were back? I'd roll with it. "Wow, that's great to have your career figured out. Are there college programs that teach gaming development? I know nothing, remember."

He grinned a little at that. "You know more than you let on. Especially if you play games yourself. I never would have thought that about you either."

Jonah looked at me, one mere couch cushion away, and my stomach did a backflip. He wasn't even touching me or anything. His dark eyes searched mine for...something. Words were difficult again. Not something I was used to. My limbs spontaneously emptied themselves of bones. I'd turned into a mumbling jelly-limbed fool.

This was *Jonah*. A totally different side of him, but still, somehow very much him.

The room felt hot all over again, so I grabbed the water KJ had gotten for me and chugged.

I stood. Something about this whole conversation needled at my skin and I wasn't sure how to deal. Jonah was supposed to be my support in making friends—which was a ridiculous concept now that I made myself face it. And yet, Jonah came. Only I wasn't supposed to be schmoozing with him. I needed to talk with KJ. How had I gotten so far off track?

"I'm going to mingle. Want to join?"

I knew Jonah would say no and he did.

After a quick trip to the bathroom, I returned to the kitchen where KJ leaned against the island talking to a group about water park horror stories.

"Hey, Elena." KJ watched me with a little more distance.

"Hey." I fit myself between where he stood and another guy I'd met earlier. A little cozy so he knew I wasn't trying to ditch him like I'd stupidly done earlier.

The door from the garage opened and two new people walked in.

Chelsea. Beside her, her friend Kaitlyn. Chelsea took in the room. When her attention landed on me, her eyes narrowed. "What's *she* doing here?"

Beside me, KJ sighed. "I invited her."

The next thing that happened stopped my heart.

KJ slung his arm around my shoulders.

Dead stopped.

Chelsea fired eye daggers at me. She stomped through the kitchen until a solid mass blocked her way. Only she didn't expect it and plowed right into that solid mass, knocking her face right into the guy's chest. Into Jonah.

Chelsea squealed. "Ahh! What are *you* doing here?"

Rude. "I invited him."

She growled in an impressive mix of Miss Piggy and a chipmunk. Everyone in the kitchen broke up laughing.

Chelsea whirled around. "This isn't funny!" She glared at me. "You. It's always you doing this to me."

She and Kaitlyn disappeared onto the back porch.

"We might have a few things to sort out," I said.

Jonah stood still in the space from the living room to the kitchen looking at me. Suddenly, KJ's arm weighed heavy on my shoulders. I didn't like this attention on me. I typically preferred quiet stolen moments where I could be alone with a guy. Or a party like this, but without everyone staring at us.

I cleared my throat. "So, uh. How's everybody's summer?"

The conversation picked up.

In my ear, KJ talked low. "I'm glad you came, Elena. Say the word and I'll get you back on our side of the park. Where you belong."

I looked across the kitchen. Jonah was gone.

Chapter Ten

♥

I had an honest-to-goodness day off and I didn't have a clue what to do with myself.

Scratch that—I slept in. Until noon. Glorious.

My parents were both at work so they couldn't bug me. I wasn't sure they even knew I'd be home today since Mom kept forgetting my schedule. With my brother away at soccer camp this week, I had the house to myself.

I ate chips and salsa for breakfast and sat on the deck off the kitchen facing our neighbor's back fence and some trees. I took out my phone to catch up.

Scrolling through my social feeds and watching video clips, my mind wandered to work. The guys would be busy today. I should be sick of Wild Adventure by now, but weirdly enough, I wasn't.

A text notification appeared. From KJ.

My heart raced.

KJ: Hey girl. What's up? Coming to the wave pool today?

Me: I'm off today.

KJ: [emoji sad face]

An overwhelming sensation filled my chest. KJ Keene sad-emojied my absence.

I let the feeling sink in. KJ liked me. He wanted me around.

KJ: Uncle Frankie's in today. Want me to talk to him about your job?

And with a word to KJ, he could get me on his side of the park. No more exhaust fumes, no more Antarctic parking (in distance, not in temperature), no more outsider status.

When I closed my eyes to imagine Wild Adventure, I pictured the Go Zone. Maybe because I was used to being there.

My fingers grazed the keys. I typed, then erased, typed and erased.

It didn't feel right to ditch the Midfits.

My last image of Jonah from Craig's party came to mind. The look on his face at seeing me with KJ's arm across my shoulders. Not shock or surprise. Disappointment? Something that held shades of hurt. A total contrast from the look he had when we'd talked about video games and his interest in working in game development. I liked that side of Jonah. I wanted to see it more.

I sent a message back to KJ.

Me: Let me think about it.

Walking through the gates at Wild Adventure the next day returned me to my comfortable routine. I liked my day off and all, having met up with Holli and two other cross-country teammates, Deja and Jasmine, but a thrill ran through me at what the day might bring at Wild Adventure.

The thrill subsided pretty quickly as I organized helmets in the racks. The helmets were a mess and a line snaked from the pit to the pathway connecting to Final Lap.

Hold up. This level of traffic matched what we brought in at night, not during the day. Business had picked up.

A group of drivers were out on the track with Nando and Audio monitoring. Jonah hadn't been in the break room and I didn't see him around, unless he drove laps with the park guests. I hurried to get helmets cleaned off and prepped for the next drivers.

Nando headed to my station. He had a fresh haircut with details shaved into the sides—little racing stripes above his ears.

"Nice hair," I told him.

His braces glinted when he smiled. "Thanks. I'm hoping to catch the attention of a fine lady."

I pressed my lips together. "Do you have a fine lady in mind?"

"She works at Final Lap. Mariela. She goes to Ginsburg East. As you know, I go to Ginsburg Catholic and my parents forbid dating."

"Jonah goes to East. Does he know her?"

"Probably not." His eyes popped open. "Never mind me, I can't believe you took Jonah as your *date* to Craig's party!"

"Um, that is *not* what happened. I asked Jonah to come with me as backup. You know, like a wing man. He told me no and then showed up there on his own."

"He and Craig go way back."

"I know that now. He didn't say anything to me at the time. Anyway, we talked a little bit. I didn't realize he was into making video games and wants to develop them as a career."

Nando's brow furrowed. He seemed confused by what I said. "I knew he played games, but not that he makes them."

"Oh." If anyone knew details about Jonah outside of work, I'd suspected it would be Nando. Possibly Blender, but Nando was way more chatty and able to get people talking. "Weird. Maybe it's a new interest."

"Or maybe he only told you that." Nando whistled as he wiped down the counter with cleaning solution.

I suspected the whistling covered up something more. "What aren't you telling me?"

"Me? Nothing." More whistling.

"Just so you know, KJ invited me to that party personally and has been texting me. He put his arm around me, and Chelsea went nuclear."

Nando stopped cleaning. "You and KJ?"

"He wants to get me back on the other side of the park." I watched for Nando's reaction.

He looked at me for mine. "Is that what you're going to do? Go back?"

"I don't know."

"Hmmm."

"Hmmm what?"

"If you wanted to go, you would. No one stays in the Go Zone if they don't have to. Do you know how many flash-in-the-pan part-timers we've had since I started?"

"At least a few based on what you've told me."

Karts zoomed by for another lap, the sound momentarily halting our conversation.

"They last a few days," he said. "A week tops. You've already been here for three."

Had it been that long? "Well, I at least wanted my first paycheck. And now I'm used to how everything works."

Nando grinned. "You like it here. You like us."

"Of course I like you guys. You're awesome."

I couldn't be sure, but it looked like color seeped into Nando's cheeks. "You're the coolest of the cool kids to ever come to our side. Most of them turn out to be jerks. Or they get out as soon as they can."

I nudged him with my elbow. "You're pretty cool yourself. Maybe there's a reason I'm not itching to get out of here."

"Oh, there is. I know exactly who he is."

"He?" Oh, wait. I got it. "You think I'm all swoony for Blender, don't you. That I want to be one of his harem. He *is* hot, I won't lie. But he's old enough that he's more like an older brother."

"Not Blender."

A tingle spread through me. "It's not...do you think, me and you?"

His eyes widened. "Elena, you're gorgeous and by far my coolest female-identifying friend, but no offense, you aren't my type."

I swallowed a laugh. "I can't wait to see Mariela so I know your type."

His eyes went unfocused as his imagination took him to another place. "She's...perfect. Anyway, quit being dense. We both know you have a thing for Jonah."

"I do not!"

"Your immediate rebuttal says otherwise."

"That makes no sense. Also, what does rebuttal mean?"

"It's like a counter-argument. Yours is weak." The karts were now headed into the pit to change drivers. Nando zipped around the counter to corral the crowd.

"This isn't over," I called after him.

Chapter Eleven

♥

Jonah appeared from out of nowhere. There he was, right when needed, to assist in moving new drivers in and funneling out those who'd just finished. He didn't look windblown so he hadn't been driving with the last batch. He must have been around somewhere.

I worked helmet distribution until the new crop of drivers had what they needed. Nando did the safety speech and ran the countdown. The new drivers took off.

"Jonah." I jogged to him. I didn't often say his name out loud and especially not to him, so it came off oddly personal. I joined him at the edge of the pit's overhang facing the merge. "Thanks for coming out the other night. It was good to talk to you. I'm sorry I didn't get a chance to say goodbye." Because Jonah had taken off without telling anyone.

He had his hands stuffed into his shorts pockets, watching the track. "You didn't need me."

"I appreciated that you came. It meant a lot since I went alone and didn't know people."

"Looked like you knew people just fine."

He meant KJ. "I think it was good of you to make an appearance at the party."

Jonah turned to me. "I'm not friends with them, Elena. I won't ever be."

Hearing him say my name sent a hot ripple through me. "Chelsea is a drama mama—ignore her. Craig said he liked seeing you there."

"Craig is different. But not that different in the end."

Maybe Jonah had a story with Craig similar to mine with Chelsea. "Have they hurt you? KJ, has he hurt you?"

Jonah bristled. "I'm fine."

That wasn't an answer. Or at least not the one I wanted. "I know what it feels like to be betrayed. It's terrible. I only want to help."

He paced the strip of concrete between where we stood and the tire barrier. "You have helped. You see that line, don't you?"

The line of waiting park guests remained as long as when I'd first clocked in, even though a whole group had just gotten into karts. "Has it been like this all day?"

Jonah nodded. "And yesterday."

I hopped up and down. "Something must be working if we're getting more park guests here."

"Nando and I went to Final Lap. Made some connections."

I mimed cleaning out my ears. "What did I just hear? You made connections with other park staff?"

He nearly grinned. "Nando's cousin works at Final Lap. Nando promised me free fries if I went with him."

"Smart guy, that Nando. So, you talked to them about promoting the go-karts?"

"Their lunch and dinner rush is busy, but they're dead in between. We worked a deal to give coupons for discount food during slow hours to park guests waiting in our line. In exchange, Final Lap will give out a priority lap pass to guests if they delay their seating request for a half hour during a rush. For traffic flow."

"We have priority lap passes?"

"We do now." He dug out laminated tickets from his shorts pocket and fanned them out. "This is a prototype I made. Blender's got a guy who works at a printing company. We'll get more."

Ignoring that these passes were unofficial at best and fraudulent on the worse end, the idea was genius. "This is incredible. And the turnstile into the pit counts each of the guests so the numbers are tracked. If this works, I bet Wild Adventure would put these into production themselves. It's a good idea."

My heart warmed that he and Nando improved on Operation Zone War when they'd originally dismissed it. Jonah may have been tricked into helping, but enlisting Blender's contact for printing meant more of them were involved now.

He headed back toward the pit. "If you want to visit the other park, it's probably good to go before business picks up even more."

I caught up to him. "I'm good. Another group got off the tram. I have the feeling you'll need me."

Jonah shook his head with a smile edging his lips.

·♥·♥·♥·♥·♥·

I ended up heading to the other side of the park after the rush eased up. I took the golf cart this time since it was faster.

To Jonah's credit, I was grateful for the practice driving the golf cart around the Go Zone with Nando before trekking off on my own. The brake pedal liked to stick. The Midfits always had their little hacks to get around our broken stuff.

I parked near the water park entrance alongside another Wild Adventure golf cart. I veered right to the shaded entrance of the Log Jam ride. Technically part of the water park since it involved water, the Log Jam seemed more like a regular ride. Groups of two sat in a hollowed-out log boat and rode through a winding river on a track. Two big dips during the ride guaranteed splash damage.

Craig noticed me and waved in a way that looked more like a salute. "Hey, Elena. Are you seeing any more visitors on your end?"

"We are, actually. Are you sending people to us?"

"Affirmative. When the line backs up to this point, I've been telling guests there's no wait at the go-karts. The tram is right there, so it's not a hard sell."

"That's great, thanks."

"Honestly, a lot of them end up staying if they're in swimsuits already. Or they say they'll come back later, but plan to stay on this side." He gave me a *what can you do?* look. "We're trying, I guess. Hey, so it was cool to see you out the other night. Are you and KJ..." He swayed his shoulders in a...I didn't know what that was.

I bit my lip to hold back a laugh. "Care to use words?"

"He seems into you. I wondered if there was more going on."

I gave him a light shrug. "Maybe." I stepped back to avoid blocking foot traffic. "We go to school together, so I've known KJ a while. Or, more like, we know common people. Anyway, he's a super great guy." Was I rambling? "Are you interested in anyone?"

"Yeah, but she's not into me."

"How do you know?"

His gaze darted in either direction, probably checking for other staff. "She's into KJ. It's Chelsea," he said in a rush.

"Hold up—Chelsea is into KJ?" Suddenly, so much of this summer made sense. Not in a logical way, but more like in a messy drama-llama sort of way. And I was no expert on pack animals.

Craig directed a few stragglers looking for the line entrance. "Chelsea seems like, obsessed with KJ, but I don't get that he's into her. I was glad to see him acting into you at my house."

Craig seemed to be a decent guy. Chelsea should give him a chance.

Then again, Chelsea had baggage she didn't seem willing to give up. Craig didn't deserve to be weighed down by whatever negativity she hauled around.

"You should go see KJ," Craig said. "I'd say I'd put in a good word for you, but I don't think I need to. If you could put in one for me with Chelsea..." He patted his heart. "I am crazy about that girl."

"She pretty much loathes me, or I would."

"Chelsea? No way. She's so nice."

"To you maybe." Shoot. Had I said that out loud? "I hate having unresolved issues with people, but there's something up with Chelsea. She and I were friends until my first day here. She's the one who tricked me into going to the Love Hut. I still don't know why."

"Pranks are kind of our thing." Craig said it like this was obvious and no big deal. "Just yesterday, KJ switched out the spare staff shirt in my locker with a kid's shirt from the Little Adventurer Zone. I can't exactly go shirtless here, so I was stuck wearing my soaked shirt the rest of the day after fixing a log jam." He laughed to himself. "We let stuff roll off our backs."

Maybe Craig and KJ could roll with those pranks, but this thing with Chelsea seemed more than a dumb prank. Burning coal simmered in her eyes every time she talked to me. She'd said I had wronged her. I felt bad about that, but my memory was like a blank spot when it came to thinking what I could have done. I just didn't know.

"I don't want to stand in your way," I told him. "Any issues I have with her hopefully won't affect what you're looking for from Chelsea."

"And same to you. All systems go if you're interested in KJ."

I laughed. "Okay, sure."

"Go get 'em, Elena."

I made my way to the wave pool. KJ noticed me and waved me closer. When I reached him, he ran his hand up my arm to my shoulder and squeezed. I sensed stares from a group of girls our age huddled nearby.

"What's up?" KJ asked.

"Nothing. Taking a break." I didn't need to be here other than putting in my appearance to keep up the friendly factor.

He grinned at me and the feeling drained from my kneecaps. "Any time."

We talked for a few minutes. An invisible clock ticked in my head. I needed to get back or the guys would think I ditched them for real.

On the way out, another sense of someone watching me made me stop and look back. Kids and their parents crossed from the pool to the changing rooms. *Come on, Elena. Nobody's watching.*

And then I saw her. Chelsea. Staring at me from behind a frozen banana stand.

I raised a stiff hand—my attempt at a wave.

Smoke curled from behind Chelsea as her glare settled on me.

Yikes.

Me going for KJ was all fine and good for Craig, but not the greatest development for Chelsea if she liked him too. Getting in a turf war over a guy landed last on my summer to-do list. Neither of us had a claim on KJ. I'd just liked him for a really, really long time.

And Chelsea knew that.

Maybe her obsession wasn't so genuine. Maybe she followed him around because she knew I liked him and was using him to get back at me. Again, for mysterious reasons. Mysterious to me.

I headed back to my side of the park.

With thoughts of Chelsea in my head and how I might have wronged her—and how she'd wronged me—my sunshiny social vibe faded to gray.

Chapter Twelve

My next Wild Adventure shift, I walked into chaos. Blender, usually cool and chill, buzzed in a frenzy between the karts beneath the overhang at the pit. Jonah crouched in front of a kart while Nando and Dad-slash-Mark carried gas cans.

I could barely focus on any one thing. "What's going on?"

Blender's hair spiked even spikier when he ran a hand through it. "We got punked."

"Huh?"

"Sugar in the gas tanks. *Idiots*."

I pressed a hand to my head. Who on earth mistook a go-kart for a stand mixer? "Sugar in the tank? That's a thing?"

"If you want to mess with somebody, it is. Thing is, it doesn't do what people think." He nodded to Nando as he crossed to me. "Because sugar doesn't dissolve in gasoline, there's this idea that putting it in the tank gunks it up and wrecks the engine. I won't bore you with the details of why that's not true, but somebody thought it would work. We found a spilled bag of sugar and a bunch of open gas caps on the karts. We're checking for potential damage."

"Sloppy work," I noted.

Nando wiped his hands on a greasy rag. "Whoever did this started their prank and took off when they thought they'd get caught."

Blender scratched at his chin. "Night security patrols the grounds. This place gets locked down."

"It had to be an inside job," I said. "Even so, it seems like they'd be smarter to avoid the night patrol."

Chelsea had motive. Only, I couldn't imagine her venturing to this side of the park at night. Let alone opening the gas tanks on the karts to fill them with sugar. I couldn't even imagine her carrying the sacks. Or carrying anything but a grudge.

"This one's running pretty rough," Jonah said to Blender. "We were having trouble with it yesterday, so could be unrelated."

I joined Blender for Jonah's assessment.

"I think we take out these three." Jonah pointed to three karts he had marked with blue painter's tape on the doors. "These had loose caps and are near the sugar spill. The rest don't look like they've been tampered with."

That was a relief. "So, if it's not a problem to have the sugar in there, are we taking the karts out as a safety precaution?"

"Yup," Blender said. "It's worse to have water in the tank, and we don't know what actually happened here until I can get a closer look."

He went into an explanation about checking fuel lines which I mostly followed, though I couldn't help question who would do this. Undoubtedly, staff from the other side of the park. But who?

"Six karts out of commission counting the others in the garage." Jonah's tone sounded grim. "With the uptick in guests, the wait time will suck."

My hands balled into fists. Right when we'd made progress, now a setback. The situation could have been worse, but we'd still probably lose some of our newly-earned traffic if people had to wait too long.

With the park now open, a group of guests moved toward us from the tram.

"You have those Final Lap discount coupons?" I asked Jonah.

"I do, but the restaurant doesn't open until ten."

I held my hand out. "Give them to me. I'll manage the line and watch for any issues."

Blender and Jonah drove the decommissioned karts to the garage while Nando and Dad-slash-Mark prepped the remaining karts.

The morning grew busier. A dense pack of kids in matching day camp shirts moved in a solid mass toward us. They came in from the water park path.

So. Many. Kids.

The day camp staff looked at what lay ahead. A line had already accumulated for our smaller fleet of karts. The guests didn't know the fleet was smaller, but I watched as a woman in a day camp branded visor counted the karts out loud to herself. There were way more kids than karts.

A sense of panic rose up. We needed the business, just not all right this second.

"Hi!" I said brightly. "Welcome to the Go Zone. I'm Elena. Can I help you with anything?"

The woman in the visor smiled. "Just here to ride the go-karts. The people at the water park said to start here first."

"Did they." I kept my smile full. Funny, because the water park didn't fill up until later. Someone decided to send guests here early.

Early on the same day we'd been pranked. Almost as if those two ideas belonged to the same plan.

"We're getting the first group started any second now." I glanced to the pit. Why weren't Nando and Mark moving guests into karts? They talked on the side. Nando's hands moved in animated expressions.

"Looks busy," the woman said as she physically pressed back two kids attempting a break for it. "Cody! Emmerleigh! Back in line." She looked at me. "Sorry about that. I thought this would be suitable for our group, but it maybe it's too grown up a driving course for our age kids."

"They just need to be tall as Paul," I told her and pointed to the height chart sign. From eyeballing it, most of these kids appeared tall enough. These were older kids in the upper elementary to middle school range.

The other direction from us, the tram let off a swarm of park guests.

Yike-o. We'd have a massive clog in no time. No food options open yet to direct them to. Even our sad pita stand didn't pop up until eleven.

Why didn't we have our own frozen banana stand? Frozen bananas could at least tide the kids over for a little while. And there was fruit under that chocolate dip so it was practically healthy. Factor in time to clean sticky hands and it offered a solid distraction.

We had no bananas. The hoard moved closer.

I could either freak, or act.

Actually, that gave me an idea.

The day camp staff huddled together with the kids in the middle for a strategy meeting. Meanwhile, I funneled the tram traffic to the lengthening line.

Finally, Nando unlocked the low gate separating the line from the pit. He waved guests through the turnstile.

"Now look at the line," the visor woman said to her coworker. "Let's go back to the water park."

"No." I ran up to them. "We have entertainment for your wait." I knew a pretty good selection of songs from a season of day camp the summer before Mom remarried. I had a not half-bad singing voice with a little skill I'd picked up from theater at school. It paid to be well-rounded after all. "You guys know this one?"

I started in with the song from a mega-popular musical I'd sang for West Ginsburg's Springtime Musical Medley concert. When I reached the chorus, I gestured to the mildly interested girls at the edge of the group signaling for them to join in.

And they did! Now we were all singing. Okay, three of us were singing. The visor lady looked at me like I'd lost a few screws. The rest of the kids appeared a mix of confused and horrified. Regardless, I had their attention.

I needed a surefire camp song. "How about this one?" I sang the opening lines of a call and response. This time, half the kids sang back. Bless those camp counselors, they joined in too.

Still singing, I led the group to the pit line for the karts.

Mark gawked at me. Nando bounded toward us and joined for the last line of the camp song.

The crowd ahead in line moved into the karts for their laps around the course. The camp kids would have to wait another round.

"Here's another song—" I started.

The visor lady tapped me on the shoulder. "You don't have to keep singing."

I tried not to take her dis personally. I had a lot more camp songs in my internal playlist, but I also recognized being played off stage.

I handed her a wad of Final Lap coupons, tipped an invisible hat, and peaced out.

Later, when the crowds finally thinned giving us a break, I ended up at the helmet counter with Jonah.

"You sang to children," he said.

"Their camp leader asked me to stop if that makes you feel better."

He chuckled. "It was nice."

Whether he meant my singing voice or the attempt to entertain, either way I'd take it. His comment came as such a surprise, I wasn't sure how to react.

I looked at Jonah. He stared straight ahead but didn't appear to look at anything. Suddenly, the air grew charged between us. This felt like a moment ripe with ruining potential. I tended to blurt weird things when no one else talked. Or I talked over them even if they were talking. Why was silence so darned loud? I resisted the urge to fill the endless void.

Jonah shifted, causing his shoes to squeak against the floor. "You're quiet."

I let out a breath I'd absolutely been holding. "It's *really* hard."

"You were trying to be quiet?"

"I didn't want to annoy you with useless blabber."

"Why do you think what you say is useless?"

"Well, *I* don't think what I say is useless. It's usually other people telling me that. Or tuning me out. Sometimes they're offended by what I say."

"Those people are stupid."

My head turned like a clock hand. "Say what, now?"

"People are stupid if they're offended by you. Sometimes things need to be said."

"Oh. Right. Okay." I swallowed back the urge to dismiss what came across as actual praise. I spent a lot of time questioning if I'd ruined circumstances by running my mouth. There had to be a balance between watching what I said and holding back entirely.

Now the silence came with more peace. I didn't feel like I had to fill the empty void. I sanitized helmets and the counter, letting my thoughts wander.

I rewound through everything I knew about the prank. "We have to find out who did this to us," I said to Jonah since he hadn't left.

"Or not."

I spun toward him. "We *have* to. What they did was dangerous. Park guests ride in those karts."

"What Blender said about the sugar is true. We only took out those tampered karts to be absolutely sure something else wasn't done to them. The rest of the fleet passed our maintenance checks."

"Whoever did this, the goal wasn't to embarrass me in the Love Hut or switch out someone's T-shirt at the pool. They could have hurt a guest. If that happened, we'd get the blame. Most likely Blender or you." My focus drifted to the garage beyond us. "I think this was more than a simple prank."

Jonah made a low grunting sound.

"This could start rumors that our side isn't safe," I pointed out. "If we get complaints... I don't want this to get out of hand."

"What are you suggesting?"

"I don't know. We need to be on guard. Maybe alert the night security about our concerns."

He nodded. "I'll do that. We have security cameras in the pit, but one is broken. I'll fix it."

"You mean you'll let Terry know to get it fixed?"

"I mean I'll fix it. So it actually gets fixed."

Jonah walked around to the outer side of the building. A camera behind a plastic cover pointed at the strip where the karts parked. He grabbed a stool and slid a screwdriver from his pocket to remove the mounted camera.

I needed to keep some of these recent events to myself. If my parents found out about tampered gas tanks and broken security cameras, I'd be pulled out of here quick.

With the sun high in the sky that afternoon, I feared total skin meltdown. Why had I thought an outdoor job would be fun? Oh yeah, I expected I'd be stationed in the kid's park where shade covered nearly everything and misters gently cooled you with light puffs of water.

I didn't have much time left on the clock and tried to stay positive. A steady stream of guests came through the Go Zone, which was great, but the fumes and the heat made me queasy. I slipped behind the counter by the helmets, but this was all open-air and the humidity wouldn't quit.

Nando handed me a cool rag. "You should take a break."

I immediately placed the rag on the back of my neck. My shoulders sank with relief. "This feels so good. Thanks. By the way, I just took a break."

"Drink some water then." He nudged a water bottle on the counter closer to me.

"We should call you Dad instead of Mark. You're always taking care of us."

Nando straightened, seeming to stand a little taller. "I do my best. You should have seen those khakis Mark had on, though. They were *pleated*. And he used one of those braided leather belts." His nose scrunched as he shook his head. "Poor guy."

That did sound pretty dorky for anywhere outside of an office cubicle. Even then.

Nando perked up. "Hey, Mariela at Final Lap gave me her number."

I gasped with excitement. "She did?"

"Actually, no. But I'm on a text chain with her and some of the kitchen staff. I saved her number. I'm working an angle to start a side chat."

"Sounds promising."

He stroked his chin. "I'm convinced if I had a beard, I'd be unstoppable."

"Have you tried to grow one?"

"I *am* growing one."

Not a single hair appeared on his bare face. I squinted past him. "Who's Jonah talking to?"

Apart from the line, Jonah knelt to eye level with a boy aged nine or ten in a wheelchair.

Beside me, Nando's own water bottle slid out of his hand. It bounced off a box on the floor and rolled past me. He scrambled to pick up the bottle, but condensation soaked the outside of the container and it flew out of his hand again.

Finally, he got hold of the bottle and stood. "That's him. That's Cayden Moore."

The kid Jonah saved. "Wow, he wants to come back after the lawsuit?"

"I've only seen him one other time, but it was by the offices." Nando seemed to be holding his breath. "His mom is there."

A white woman with dark hair pulled into a ponytail stood farther back checking her phone.

The kid, Cayden, had sandy brown hair spiked in front and wore a bright orange T-shirt with a character from a popular video game. He talked excitedly and handed something to Jonah.

Jonah, who'd been laughing, shifted his expression to more serious. He nodded, reading the papers Cayden handed him. Then he leaned in to hug Cayden with one arm, half standing, half crouching.

Cayden beamed.

"Seems like things are okay between them," I said to Nando.

"Yeah. He doesn't talk about Cayden much."

No surprise there.

Another hour later, Jonah and I ended up clocking out at the same time. Instead of ignoring me like usual, he waited for me at the gate and held it open for me.

My heart danced a little jig. As corny as it sounded, I liked when guys did the polite good manners thing. Most guys at school were so busy belching and being gross the idea of holding open a door for anyone didn't occur to them.

I'd never seen Jonah burp loudly or do much of anything loud.

I passed by him through the gate.

"So that was Cadyen Moore," I said once we were out of Wild Adventure and in the parking lot.

He blinked, then understanding seemed to set in. "Nando?"

I confirmed in a nod as we walked toward our cars. "How is he?"

Jonah gave the faintest grin. "He's good. He doesn't get out here much, but he's been begging his parents to come. He always says he wants to see me in action." He shook his head, his cheeks a little flushed.

"So, you talk to him often?"

He half-shrugged. "Mostly we talk through an online forum. He's helping me with my game."

"Your video game? *He's* helping *you*?"

He laughed. "The kid's practically a genius. He told me he liked making web games, so I looked into it, figuring I could help him out. He's way past me in that department. He's the one who showed me the forum."

"Oh wow. I thought your aunt is the one who inspired you to make video games."

"She's part of it. Cayden, he's a cool kid. He gets an idea and just goes for it. Even if he fails, he shrugs it off." He slowed so our strides matched. "His whole life changed last year. He used to play sports. Soccer and baseball. He's still active, but life is different for him now."

I had so many questions. But like Nando and everyone else said, Jonah never talked about Cayden. Assuming what he'd told me was common knowledge, I doubted I'd get much more.

"Is that you?" Jonah asked, nodding toward my car.

He'd remembered. "Yup."

"You've got a flat."

"What?" I looked closer at my car. The back slumped a little to one side. The rear passenger tire, sure enough, showed a flattened section along the bottom. *"Dangit."*

I took my phone out and swiped through my contacts to call Mom. Except she'd tell me to call my stepdad. No way could I do that. Besides the fact he was probably in some meeting and wouldn't respond for an hour, I didn't need to give him yet another tally mark in his hot mess tracker. I was certain he had a tracker—he was an organized guy. The more irresponsible he saw me, the greater chance he might regret tying himself to our kooky little family.

Which was a lot to think about when dealing with a flat tire.

Two spaces over, Jonah opened his SUV's trunk. He took out a jack and small black duffel bag. "Can you pop your trunk?"

"Why?"

"For the spare."

I sighed. Jonah was here and offering. It would be stupid to turn him down. "Fine."

Scrambling for my keys, I hit the trunk unlock button. I followed Jonah and swung the trunk open wider.

Jonah whistled low. "That's a lot of stuff."

I grabbed two sweatshirts and an old cross-country T-shirt and jammed them into a decorative soft-sided cloth bin intended for keeping those very things contained. The bin was full of other junk, so I smooshed everything down farther and set the bin on the ground behind my car.

"What's...this?" He held up the top half of a cardboard cut-out of a famous Korean boy band.

I took the beautiful boy faces from him and set the cutout against my bumper. "I won that fair and square."

Pushing aside notebooks from last semester, a blanket, old running shoes, and a plastic super soaker gun, finally we could see the outline of the secret panel. At least that's what I called it.

Jonah lifted the panel...to nothing.

"Where's the spare?" I nearly shouted.

He looked at me. "You don't know?"

"I've never had to use it before." I ran a hand through my hair which felt mildly crunchy from dried sweat. "I'm such an idiot. Driving around with no spare tire."

He reached in. "There's a patch kit in here. You're not an idiot. A lot of newer model cars don't come with spares anymore."

"Really? My parents would freak if they knew. I don't know if they'd even thought to check for one."

I'd classify my family as busy and well-meaning, but not always one hundred on the finer details. I'd never minded since Mom was holding down the fort after Dad left and if things were forgotten, that was just part of life. I'd learned to pick up slack where I could.

Here was slack I'd left hanging.

When she married John, a whole corner of my life fixed itself. Some kids I knew with stepparents were salty about it, but for us, it was like winning the lottery. John had money. Knowing we had stability meant less worry about the day-to-day stuff. The first time we grocery shopped after moving in with John felt like Christmas. We bought everything on our list plus fun snacks—even the name brand ones.

Once I'd gotten to know John more, I grew to trust him too. He wasn't magic or anything. He just really loved my mom and I believed he loved me and my brother too.

I couldn't blame anyone but myself for not knowing about the spare tire. I just couldn't keep track of every little thing all the time.

"I'll run back to the garage and get a manual pump," Jonah was saying.

The heat ramped up my embarrassment and sent sweat beading at my hairline. "I'm sure you have better things to do. Actually, I've got a laminated card in my glove box with the roadside assistance number. Let me get it."

"I can fix it faster than someone can get here."

"This is my mistake. It's not yours to fix."

His dark eyes softened at the corners. "You didn't make a mistake. It's just a thing that happened. And I want to do this. Will you be okay waiting while I grab the pump?"

I found myself nodding. Jonah turned sharp and jogged back to the staff entrance. He went fast, on a mission. A mission to help *me*.

I unlocked the driver's seat to air out my car even though I wouldn't be going anywhere soon. I couldn't help feeling super lame that I needed a rescue for something so basic. I worked at a go-kart track and I couldn't even take care of my own car.

Jonah returned more quickly than I expected. I joined him at the back of my car.

"Here, let me show you."

He set the pump aside and crouched closer to the tire. I crouched too and my knee grazed his. I backed up.

He ran his finger along the inside edge of the tire until he found the nozzle for the air. I watched him work. I found myself impressed by the precise actions with his fingers and how he adjusted his large frame easily to manage the angle.

His hair swung across his face and he brushed it back behind his ear. His skin was smooth and not blotchy like mine became in the heat. He barely broke a sweat out here doing physical work.

"You want to apply the patch?" he asked.

A small thrill ran through me. "Sure!" I tamped down my excitement. "I mean, yeah. I guess."

He watched me apply the patch and didn't say anything unless I asked for direction.

After I finished, we both stood.

"When your parents get your tire replaced, you can ask them to put a new patch kit back here," he said. "Probably get you a portable pump too."

A pang of worry hit. "I don't want to bother my stepdad."

Silence filled in between us.

"Is he...a problem?" Jonah asked finally.

"What—John? No, he's not a problem." I waved him off. "Sorry, that must have come out weird. John is great. Truly. If anyone's the problem, it's me."

"I don't think you're a problem."

I tapped my foot, my nerves expressing themselves physically. "I feel like I should deal with this myself. I'm trying to show my parents I'm responsible. You know, sticking with the job, taking care of what I've been given. That sort of thing. I was lucky to have you here for the help."

Jonah looked at the pavement. "I'm glad I was here too." He cleared his throat. "The place my family uses will give you a good deal. We could go now. If you have a credit card or something to pay for it."

I shook my head. My family may have had money now, but not granting-Elena-her-own-credit-card level money. "I should probably head home, but I'll take the name of the place so we can get the tire done there."

Jonah put his tire changing gear back in his trunk, including the pump borrowed from the Go Zone garage.

"It's Edmonds on 55th Street. Out by the municipal airport."

I had no idea where any of that was. "Maybe you can text me the name. Here." I slipped my phone out. "What's your number so I can give you mine?"

"Oh. Um." Jonah fumbled to remove his phone from his shorts' back pocket. "I could just write it down on some paper."

"Did you see my trunk? That paper will immediately disappear into a vortex. What's your number?"

Jonah gave me his number.

Geesh. Wasn't he used to number trading? I bit my lip. Maybe he wasn't. And especially from someone like me. An outsider who ran with the popular kids. Okay, perhaps *ran with* defied accuracy. Ran *adjacent* to.

I sent him a message: *It's me! Elena!*

A moment later, a new text appeared with the name and cross streets.

I added his name to my phone's contact list. My finger slipped to the emoji keys which accidentally added a smiley with heart eyes after the "h" in Jonah. I backspaced, saved, and slid the phone into my purse.

"Hey, thanks again, Jonah. This patch will last until I get home, right?"

He leaned back against his SUV. "Are you doubting my skills?"

"I put the patch on, remember?"

"I supervised. I don't sign off on shoddy work."

I grinned. I liked the saucy side of Jonah. The saucy side where he didn't grumble and sparks shined in his eyes. "But do you have a mechanic's certification with the Midwest Wild Adventure logo on it?"

"Paul Bunyan's certification? No, sadly, I do not."

"You should. You're Blender's go-to back-up."

"Eh, not really. Blender's like an engine whisperer. He knows cars on another level. He has a psychic connection to the karts."

"That's funny." I liked funny Jonah too. Why were people afraid of him again?

"If you're concerned, I could follow you home." Jonah coughed. "Drive behind you, I mean."

"You don't have to," I said quickly. "Then I'd really feel helpless and dorky."

"It's not dorky to ask for help. The only reason I know stuff about cars is I ask Blender a million questions."

"I bet he *loves* that." I laughed. "I can't even imagine you asking a million questions."

"Oh, I did. When I first started, I didn't know jack." He pushed his hair back behind his ear.

I imagined what it would feel like to push that hair back myself.

Wait, no I didn't. Pushing back Jonah's hair would be a severe invasion of personal space. Jonah would *hate* if anyone attempted to touch his hair.

I tingled all over. I was either having an emotional reaction to the idea of touching Jonah's hair, or mild heatstroke had settled in.

"So, uh, do you know about any other parties you've been avoiding?" I asked.

"No. Why?"

"I thought it might be fun to hang out again."

"I'm sure the new parkies would like that."

"I meant hang out with *you*."

His face clouded. "I don't think KJ would like that."

"KJ isn't my boyfriend, you know."

"But don't you want him to be?"

I started to deny it, but no words came out. I *did* want that. Only right now, standing here with Jonah, KJ was the furthest person from my thoughts. "I don't know," I ended up saying as my answer.

It was true. Something about KJ didn't feel as right as I'd once imagined. Almost like the KJ in my mind, the one I'd dreamed about for so many years, didn't match up with reality. Obviously, I knew KJ wasn't perfect—nobody was perfect. Maybe the truth of it was, the real KJ didn't match up with me. The me who didn't have to try so hard to say the right thing and be the right type of girl.

All I knew was for the moment, I wanted to keep talking to Jonah. I wanted to know more about him. About his video games, his unlikely friendship with Cayden Moore, and this funny side I only recently uncovered.

"Well, now you've got my number in case you find any trouble on the road," Jonah said.

He gave a chin nod as his exit.

I watched as Jonah entered his SUV. I returned to my car with the open driver's side door, where inside the car had leveled down from sweltering to mildly volcanic. I imagined Jonah following behind me home to make sure I made it safely. I smiled.

Maybe I'd already found my trouble.

Chapter Thirteen

♥

A totally unexpected text hit my inbox on my phone an hour later.

Jonah.

Jonah: Party tonight. Wild Adventure crew. You probably know already, but said you wanted a heads up.

A Ginsburg address followed.

Me: Are you going?

Jonah: No. Are you?

I'd just found out.

Me: Not by myself. If you wanted to go, I would go.

Jonah: You know I don't want to go.

Me: Then why are you telling me about it?

Jonah: You wanted to know about parties. I'm telling you about a party.

Ugh, so difficult! If he thought I knew about the party already, why bother with the text?

Me: I'd like to go. Last time I told you I didn't want to go alone and you showed up. What are the chances of that happening this time?

The little dots showing Jonah mid-type danced along the screen.

Jonah: I've got my magic 8 ball right here. It says: Outlook cloudy.

Me: Dang it!

Jonah: haha. Okay, maybe outlook not so cloudy.

This would be a toss of the dice. I could end up facing off with Chelsea again with no ground support from KJ, Craig, or Jonah. Or, I could trust Jonah texted me for a reason. Not solely to let me know about the party, but to check up on me. Maybe he secretly wanted to go but needed a reason. Or a nudge.

I was real good at nudging.

I ditched the couch and thundered up the stairs to my room to get ready. Before setting aside my phone to change my clothes, I sent a final text.

Me: See you there.

I waited for Jonah outside the house at the address he'd given me. Sure enough, Jonah showed up.

He parked behind my car and met me in the driveway. Shock hit my body like a dunk in the wave pool.

He spoke before I could. "You're wearing a skirt."

It wasn't an insult, but it did seem a little like an accusation. "I occasionally wear clothes that aren't greasy shorts and Wild Adventure crew T-shirts."

"Sorry. I should have said you look nice."

"Oh. Thanks." I would process this revelation in a second after I processed what I saw in front of me.

Jonah laughed at my expression. "I clean up when I can."

Clean up? Was that what he called this?

The Jonah in front of me was unlike any version of him I'd seen. He wore a short-sleeved button-down shirt in a faded dark denim material. Not as thick as denim, but rough textured with a black T-shirt underneath. Dark well-fitted jeans. No ratty cargo shorts and no Wild Adventure branding.

But most noticeable? His hair. The strands had a sheen to it, freshly washed, and swept across one side to tuck behind his ear. It appeared shorter on the other side. A definite cut since I'd last seen him. Earlier *today*.

"Did you get a haircut?" I blurted.

He ran a hand across the shorter side. "Yeah. I wasn't trying to grow it or anything. It just sort of happened."

"Like getting older."

He blinked.

"It happens without trying. Anyway, you look good." I coughed. "Your hair, I mean. It looks good. You...also look nice." Weren't we the awkward bunch.

I stepped closer, examining the cut. His hair still looked shaggy, but now with purpose instead of dark drapery parted in the middle to sometimes reveal a breathing face behind it.

Jonah looked at the ground. "I'm not used to attention like this. Are you done yet?"

I clapped a hand across my mouth. "I didn't mean to. You're not a roadside attraction or something. It's just a haircut, right?"

"Yeah. So, thanks for coming." Jonah moved toward the house and I followed. "This is Oscar's place. He used to work at the pit."

We knocked at the front door.

"Door's open," someone called out from inside.

"Jo-nah," a chorus of voices chanted when we walked in.

"Hey, guys." Jonah didn't sound exactly enthusiastic, but the sense of dread and loathing often present in his tone had vanished. "This is Elena, for anyone who doesn't know her."

Right away, I could tell this wasn't a usual high school party. Besides some of the faces looking older, the house itself had a *no parents allowed* vibe with the decor and furniture. It looked like the pictures of my cousin's apartment who was a senior in college.

But instead of light-up beer signs and movie posters like my cousin had, this place featured a shelf of action figures and posters with video game characters. The TV was the focus of the room with three different gaming systems hooked up on the shelves beneath it. Bean bag chairs and a ratty plaid couch were taken by a handful of people, some of whom seemed familiar, but I couldn't name them.

"I'm Oscar." A guy waved from the couch. "Come on in."

The TV, apparently on pause, un-paused and blared with the sounds of a video game trailer.

We made our way farther in. A girl with deep violet hair and multiple face piercings jumped up from her bean bag. "You can sit here. Or raid the snacks first."

Jonah made a beeline for the snacks.

"Thanks," I told her. "I'll be back."

On a folding table set up off the kitchen, a spread of all the major junk food groups from salty snacks to toxic-colored candy awaited. On the other side of the table, a familiar voice called out. "Hey, pit crew."

"Blender?" I did a double take seeing him outside of work. "Do you live here?"

He shook his head. "Naw. Oscar and those two guys out there do. I fix their cars."

"I heard that," Oscar yelled from the front room. "I changed those brake pads myself and you know it."

The violet-haired girl joined Blender and whispered in his ear, then gave him a kiss.

I turned to Jonah. "These are your friends. Why didn't you want to come?"

Blender laughed. "Jonah never comes to parties. Even with his friends."

"But you thought I'd want to come even if I didn't know anyone?" I asked Jonah.

Jonah grabbed a paper plate and stacked it with nachos and the pre-packaged seven-layer dip I'd brought and opened. "You know Blender."

Blender had already moved on to the kitchen with the violet-haired girl. I'd be a total third wheel if Jonah hadn't come with me.

"I don't know him well enough to hang out with outside of work. These are...adults. I'm seventeen."

"Just a few years older," Jonah said. "Besides, you get along with anyone."

My heart warmed. I definitely recognized a compliment. "Thanks."

Two more people came in through the front. More girls, but I didn't know them.

"Do they work at Wild Adventure?" I asked Jonah as I gathered a sampling of snacks on my own plate.

"No. They graduated from East last year."

The girls waved to Jonah and he raised a hand back.

Look at Jonah, being all social. "You've got *friends*, Jonah. You always act like the loner type, but you have a crew."

He grunted, but it didn't come off angsty.

"She's cute. The blonde." I covertly gestured toward the girl with a fantasy art print shirt and shredded jeans. I elbowed Jonah. "How well do you know her? Do you want to know her more?"

"That's her girlfriend with her. In case you think you're Emma."

"Oh. Well, she's still cute." I did a double take. "Wait, Emma who?"

"Emma Woodhouse."

I bit into a sour cream coated chip. "Huh. Don't know her."

He laughed. "She's pretty famous. Really old too."

"She's old? Like what, thirty? Did she used to work at the pit?"

Jonah's shoulders shook. He was still laughing. "You're killing me, Elena. I'm talking about Jane Austen's character Emma. She tries to be a matchmaker."

My brain formed several responses that never materialized. "You're making English Lit jokes at me?" I swatted him. "I've seen the *Pride and Prejudice* movie. I just didn't know about Emma. That old timey stuff isn't my thing." I studied Jonah's face. "Is that old-timey stuff your thing?"

"It was assigned reading. I didn't hate it. I liked the Merlin fantasy series better, but I'll give anything a shot. I like to be well-rounded."

Funny, I enjoyed knowing a little bit about everything too. Just in different ways than classic books.

We joined the rest of the group—minus Blender and the violet girl who'd disappeared. The TV streamed on-line videos of gamers doing what Jonah called speed runs.

"These players are intense about it," he said from his spot on the floor beside where I sat on the vacated bean bag. Of which I had to sit with my legs folded to one side since I'd worn a skirt. "It's not simply playing fast but exploiting hacks in the game to beat the whole thing with as minimal play time as possible."

"My brother and I used to do the opposite when we were bored. With this racing game, we switched it up so whoever came in last place won. But your car still had to be moving." My cheeks grew warm. "Obviously, it's not the same as those pro gamers. I mean, we were kids goofing around."

"It's the same idea," Jonah said. "Testing the limits of the game and of yourself as a player."

The video switched to clips of movies with funny songs edited on top of them. All of them were new to me and completely hilarious. Oscar and Jonah sang along to several of the songs, knowing all the words.

At one point, my side hurt from laughing. Even Jonah laughed so hard he wiped at his eyes.

Oscar hopped up. "We've got firecrackers. Let's go set them off out back."

The group moved outside. A pathway from the back door led to a detached garage connecting to a weathered stone patio. I stood at the edge of the group watching smoke curl from a smoke ball. I noticed Jonah beside me. "This is fun. Thanks for inviting me."

"Is that how it happened?"

"Come on. You wanted to come. You needed an excuse."

He made a non-committal sound.

"You can use me as an excuse to socialize," I said. "I don't mind."

Jonah grimaced, but the bite was gone. "I can't tell if you're teasing me."

"Why would I tease you? I like socializing. I like meeting new people and learning new stuff. Check to all of that tonight. After watching these videos, I can have a conversation with my brother where I understand sixty percent of what he says."

Jonah laughed. "He's a gamer?"

"He plays some. Mainly he and his friends watch those videos of better players going through their favorite games. I make fun of him for that all the time but now I sort of get it."

Oscar approached and held out an open box. "Pick one. Everyone gets a pick."

I chose a cone shaped thingy with the Statue of Liberty drawn on the side. I lit the top with a lighter Oscar handed me and set it on the stone. I stood back. Colorful sparks sprayed up and out.

I may have squealed in delight. Something about a summer night and lighting off sparks made life extra good.

Turning to Jonah, my stomach did a gymnastics routine. The look on his face caught me by the collar and pulled me in. It was like he *saw* me. This wasn't a look at me or past me or down his nose. It was like, *into* me. A connection had formed. Our own trail of sparks. I found myself moving closer.

"Do you want to light one?" I asked, my voice coming out quieter than I'd intended.

"No."

A soft laugh came out. "Okay then."

He blinked. "I'd rather you have my pick."

I returned to Oscar and the Box of Doom—those were the words actually written on the side—and chose a tube firecracker that said it sprayed fountain sparks. I lit it and stepped back by Jonah.

It popped loud and I shrieked, grabbing hold of what was nearest. Oh dear. That would be Jonah. I had a grip on his arm. His very muscular arm.

I jumped back from him.

The firecracker was still popping off, making me flinch with each loud crack.

Jonah placed a hand at my back. Maybe dumb, but I felt safer. If this cracker went rogue, no doubt Jonah would shield me with his solid body. I imagined a dire scenario—the garage exploding—and Jonah pivoting to grab me and turn his back toward the smoke and flames. One swift move and he'd shield me from danger.

"Everybody get down!" he'd shout. And they would.

"You okay?" Jonah asked.

Snap out of it.

We were close now, me and Jonah. He smelled good. Like aftershave and Ivory soap. Basic stuff, not fancy or trying too hard.

A different firecracker whistled like a shrieking banshee which you'd think would ruin the unspoken thing happening between me and Jonah, but it brought to mind my danger fantasy and Jonah lifting me out of harm's way. I breathed low and shallow.

What was wrong with me?

Jonah? Really?

My gaze settled back on him as he looked at me with intensity. With admiration, maybe. For what, I didn't know. I found I wanted to know what lay behind that gaze. What he found so fascinating about me. Because I found him fascinating. He wasn't at all the closed off, hardened beast people accused him of being. Not once you got to know him.

Yes, Jonah. *Really.*

My heart thundered in my ears louder than the fireworks on Oscar's back patio. For some reason, Jonah was telling me the time.

"You have a curfew, right?" he asked.

I blinked out of my stupor. "What time is it?"

"After eleven-thirty."

With the drive back, I'd be cutting it close for twelve. "I guess I should go."

I didn't want to go.

"I'll walk you to your car." Jonah nodded toward the side of the house where the driveway led to the front.

I waved and said my goodbyes to everyone at the party. Oscar tried to send me off with a parting package of fireworks, but explosives were the last thing my trunk needed.

The violet girl and Blender appeared at the corner of the house along the driveway. "You're leaving already?" she asked. "We didn't even get to talk. I'm Tyra."

"Maybe another time," I said. "Curfew."

"They're in high school," Blender reminded her.

She nodded. "I'm just glad Jonah left his dungeon. He finally brought a date to one of our parties."

I cringed knowing this would brutalize Jonah. "It's not—" I stopped myself. Denying this was a date could potentially brutalize him further. "Yes, totally. I told Jonah to clean up, look good, and take me out like a girl deserves."

Her jaw dropped open before she cackled with laughter. "Jonah! I love her." She slung an arm around me. "Please come back."

Blender shook his head, grinning. "You're something else, Elena."

Jonah and I continued on the driveway to the front side of the house. I only now dared to look at Jonah.

"Look," I told him, "I only said the date thing so it wouldn't be embarrassing. If I was all, *this isn't a date! Yada yada* it comes off worse than owning it, you know?"

Jonah focused on the ground as he walked through the dark. "This isn't a date."

A corner of my hope crushed inside me. "Oh. Right. I didn't mean that it was. Obviously it's not."

Only the sounds of our feet against the rough blacktop sounded until we reached my car.

"Um, thanks again for thinking of me." I fumbled for the keys in my purse.

"It's not a date because of KJ." Jonah's eyes were closed when it said it. He opened them looking everywhere but me. "I would never ask you out knowing you're with someone else. That's not the kind of thing I do."

That corner in me un-crunched a little. "I'm not with KJ. I told you already."

"But you want to be. I told *you* already."

He had. And I'd waffled on my response. Same as I was waffling now. And I was a pancakes girl.

"KJ's not here, and I don't miss him." It was a relief he hadn't shown up. He or Chelsea. I wasn't quite sure where I was going with this but spoke as truthfully as I could. "I haven't thought of him this whole night. Instead, I laughed until my sides split, I ate deliciously gross food, and lit the kind of fireworks my mom warned would blow my fingers off. This was a pretty great night. That's thanks to you."

Jonah shifted his weight, his hands in his pockets. "I'm not like KJ."

"You don't need to be like KJ. You're you. I'm liking getting to know you."

"Yeah?" He looked at me again. "It's hard to believe coming from you."

A pang hit my chest. "Why? Because I'm a loud mouth who says dumb stuff?"

"No. Because you're…funny and fearless and beautiful."

My breath left me. I'd never been told I was beautiful. Not by someone outside my family. I mean, those people shared genes with me so a compliment on beauty was self-serving. This, from Jonah, this meant something. The way it came off Jonah's lips was like a solemn truth spoken earnestly. Not something to say because it seemed the right thing to say.

He was splitting himself open right now. The nervousness rolled off him so thick I wanted to wring it dry and toss it out back with those fireworks.

I moved closer. "I wouldn't mind if tonight was a date."

"Really?"

"Really."

"I've never gone out with someone like you." He held up a hand. "I know that sounds weird. You're just you. Not some category of girl. I just mean someone who is outgoing and...bubbly."

"What do you have against bubbly?"

"Not against bubbly, I'm just not familiar with it. It's hard to grasp how we're here together. That you're talking to me."

I followed what he meant. "I've never gone out with someone like you either. Quiet. Distant. No hint of carbonation. I wish people at the park gave you a fair chance."

"I don't care about them." He swallowed. "I care about you."

Heat flushed my face, but I didn't look away. Jonah's eyes pulled me in. That deep darkness that shone with light when the right angle caught hold.

Like a magnet, I drew closer until my hands met his arms, my fingers against the skin below his sleeves. Solid, strong arms. I looked up at him as he gazed down at me.

Both of us moved at the same time. Jonah's lips met mine with a gentleness that sent sparks across my skin. He felt warm and welcoming. I breathed his scent and returned the kiss.

I pulled away and rocked back on my heels. My insides thoroughly cooked.

I smiled. "You *like* me."

Jonah shook his head in silent laughter. "You're the worst."

"You like me!" I sprung forward, landing in his arms. "And I like you."

Chapter Fourteen

♥

I'd kissed Jonah. I'd *kissed* Jonah.

For the whole ride back and when I prepped getting ready for bed that night, I replayed the moment in my head. These unexpected turns of events and how completely...perfect they were.

Something about Jonah made me feel safe and cared for. I hadn't realized I'd wanted to feel safe and cared for. I was kind of a take-care-of-things-myself type of gal. This was a new experience to enjoy the sensation of someone big and strong who could save me from a wayward bottle rocket.

Yeah, I was still having those little fantasies of Jonah jumping in front of exploding things to protect me.

Even for being a big guy, Jonah wasn't the macho type. What had my mom called it? Alpha—that's right. Back when she'd been dating—a horrible year I'd prefer to wipe from my memory, she'd said she couldn't stand alpha guys who knew they were alpha. She wanted an alpha in beta clothes. I'd just wondered why she talked about the alphabet so much.

But I was starting to understand. Jonah had the big guy presence and a reputation of being dangerous and scary, but he was kind, interesting, and thoughtful. Physically strong sure, but he seemed strong on another level too. Like strong with purpose. He mentored a kid to develop video games and admitted to being the one who was mentored. At the same time, he fixed go-karts and repaired my tire.

And he'd saved Cayden.

I wanted to know more about the Cayden Moore incident. Maybe another night when I wasn't buzzing with emotions.

We'd kissed.

I'd let this feeling linger some more. I liked it.

Jonah wasn't at all like I'd assumed. Honestly, he'd been one big question mark from the jump. Now that punctuation was filling in. And I liked what I found.

I liked Jonah.

It wasn't until I checked the alarm set on my phone moments before crashing to sleep that I saw the texts.

Jonah: *Did you get in OK?*

Me: *Yes. Home now.*

He responded nearly instantly.

Jonah: *OK. Good night.*

I smiled. Simple and to the point. Almost like he'd been waiting for me to write back before signing off for the night.

An unread text remained.

KJ: *What's up girl?*

My breath stilled. This was the guy who should have had my skin electrified and my heart doing wind sprints. Only I didn't feel energized or breathless looking at KJ's text. I felt something else. Something more undefined.

Right now, I was tired. It was late enough after my bedtime routine that I could save a response for tomorrow.

My brother Eli would finish his last day of soccer camp today, so for now, the house remained blissfully free of his pestering. Except, I wanted to talk to him about video games. About speed runs and the streamers we'd watched at the party.

"Morning, Miss Elena," my stepdad, John, called to me from the kitchen. He had on a plain T-shirt and jeans which made me do a double take. He wore business casual more often than not. "We're practically strangers these days with you working so many hours."

I wandered from the family room to the kitchen. "You work a lot too, you know."

"Eggs?" John held up a pan. "I wasn't sure if you'd be sleeping until noon." He grinned as he said it.

I glanced at the clock on the microwave to calculate how many hours until I needed to go in. "I'm working this afternoon. Plus, I couldn't sleep."

That wasn't totally true. I'd slept well but woke up to garbage trucks rumbling outside. My mind kept me from falling back asleep. Rewinding to my night with Jonah, our kiss was hard to put out of my thoughts.

"Yes, to eggs," I told him.

He cracked another egg into the pan. "You're right, I've been working a lot. I didn't imagine this summer going this way, to be honest. My company has been through a lot this past year and we're doing our best to come out ahead. I'm sorry if I haven't been around much."

I found juice in the fridge and poured us each a glass. Good old-fashioned orange juice and not the midnight green concoction with a homemade label that Mom drank. Blech.

"How's your tire holding up?" he asked.

"Oh, it's good." I'd had to tell him and Mom about the tire patch since it was meant as a temporary fix. "Thanks, by the way. For the tire."

"Not exactly the dream gift you were hoping for, huh?"

My family buying a new tire pre-John would have set us back. One single tire cost *hundreds* of dollars. If not for John, I wouldn't have my own car to drive in the first place. More things meant more money spent taking care of them.

I took out plates and forks for the eggs and dug out the bread loaf for toast. "It's appreciated all the same."

"Lucky you had that fellow there to repair it. What did you say his name was?"

"Jonah."

"Jo-*nuh*" He annunciated his name, trying to make me laugh. "He works in the water park too?"

"Uh, no the go-karts."

"Hmm, aren't those all the way over on the other side of the park? It's been a while since I've been out to Wild

Adventure, but I remember those karts. Dangerous, but fun."

"Yeah but we—" I stopped myself as the first round of bread jumped up from the toaster. This was not great. John assumed I still worked in the water park. That was day one and done stuff and he didn't know? Why hadn't mom told him I'd gotten the boot? She'd said no secrets.

No, this didn't bode well. If Mom kept this under wraps, she must have not wanted to stress John with my drama with him working those extra hours. The last thing he needed was to worry his stepdaughter spent her days with a bunch of gearheads on the neglected side of the park.

Mom wasn't around to ask. I needed to say *something*.

I could either go with his line of thinking or 'fess up I'd been working the go karts all these weeks. I couldn't believe it hadn't come up. Or that he hadn't smelled the gas fumes on my clothes.

Before I could decide which way to go, John served up the eggs on our plates on the kitchen island. "I meant to ask you. Do you know a boy by the last name Keene? He'd be your age or a year ahead at West Ginsburg."

"KJ? Yeah, why?"

"I've got a business deal going with a new company and met his folks. Nice couple. They said their son works at Wild Adventure."

"He does, yeah."

"Excellent, so you already know each other." He wiped his hands on his jeans. "They'll be at the company picnic next weekend."

"Company picnic? Sounds interesting. How does that work?"

He looked at me, puzzled. "You'll see for yourself. It's a family picnic event at a park. Food, games, prizes. You know, that whole thing."

The eggs hung out on my fork halfway to my mouth. I didn't know that whole thing. My Mom, and Dad before that, hadn't worked places where companies offered summer parties for their employees and their families.

"I probably have to work. KJ probably does too."

I rewound the conversations I'd had recently with Mom and winced. She *had* mentioned something about John's job having an event. In my head it went *something something* company picnic *something something* ask for the date off. *Crap.*

"I'll figure something out," I added quickly. John bought me a tire and now I was withholding the details about my job. The least I could do to not be a problem was to go along with this family picnic thing.

His shoulders eased. "Hopefully, you can swing getting the date off. It'd be great to show the Keenes how our merger would be good not only for their business, but their family. Having you there and knowing KJ, even better."

"I doubt I'll do much good for a business deal."

John shook his head. "You'd be surprised how much a family can influence business." His eyes crinkled at the corners more than my mom's since he was older than her. Six or seven years, which had seemed like a lot when I'd first heard.

To me, older was KJ, being a graduate and me still being in high school. Or however old Blender was.

"Your mom might not have told you this," he said, "but she was held back from a promotion at her last job. The manager said she was too stressed raising you and Eli on her own. Which is ridiculous."

"What?" I nearly spit out my juice. "Who does that?" She'd been stressed because she barely made enough money to pay our bills. A promotion would have solved so many of our problems.

"I'm only telling you because she's out of that place now. They wanted someone who would work nights and weekends but not pay her a competitive salary. Good thing for her, she found a better company."

"And she found you," I added with extra cheese in my tone.

My mom worked for a company that John's business networked with—whatever that meant—so she didn't work directly for John or anything.

"The irony is she ended up remarrying anyway." He smiled a bit self-satisfied at that. He was so goo-goo eyed about my mom same as she was about him. "What I'm talking about with the picnic is to show families we support them. We don't want people working endless hours at the expense of seeing their loved ones." He held up a finger. "I know this sounds like I'm being hypocritical since I'm the one who's been working a lot." He sighed. "My hope was I could do this so other people wouldn't have to. At least until we got back on track."

No wonder Mom didn't want to pester John with details about which zone I worked in at an amusement park. The guy shouldered a lot of responsibility. And here I thought kart safety checks felt like a big job.

"I'll be at the picnic," I told him. "Wait, Eli has to go too, right?"

"He does."

Ha. If I had to suffer, so would he. "Don't worry. We've got you."

Rain pelted down, preventing riders from driving the course. Mark-slash-Dad and I hung out beneath the pit's overhang listening to the rain clash against the metal roof. A small group of park guests huddled beneath it with us, a few wearing the temporary plastic ponchos sold at kiosks on the other side of the park.

"We'll start the karts when the rain lets up," Mark told them.

Wild Adventure remained mostly dead today because of the weather. Time passed slower than a Friday afternoon in Earth Sciences.

Nando appeared. "Did you see the latest numbers?" He slid a flyer across the counter. "We're in second to last place in the park with guests."

I snatched the paper. "Where did you get this? Who verified these numbers?"

"It's from Terry," Mark responded. "We had an opener meeting today before your shift started."

"But the passes and all our work with Final Lap." None of it was working. The water park still had double the number of park guests going through their gates and buying food at their stands. "Someone is messing with us and with those numbers. First, sugar in the tanks. Next, who knows!"

"*But*," Nando pointed out with emphasis. "Terry is happy because the surges to the water park are evening out. Here are more charts." He flipped this sheet over. "The whole point of the initiative was to reduce clogged lines and overcrowding, which is already happening. It *is* working."

I scanned the data which displayed in bar graphs and point plots on a grid. "This is way more detailed than I expected."

"Terry is in grad school," Nando said. "He took a stats course last semester and is stoked about using charting software at the office."

I looked up from the paper. "How do you know that?"

He leveled a look at me. "I make it my job to know." He winced. "Ah, my lip got caught on my braces."

My fingers flew to my own lips in empathy. "Braces are the worst. I had mine in eighth grade."

Nando sighed with the collective drama of a theater camp on opening night. "People *love* to remind me how much younger they were when they wore braces. I'll add you to my list."

"Do I go on a plotted graph?"

His eyes narrowed. "I would shove you but I fear you now that Jonah's on your side."

"He was your friend first."

"As a friend, sure," Mark said with a fair amount of sass. Mark rarely commented in our conversations, so this surprised me enough to stare incredulously at him. "What? I'm part of the group too. I can be part of things."

"So anyway," Nando continued. "Your plan is working. We have more guests on our side. Brav-o."

Only it didn't feel like winning. It didn't feel like nearly enough. "I want the Go Zone to be at the top. I want the rest of the park to remember us, that we're not forgotten. If we aren't last, who is?"

"The pita stand."

Also in the Go Zone. Great. We were dead last in popularity with the park guests and the park staff.

Mark paced toward the track, then circled back. "If Terry's happy, he stays off our back."

"I guess." I'd been thinking Terry needed to be more on our backs, or at least take a trip to see us. Maybe fix a broken security camera so an hourly wage worker didn't have to do that on his own time.

Speaking of, Jonah arrived through the employee gate to start his shift as Mark switched out. He crossed to us, his hair wet and back to covering his face, though less than usual coverage given the haircut.

"How many guests are waiting?" he asked as his greeting.

I gave him the number without looking at the line. I'd already counted them in the span of time we'd been standing here.

"Once it lets up, let's get two of us out on the track to check conditions."

Nando saluted Jonah. I watched Jonah for a sign of change since *hello*—our lips had mashed together and now we were talking as if that hadn't happened.

He caught my eye and smiled a very Jonah smile, so subtle I almost missed it. "Hey, Elena. How are you holding up?"

"Good."

I gripped the counter to ground myself. The urge to run to him and throw my arms around his neck came strong enough that I had to hold on to something.

Get a grip, lady! Literally!

Jonah headed inside to the break room leaving Nando and I alone. Well, alone except the park guests, some of whom were ditching the line and making a dash for Final Lap.

Nando leaned an elbow against the counter. "So, you and Jonah, huh?"

"How do you know everything? I haven't even... who would have told you?"

"You just did."

I pressed my lips together. "I told you nothing."

"I watched your face when he came in. Don't ever play poker. You'll lose."

I rolled my eyes. "What did my face look like?"

He made his eyes go dreamy and his gaze all dopey.

I folded my arms. "I did *not* look like that."

"No, you're prettier than me. But you definitely had a la-la look on your face. And he's definitely into you."

I scrunched up my nose. "I don't know how you got all that from our interaction. He barely acknowledged me."

"Are you kidding? He asked how you were doing. By name. What more do you want? I didn't even get a passing grunt."

The sound of a motor coming toward us caused me to turn. A quieter motor than the karts. A golf cart.

With KJ driving.

He hopped out effortlessly and sauntered toward us with a big wide grin, scanning the area as he approached. "Hey, Elena. Want to get out of the rain?"

"I'm already out of the rain." I pointed at the roof.

Nando snickered from behind the helmet counter.

Shoot. That came out snarky. "What are you doing here?" Dangit—not better. "I mean, it's nice to see you here in these parts."

He slipped a hand through his dark hair. "We need someone at the wave pool after a call-in. It's under a shaded stand. I thought I'd rescue you and bring you back with me."

"Oh. Thanks for thinking of me, but I'm on shift here, so...."

He nodded toward the parked karts. "None of them are running."

"They will be when the rain lets up. Are people in the wave pool?"

"Yeah. We don't kick them out unless there's lightning. Not as many people are swimming, but since they're already wet, a lot of them don't care. It's still hot out."

If I left with KJ, I could work an angle directing guests here when the lines grew long. Going to the other side helped fulfill OZW. It would get us moving up those ranks.

Also, this was KJ. He'd offered to rescue me. Hadn't I just been daydreaming about being rescued?

Yeah, by Jonah.

I never even texted KJ back from yesterday. I couldn't think of what to say. And to be honest, his *hey girl* left a lot to be desired.

Or maybe I desired someone else.

KJ's bright expression began to lose footing when my response stalled.

"It sure is nice to see you," I started. "I don't think it's a good idea for me to leave." Because I didn't want to. Logic told me to go. I didn't care about logic at the moment.

KJ lowered his voice. "Elena. I told you I'm working on getting you out of here. Don't you want to?"

"She said she doesn't want to go," Jonah spoke up, now back from the break room.

KJ straightened. "I think Elena can answer for herself."

Jonah stepped beside me. "She did. You didn't listen."

A low whistle came from Nando, lurking nearby.

KJ let out an exasperated breath and looked at me. "Maybe I misunderstood what's going on here."

I couldn't miss the hurt in his voice. I reached for him as he turned to leave. "Wait, KJ. I'm sorry. It's just, I take my job seriously. I don't want to leave our crew short. When the crowds pick up, we'll need to shift out for breaks. We're already on our own enough without any support."

"That's exactly why I'm trying bring you with me," KJ said with more intensity. "We want you on our side. I feel bad about what happened that got you sentenced here. It was a prank gone wrong. It shouldn't have happened."

"It's not jail. It's a job." My heart raced. "KJ...maybe it's best if you—" I wasn't sure I could say what I needed. "Maybe we can talk later. Please."

KJ looked from me to Jonah and back again. His eyes sparked. "And I'll see you next weekend." His fingers formed little handguns he fake shot. "Company picnic thing?"

"Yes. Right." I fake shot my own finger guns back.

He returned to his golf cart and drove off as the rain dwindled to a light mist.

I let out a breath and turned to Jonah. "Awkward."

He watched me with shifting expressions that would have seemed minor on anyone else but came across as hugely significant on Jonah. Reserved, confused, relieved, a little angsty. I was for sure catching some angst.

Chapter Fifteen

♥

Even a drive around the track couldn't shake off the feeling I'd hurt KJ. I'd been following him around for months, watching his baseball games, hanging out with his friends. I could have worked anywhere, but I'd interviewed here because KJ worked at Wild Adventure and I'd wanted to be close to KJ.

And now? I'd sent him away.

What was wrong with me? I finally had a taste of what I was aiming for, and I'd reversed course to a guy who barely spoke and whose life remained mysterious.

I clearly needed a kick in the pants.

My trip around the track wasn't intended for racing, so I kept my eye out for debris or large puddles hazardous to park guests. I noted three puddles of concern and memorized markers near each.

Back at Pit HQ, our crew devised a plan for managing guests and the rain for the remainder of the day. Focusing on work kept my mind off everything else.

At closing, Jonah walked me out to the parking lot. My words gummed up and I couldn't think of a single thing to say.

"Is everything okay?" Jonah asked.

I made a sound that wasn't an answer.

"Today was a weird day."

Tension left my shoulders. "It was, wasn't it? Totally weird." Something about having him acknowledge this made talking easier. "Earlier, when KJ came around...I'm sorry for how that played out."

"He likes you, Elena," Jonah said.

"Yeah, I think he does." It felt surreal to admit.

"And you?"

My crush on KJ felt almost like a memory, like he was someone I used to like. Only I wasn't sure I was ready for that to be past tense. At the same time, I couldn't mislead Jonah. "I'm not sure how I feel about him."

"You guys are going to a picnic?"

I fluttered a hand. "I guess our parents know each other. It's some business thing." I stopped walking. "Look, Jonah. If you think I'm all over the place and a train wreck, I get it. If you want to forget everything from the other night and cast me off into the sea, I get that too." I stared at my dirty shoes, unable to face him.

"Which sea?"

My head shot up. "What?"

"If I get to cast you into the sea, which one?"

I let my head fall to one side. "The Aegean? I don't know. I know this is all weird and I'm annoying."

Jonah took a beat before speaking. "You're not annoying. Do *you* want to forget about what happened? Between us?"

"That we kissed? No."

He studied the ground. "I don't want to forget either. I wish you'd stop doubting yourself. When KJ comes around, your confidence disappears."

My skin pulsed. "You think I doubt myself when KJ is around? That can't be true."

"From what I've seen, it is. And with that Regina girl."

"Regina who?"

"The water park girl who's like the head of the squad from *Mean Girls*."

"*Chelsea*?" I busted out laughing. "And for real, *Mean Girls*?"

"I watch a lot of movies." He shrugged. "Tends to happen when you don't play sports as a kid and aren't the life of the party when you're older."

He didn't say it in a pitying way. More as a fact. And I didn't feel sorry for him either. I was starting to see how some of my own supposed friendships had been built on unsteady ground quick to crumble.

I stepped closer to Jonah. "I don't want to forget what happened."

"Then let's not."

Gone was his shyness. He made his move and his lips met mine.

The clatter in my head fell away. This moment with Jonah mattered right now. He grazed his hands across my upper back in a way that made me feel secure but not trapped. He tasted minty and warm. Heat pooled in my fingertips and electric current ran in my veins.

I had to step back to catch a breath. "Where did you learn to kiss like that?"

He shook his head, laughing nearly silently. "That probably came from movies too."

I stood on my tiptoes and wrapped my arms around his neck, pulling him in again. "What's your favorite movie?"

"*Star Wars.*"

"New or old?"

"The old ones, obviously. I like the newer movies okay."

"I'm trying to remember how the characters kiss. Are there any good kisses in *Star Wars*?"

"Han and Leia." He kissed me again, long and sweet.

We broke apart. "Was that their kiss?"

He laughed. "I have no idea. I watch those movies for the space fights and the droids."

In the distance, cars exited the park, their red taillights dotting the horizon. We were last out on our side with no one else around.

"This parking lot is pretty big," I said. I sure knew how to ruin a romantic mood. "Those concerts Wild Adventure used to have. Could we bring those back?"

"Uncle Frankie isn't into it. They didn't make him a profit so, no."

An idea still rattled around in my head, but for now, another kiss would do.

I'd switched a shift with Nando which sent me back to Wild Adventure the next day for an opening shift. Which put me on with Jonah. Not like I'd planned that or anything.

Okay, I'd planned it. As part of a larger deal with Nando to cover for me on the company picnic day, and it just happened to work well for me.

The skies held hazy clouds making the temperature a little cooler. Nearly perfect weather. Jonah and I ate lunch together in the break room and talked more about video games and my hatred for running.

"But you ran cross-country," he said, looking up from another incredible looking sandwich. "That's all running."

"Obviously, hating running is a big reason why I'm not on the team anymore." I gestured in the air with a sweet potato fry courtesy of Final Lap. "Yes, I knew joining the team meant I'd be running pretty non-stop, but I didn't hate running when I joined. I think hated the competitions. And all the training to shave off time from my mile. Like, who cares?"

He laughed silently and his shoulders shook. "I know I never cared about being fast. Flexibility and mobility, that's more important."

"Like yoga?"

"Like being able to slide under a car and fix it without hurting myself. Keeping in shape so when I'm sitting for hours programming games, I'm not stiff with back pain. That's why I like being here. It gets me moving around."

Behind me, the vending machine made a mechanical burp and Combos fell out. My eyes grew wide as I whipped my attention from the machine back to Jonah. "Did you see that?"

"It happens sometimes."

"That machine is possessed."

Audio entered the break room, his only sounds footsteps and the faint, tinny sound emitting from his headphones. He walked to the vending machine, plucked out the Combos, and returned outside.

I looked at Jonah. "Did he *summon* the Combos?"

Jonah stilled. "I don't know. I think you're right. Something is controlling the machine."

We theorized about the potentially possessed, haunted, or controlled-by-remote access vending machine as we finished lunch and returned to our shift.

When late afternoon hit, Jonah and I both clocked out as Mark arrived to work alongside Audio until closing.

"What are you up to the rest of today?" Jonah asked as we approached our cars.

I beamed at him. "No plans. It feels like absolute bliss."

"So, you'd probably rather go home and like, bliss out?"

I laughed at his phrasing. Then reconsidered. "Rather than what?"

"Oh, just, it's Summerfest in downtown Ginsburg." He scuffed a foot against the crumbling pavement.

"You're right. I forgot." The festival offered carnival rides, concerts, and kid's programs for nearly a week each summer. "Since we're near rides all day, it seems less exciting. Why, are you going?" A burst of energy hit. "Are you looking for someone to go with? Like now? Today?"

"I was thinking about asking."

"Ask. Go ahead and then see what I say."

He shook with laughter. "Will you go to Summerfest with me?"

A date! A right now date. "Yes. I'd love to."

"If you need to stop home first to change—"

"Nope." I popped my trunk open. "I refreshed my trunk stash after the whole tire thing. I've got like three extra outfits, a clean blank notebook, and a case of bottled water." I held out a water bottle. "My mom is obsessed with my hydration. Here, take one so she won't think I'm not drinking any of this."

Jonah took the bottle. "We can meet at the north end parking garage. The one by the library."

I grabbed clothes which I'd change into inside my car once I aired it out from heat. "Sounds like a plan. This will be fun. It's not like I go on any rides when I'm working. Except the karts."

"That feels like work now, I bet."

"Yes and no. I still think it's fun. Plus, if we go to Summerfest, we won't have to deal with the new parkies."

Jonah, he couldn't have looked prouder. "Shunning new park staff? Maybe you're one of us after all."

I grinned. "Maybe." I hoped.

I let Jonah take off first to allow me time to switch clothes. I was a pro at changing in the car. Clean drapey tank top, clean shorts, cute sandals. I peeled out of Wild Adventure and headed downtown.

Parking where Jonah suggested, we met on the street by the library. He had on a soft black T-shirt now, so he must have done a quick-change in his SUV. The sleeves hugged his biceps—not tight, but enough to show off how strong he was.

Joining him, I grabbed his hand. Jonah flinched. "Sorry—I shouldn't have—"

"It's okay. I like it. Just surprised me is all."

A wash of heat coated me. Maybe Jonah was so used to being shunned, my sudden physical touch came like a shock. How sad. It made me furious at the same time.

Gaudy light-up palm trees flanked the entrance to Summerfest. Who were they kidding? Palm trees did not exist anywhere near here.

A thought struck and I stopped short of the entry gates. "I don't want you to think I wouldn't walk around Wild Adventure with you. That I came here so we could avoid our coworkers. I mean, we *are* avoiding coworkers. The point is to get away from work."

Jonah nodded slowly. "That makes sense. I'm not embarrassed to be seen with you either."

I gasped with added drama. "How dare."

He grinned and squeezed my hand.

The evening flew by. Carnival rides, festival food, and skill games on the Midway. I held a plastic gun and aimed it at a row of targets on the far side of a counter, hoping to win myself a plushie.

I missed another shot.

The plushies with their beady plastic eyes taunted me from the prize shelf.

"One more shot," Jonah said.

I focused, steadied my breathing, and clicked the trigger. *Blam!* Hit the target right in the middle.

"Woohoo! Eat it, sucker!" I danced in victory.

Jonah took in my dance without comment. "Unfortunately, hitting one target doesn't get you a prize. But I'll win you one if you want."

"Eh." I shrugged. "*Let the guy win you a prize*. It's so expected. I'd rather you win a prize for yourself."

"I don't want a stuffed animal."

"Okay, forget what I said. I want that pink one right there. The one with the mocking expression. It was eyeing me the whole time."

Jonah handed the guy his tickets and took the plastic gun. As if expending zero effort, he hit each target for each turn at the shooting gallery. The booth lit up with sound and light.

"Winner," the bored carnival staff announced after the congratulatory siren waned. "Pick your prize."

Jonah swung his head to me.

"The pink one." I pointed.

The bored guy sighed. "There's like, seven pink ones."

Finally, my communication came through enough for him to award me the pink plush animal with cat ears and stuffed fairy wings. I hugged it to my chest. Why had I said having Jonah win me a prize felt expected? This felt great. I had just the spot for this round cutie in a cupholder in my car.

"You seem to like it," Jonah noted.

"Yeah. It's cute. Thanks. Ooh look. A photo booth!" I took Jonah's hand again and directed him to a short line in front of an automated booth that took four successive pictures and spit them out shortly after.

"Pictures? Are you sure?" Jonah hung back when the line moved forward.

"Don't you want to show off your new haircut?" I reached up, tentatively, to move a strand from his eyes. He didn't flinch, so I did just that. Strand moved. My heart backflipped when my fingers made contact.

His breathing came shallow. We stood close now. The festival sounds fell away as dusk wrapped around us. On tiptoes, I landed a soft kiss on his lips.

The booth emptied out for us. "The things I do for you," Jonah said. He took my hand and led me inside the enclosed space.

I slid the curtain shut behind us. Jonah sat first and well, he took up most of the bench so I landed sort of half on the seat and half on his lap. My chest thrummed. We kissed, turning at the same moment toward each other. The camera *click click click clicked*.

We left the booth grinning like fools.

Chapter Sixteen

♥

I sat at a barstool in Final Lap waiting on curly fries and a deluxe onion dog.

"It feels so good in here." I ran my hands up and down my arms, loving the chill from the air conditioning. "And it's like this all the time?"

Mariela laughed, having set down her serving tray along the bar top. "I don't know how you work out there in the heat. And with the exhaust fumes."

I was supposed to be chatting her up about Nando, not marveling over nature's man-made wonder: air conditioning. This was my part of the bargain with Nando in switching shifts so I could attend the company picnic.

First of all, Mariela was adorable and cool. Nando had excellent taste. And Mariela would be lucky to have someone as amazing and devoted as Nando if she was interested.

Which I wasn't able to tell at the moment. Because I couldn't get over how ninety-degree heat molecules weren't clinging to my skin. And I couldn't smell any gasoline or sunburnt rubber.

"It's not so bad," I said of my working conditions.

My food arrived at the bar where staff picked up orders. If the bar was full, then we entered through the back by the kitchen. I'd come in through the front to talk with Mariela. I didn't care about the food.

"Anyway, Nando's going to love these fries. You know Nando, right? I hear you guys are on a group text."

Mariela, shorter than me with arms more sculpted than mine, tossed back her long dark hair. Hair she could leave down from a ponytail since it wasn't so hot—okay I needed to move past the heat vs. A/C conditions. "Nando? He's so sweet. He's Chico's cousin. I'm surprised they let someone so young work here."

"He's sixteen."

Her eyes popped wide. "He is?"

"Confirmed—I've seen his driver's license. He makes up for his height with excessive personality. Excessive in a good way."

Apparently, I'd taken on the role of Nando's mom buttering up this nice girl his age or something.

I traced my finger along the dulled wood of the counter. "Look, let me level with you. Nando is my buddy and I'd be lost working here without him. He has a crush on you. I think he was hoping I could help move things along, but I know that gets awkward. If you see him, please be kind. He gets heat at school and—" and from the new parkies, but I didn't want to give details in case she hadn't seen. "Anyway, he's a great guy."

Mariela considered what I said. "He does seem sweet. I'm seventeen, so I'm not much older. I just assumed he was younger. I didn't know people were rude to him."

The Final Lap staff weren't required to attend most Wild Adventure staff meetings since they had their own management at the restaurant. "The whole old park versus new park thing is so stupid," I said even though we weren't talking about park rivalries.

"I know, right? Don't those other park kids get to you? They're so snooty." She turned up her nose to demonstrate and laughed. "Like, there's a girl who actually walks around with her nose in the air."

The temptation to ask whether that girl's name was Chelsea nearly overtook me. I didn't need to add fuel to an already-fuming trash fire.

She looked past me and picked up her tray. "Sorry, I have to look like I'm working."

I stood from the barstool. "No, it's okay. I should get going."

She handed me my take-out bag to keep up the ruse of serving me, though I could have plucked the bag from the counter myself. "Thanks for letting me know about Nando. He seems like a good guy."

I waved goodbye to Mariela and delivered the food to the Go Zone break room.

Since things appeared under control, I detoured to the water park. I had damage control to do with KJ.

The Go Zone still ranked last. We needed to change that. I hated being last in anything. We needed to play this game better.

At the water park, KJ manned the lifeguard stand. I kept my distance to avoid distracting him.

In keeping that distance, I ran into Chelsea. Full-on body contact.

She dropped whatever she'd been carrying and it tumbled to the pavement and splashed against my legs.

"Oh! I'm so sorry." I knelt to pick up two yellow plastic cups that moments ago were filled with lemonade based on the tart smell and stickiness against my skin. Now my shorts and socks had their own personal tasting event.

"You," Chelsea growled. "Looking to hang all over KJ again? He's working and can't be bothered."

"I wouldn't *bother* him. I'm intentionally staying away." Distracting a lifeguard was asking for trouble. Especially at a theme park with a history of lawsuits.

She snatched the empty cups from me. "Go back to your hole."

"It's a pit, *thankyouverymuch*." I stood. "By the way, we're onto you and those sacks of sugar."

She gave me the dirtiest of looks. "I have no idea what that's supposed to mean."

"Let me clue you in. Gas tanks. Late night. The fine white grainy stuff."

"Nope. No idea."

I tried to match the dirt in her look. "Yes, you do. You and your prank-loving friends tampered with the go-karts. Turns out, sugar in gas tanks doesn't ruin the kart, but we took some karts out of service anyway. For *safety*."

"We're not the only ones who don't like you greasers, you know. The dry ride kids have their own agenda."

The dry ride kids. Well, son of a mother's uncle. This was bigger than we'd thought.

"Always quick to blame someone, aren't you?" Chelsea glared at me hard.

Ugh. This was getting so old. The rivalry. The unknown offense I'd caused her. "Chelsea, can we please just talk? I don't like what's happened between us."

Chelsea brushed her hand against her shorts and shook out the cups. "So you get to decide when to talk? Whatever."

Comebacks fired fast in my head like the shooting gallery carnival game. All intended to hit and hurt Chelsea. Only like my actual shooting, each of my imagined insults would likely miss their pop-up targets.

I was tired of messing up with her.

She didn't storm off or yell at me. Instead, she stood there motionless, maybe experiencing her own invisible battle in her head.

"When you're ready to talk, I'll listen," I said. As much as Chelsea annoyed me, I hated how I'd done something to her and didn't even remember. Regardless of setting me up in the Love Hut, I wanted to close the loop that started our rivalry to begin with.

Chelsea crossed her arms, still holding the plastic cups. "You embarrassed me in front of everyone in the theater crew. I was terrified to audition, but I did it anyway because I've always wanted to be in the school stage production. Then you got up on stage and did your thing like it was so easy. You told everyone you never practiced and didn't spend hours in front of the mirror like I did, practicing facial expressions."

I itched to interrupt, but I couldn't. I remembered now.

I'd caught Chelsea once in the school bathroom practicing different expressions in the mirror when she thought no one was watching. I did the same stuff at home and didn't find it all that embarrassing, honestly. I'd rambled about it in some random commentary to get a laugh or two backstage, trying to feel more confident at the time. All of us were nervous to audition, even if I hadn't seemed like it.

"It wasn't just that you said that." She unfolded her arms and slammed one plastic cup to stack within the other. "You demonstrated the faces as part of your little show. You made me look insane. *Everyone* laughed at me."

I didn't remember that part. "I'm sorry."

"The worst part is, it all came *so* easy for you. You got the part and bragged about not practicing while I'd rehearsed for weeks. My assignment was default chorus. I had to watch you week after week do the part I wanted. You barely seemed to care. You spent more time socializing and cracking jokes than learning your lines."

I chewed at my lip. The line learning had been hard for me. There was so much to memorize. Remembering the songs came easier than the dialogue. In the end, I figured I wasn't cut out for theater since it required so much work. Another thing I'd quit like the cross-country team.

"The whole semester I watched you not care about the thing I cared about," Chelsea said. "And you didn't even *notice*. When you told me about your crush on KJ this spring, I decided to use it against you."

I could see where one dumb thing I said snowballed into something worse.

The whole wild virgin queen scenario ran though my head again. I probably would have laughed if it had happened to someone else. I'd feel bad for them, but I might laugh. Assuming Chelsea could shake off how I'd made fun of her in front of people she cared about, that was as unfair as KJ saying I should brush off feeling set-up by the Love Hut stunt.

"I'm sorry, Chelsea. For saying it and for not noticing how what I said affected you."

Around us, park guests sloshed by in soaked flip flops going about their day. Chelsea watched them, saying nothing. She wouldn't look at me.

"I'm glad you told me," I said. "Sorry. Again."

Now I was the fool still standing when Chelsea appeared annoyed at me again. All this little chat had done was dig up buried memories that hurt her again.

I felt mentally exhausted by the time I returned to the pit. Two busted karts had been pulled aside. The line grew longer as the afternoon dragged on. Jonah had the day off, so he wasn't a distraction. I only had my own thoughts and the job I'd fought for—in a go-kart pit—to deal with.

Chapter Seventeen

♥

The good news was Chelsea hadn't tampered with the karts. If I believed her, and after our last run in, I did believe her. I didn't think her anger transferred into pranks intended to hurt the park.

The bad news? Somebody *had* messed with us, which meant deeper layers existed in this competition. The dry ride kids spanned ten rides. Some of those rides were old too, and not as flashy as the newer water park. All of which pointed to how the water park reigned supreme at Midwest Wild Adventure. And with prize money on the line, everyone at Wild Adventure was suspect.

The following days blended into one another. We worked our deals with Final Lap and on a new social media account Nando created called Midwest Wild Adventure Fan Account, where he reposted official Wild Adventure posts along with some of our own to gain interest in the Go Zone. So far, he had dozens of followers.

Dozens, not thousands. But hey, he put in good effort.

The Go Zone saw a noted uptick in guests, keeping us busy. The drawback of busy meant less time to side chat. That included with Jonah, who was becoming increasingly chattier.

"You're kind of chatty," I told him in the break room later that week.

"I am not *chatty*."

"Okay. Not the right word. Talkative. Full sentences that connect together multiple times. I like it."

He unwrapped another one of his delicious looking sandwiches. I ate a few of the extra fries Nando left for us from his recent trip to see Mariela. Who was I kidding—I ate all the fries. Nando hadn't gone there for the fries.

"Do you make your own sandwiches?" I asked Jonah.

"Mmhmm." He bit into it and a tomato peeked out.

I sifted through the recent stash of vending machine loot on the table including dry as desert pretzels and a slimy cinnamon bun.

"Are you sick of fries and junk food yet?" he asked.

"Not really. My mom makes us eat ultra healthy at home. She'd freak if she saw what I ate at work. But I sweat it all out."

"I don't think you can sweat out heart disease."

I swatted him with a paper napkin. "I don't have heart disease."

"A diet of highly processed, salty food is what gets you there."

I gulped from my water bottle. "Forget I said the thing about liking your chattiness."

His shoulders shook from a quiet laugh. I loved when I got him laughing in full body mode.

We ate for a little bit. I only mildly regretted the cinnamon bun. It tasted extra slimy and full of chemicals.

"So, you're going to a picnic with KJ this weekend."

Jonah's statement landed with a thud between us.

"I'm not going *with* him. He's going to be at a picnic with his family and I will also be there with my family. Big difference."

"Mmhmm."

"It is. He and I are friends, you know."

"He likes you and you're not sure how you feel about him."

Fair point. "You remember too much."

"Were you hoping I'd forget?"

I sat back. "No. When I said I don't know how I feel about KJ, what I should have said is I like you more." I tore at the edge of the cinnamon bun wrapper. "I had a crush on KJ for a long time. Since middle school. The ideas seventh grade girls get in their heads about cute older boys are hard to break. We're talking boy band obsession levels."

He leaned his elbows against the table. "You had a boy band cut-out in your trunk. It sounds like you might be hanging on."

I couldn't deny I hovered in an in-between place when it came to KJ. The idea of him and who I wanted him to be still held tight in my mind. Seeing him in person and having him pay attention to me, what I'd wanted for so long, it felt good.

But even more, I liked how Jonah paid attention to the words I said. He remembered things about me. And I liked the way he kissed.

I sneaked a look at him. I imagined crawling beneath those large arms taking up space on his side of the table. I wanted him to hold me. A solid hug that felt safe and grounded. And more of his kisses. I grinned at the thought.

I looked up to find Jonah staring at me. All playfulness gone.

The last thing he'd said involved me hanging onto boy bands and KJ crushes and now I probably looked all dopey-eyed.

"Jonah, you have excellent biceps. I was admiring them. That's where my mind went."

"My...biceps?" He flexed one and my neck sweat.

I gulped. "Yes."

The corner of his mouth twitched up. "Would you like to touch it?"

I stilled my breath and reached across the table, running my fingers down the cool skin of his arm.

The door to the break room closed and Audio stood in the doorway. "Gross," he said, and walked past us to the fridge.

Saturday morning. Company picnic.

I really did not want to go to this picnic. But I'd barely spent time with my family since school ended. My job conveniently took care of any free time and I'd found I hadn't minded.

Our family arrived early since John had some big-wig company title. He wanted to be there ahead of the rest of the guests.

A large tent held rows of tables with what looked like catering staff setting up. Two jump houses, horseshoes, and other games were set up along the shaded grass.

"Please meet my family," John said to a Black man in a polo shirt with the company logo. "My wife, Jen; her daughter, Elena; son, Eli."

We exchanged pleasantries. I was already bored but did my best to not look it.

"It's only one day," Mom whispered to me when John and the man he introduced us to immediately launched into work talk.

Eli already had his handheld game device out.

"*Away. Now,*" Mom hissed.

Eli slid the compact device into the pockets of his baggy cargo shorts. The second she turned her back, he'd have it out again. Or he'd find a treehouse or something to climb up and disappear.

Sounded like a good idea. "Do you know if this park has treehouses?" I asked Eli.

He gave me a stink face. "You're so weird."

"Looks like the Keenes are here," John announced.

I turned and my eyes locked onto KJ's frame loping toward us with a picture-perfect family. Seriously, the genes on these folks. His mother's black hair fell sharply along her shoulders, not a wave in sight despite the humidity. She wore light layers in varying neutral colors like you'd see in an Instagram fashion post but never quite get right when you tried the look yourself. His dad had thick dark hair the same as KJ's. A sharper jaw and seasoned skin made him look worn in a comforting way. Two beautiful younger girls Eli's age flanked their mother.

Eli stood frozen like a crashed screen on his game device. He recognized their power too.

"Here we go," Mom said beside me, bracing for impact.

It was the same tone and inflection I had when I assessed something.

The Keenes smiled at once like floodlights lighting up the racetrack. I swore I heard a "Dear God," come from John, but odds were I was hallucinating at this point.

KJ came up beside me and rubbed a hand along my arm and shoulder. "Hey, Elena. Good to see you."

Mom gaped at me. Hadn't John told her I knew KJ? What kind of secrets were going on this family?

"These are my sisters, Kassandra and Katherine," KJ said. "They're in sixth grade. And twins, in case that wasn't obvious."

"Do you know them, Eli?" I asked my brother. "He's the same age," I told KJ.

Eli shook his head, still looking glassy-eyed.

"Oh, my sisters go to private school," KJ added. "My parents wanted to move me to private once their business took off, but I didn't want to."

How easily our fates could have changed with one decision. If KJ hadn't gone to school with me, I wouldn't have ever crushed on him. I probably wouldn't have applied to Wild Adventure. I wouldn't have met Jonah. *Jonah*.

I snapped out of my daze. "It's good to meet you," I said to his sisters who smiled politely. They looked mildly interested in Eli but even more interested in Eli's handheld game system he'd taken out of his pocket. Show-off.

KJ leaned close. "We should find some place to hide out."

"I said the same thing. I was thinking a treehouse, only I'm realizing that would be pretty strange to find in a public park."

He looked toward a cropping of trees. "We could hide in the woods."

"Were you dreading this as much as I was?"

He scratched at the back of his neck. "I do a lot of appearances with my folks. Charity events and stuff like this. They've been courting businesses to merge with."

My skin tingled as I connected what he said to what John told me last weekend. This merger would mean a lot to his company and a boost after a rough period.

"Maybe we should stick with the fam. For appearances and all."

"Sure. I'm just glad someone's here I can talk to. Hey, I wanted to say sorry if I put you on the spot the other day. It was stupid of me to like, bust in and say I want to get you on our side of the park right in front of those guys you work with. Forgive me—I'm a dude and sometimes I don't get it the first time."

I smiled to cover the millions of thoughts warring to be heard first. He was right, I'd felt uncomfortable. Only I knew if he'd approached me without Nando and Jonah there, I wouldn't have changed my mind.

"Thanks for saying that," I finally said as we moved as a two-family unit toward the tent. The tent I dearly hoped provided food since my stomach led a revolt. "I've gotten used to where I work and I'm okay with it."

KJ's mother turned around then, slowing her walk so she evened up with us. "Elena, so good to meet you." She spoke with a lovely, light Ecuadorian accent. "I've been chatting with your mother. I insisted you join us at our home any time you'd like. You're such a beautiful girl."

"Mom." KJ waved her off. "Too much."

She waved at him back. "I know I'm too much. I'm your mother." She looked back at me. "KJ is headed to University of Michigan this fall. Less than a one-hour drive. Not too far, hmm?"

"Not at all," I said for the sake of the conversation. I slid my gaze to him. He smiled while also checking for my reaction. *Did* he want me to visit? I'd never visited anyone at college before. I'd never long-distanced any-thing...but this wasn't a relationship. No. I had the start of one with Jonah.

I had to remember that. Today I played nice for the sake of John's business and because I liked KJ. As a friend.

His mother absorbed back with the adults so we were left alone, now in front of a table filled with appetiz-ers. More families had arrived and lined up with plates ready to go.

"Sorry about that," KJ said. "I feel like I'll be apologiz-ing a lot today."

"And we haven't even gotten to horseshoes."

"I'll need to apologize for horseshoes?"

"After you lose." I flashed him a grin.

The picnic officially began with a word from the com-pany president from a small stage. KJ and I huddled close predicting which departments people worked in.

I pointed to a woman with frizzy gray hair wearing a long linen tunic. "She's head of HRN—that's Human Resources Nonsense."

KJ covered a laugh. "How about that guy. Bald in a sports jersey. Regional Associate Systems Coordinator Assistant."

"Nice. Or Assistant *to* the Regional Associate Systems Coordinator."

He did the finger gun motion at me. "*The Office?*"

"Yeah. My brother is obsessed with that show. John thinks it's hilarious because Eli is twelve and doesn't understand how boring offices are."

I thought I heard a shush from behind us, but who cared?

"I never want to be stuck in a cubicle," KJ whispered. "Working outside is great. I get sun, can stretch my legs, go for a swim."

"And I get go-kart fumes." I laughed.

His look turned serious. "I'll get you out, Elena. You won't have to go back there. I know you're being modest about keeping your commitment, but you've done your time."

"That's not what I meant. I was just joking." The rest of what I said became swallowed by clapping now that the speeches had ended. The masses headed to the food tables or funneled from the tent to fresh air.

"Let's get food." KJ grabbed my hand.

His skin singed like lava. I jerked my hand back. "Sorry," I said in a rush. "I just...I'm dating someone."

KJ straightened, sending his hand to his side. "Oh. I didn't know."

"It's new. And not very defined, but it's something. More than nothing. Actually, very much something." I blew out a breath. "I don't want to lead you on. I mean, friends can hold hands too, but your mom suggested visiting and…"

"You don't have to explain." KJ put another step between us. "My mother is a different story, but for me, I'm sorry I assumed."

We filed in line behind a family in matching company picnic T-shirts with last year's date. Beyond the line, tables were stacked with T-shirts I guessed featured this year's date and theme.

"Anyone I know?" KJ asked.

I focused on the T-shirts. There had to be hundreds of them. "Um." My face heated. If I kept the truth from him, he'd find out. If I told him, things would go from semi-awkward to holy tension soup in a flash.

I wasn't ashamed of Jonah and hiding that we had something would imply that.

I kept my voice light. "It's Jonah."

KJ laughed easily. "Good one."

I stared at him. He thought I'd made a joke. "No, really. We hung out at a party. Someone who used to work at Wild Adventure—Oscar."

"I've never heard of an Oscar working with us."

Why would I make up a guy named Oscar who used to work at Wild Adventure? "He worked at the Go Zone. Anyway, Jonah's a great guy when you get the chance to talk to him."

Now KJ gawked at me. "You're serious. Jonah? The beast?"

My muscles tensed. "Don't call him that. It's beyond rude."

"Elena, I told you. You don't know him like I do. Like the rest of us do. He's not a good person."

"No. He's kind and thoughtful and not because he'll get credit for it. He does those things because he cares about people. I've seen it again and again."

KJ looked ahead as we inched toward the buffet. "I believe you've seen some good, but there are things you don't know about him. He's not someone you should spend time with outside of work. I thought I made that clear."

I did not miss the parental tone creeping into his words. *I thought I made that clear* was part of the opening statement in a Mom or Dad lecture. I would not be lectured by KJ.

"What's clear is you have a grudge against Jonah."

KJ's lips thinned to an even line.

I stared at the enriched dinner rolls piled high in a bowl ahead of us. I imagined setting them on fire.

"He's hurt people," KJ said in a chilled voice.

"That's it." I left the line before I did set flame to bread.

I left the tent and aimed for the parking lot. I'd text mom an SOS and camp out by our car until my parents agreed to leave.

"Elena, wait." KJ jogged after me. "I know you don't want to hear this, but it's true."

His heat registered next to me. "Go away."

"Jonah caused the accident at the park. The one with that boy Cayden."

I stopped and faced KJ. "No, he didn't. He saved Cayden."

His head hung and he shook it slowly. "You weren't there. Saving Cayden is what people think happened. Do you ever wonder why Jonah refuses to talk about it?"

Dread pitted in my gut. "Cayden almost died. He's unable to walk on his own. It sounds traumatic and he probably doesn't want to keep explaining it."

"Or, he doesn't talk about it because he's lying about what happened."

"Jonah is in regular contact with Cayden. I saw him at the park myself."

KJ inched back. "You saw Cayden?"

"Yes. He came with his mom. Jonah and Cayden work on making video games together."

KJ let out a laugh missing any humor. "That's rich coming from him. He's lying to their whole family."

The dread grew deeper. "I don't understand. It was an accident. Jonah saved Cayden."

KJ's breath came shallow as he looked at me. "I wish that was true, but it isn't. I was there, Elena. I saw all of it. Jonah is the reason the safety feature wasn't secured. His carelessness is what hurt Cayden."

Chapter Eighteen

♥

It turned out tension soup would be served after all. While KJ convinced me to return to the picnic and eat a plate of food, I lost myself to inner thoughts for the rest of the time. I smiled when needed, but I couldn't wait to get out of there.

How could it be true? I couldn't imagine Jonah ignoring safety measures. Dude was all about safety measures. But maybe the accident was the reason he paid such close attention. And the reason he didn't want to talk about it.

He'd told me sometimes mistakes just happened. What if his biggest mistake almost cost someone's life?

It explained why the other staff acted so scared of him. Well, everyone but the pit crew. And they were the ones I trusted. But how well did I know any of those guys?

I couldn't fully believe it. Not without talking to Jonah.

By late afternoon, we headed back home. Jonah texted to check in, but I couldn't bring myself to respond.

"That KJ sure is a cutie," Mom said to me in the car. "I noticed you went off with him for a while."

I scowled. "Mom, please."

"And his family is lovely. I had the nicest talk with his mother. Their girls are Eli's age—how about that?"

I nodded to keep her off my back.

At home after a shower, I shut myself in my room. I had texts from Holli asking to go to a movie, KJ checking in, and Jonah texting again. The conversation I needed to have with Jonah couldn't happen via text. Calling him? Too awkward.

I had to do something.

Me: *Can you meet up?*

Jonah: *Just clocked out. Sure.*

Maybe this was a bad idea. Jonah could be the one lying and I'd just be setting myself up for more lies. I fell back against my bed. This was Jonah. Just because KJ put these thoughts in my head didn't mean they were true.

I pressed my fingers against my forehead. I didn't know what to believe.

Jonah: *There's a great Mexican place halfway between Wild Adventure and your side of town*

He texted the address.

Me: *I'll be there in twenty*

I pulled up to the restaurant which had an outdoor seating area filled with families and young couples. String lights sloped overhead for a backyard patio vibe. I could already smell the roasted peppers and spices coming from the open order window.

Too nervous to go farther, I hung out at the back of my car until Jonah rolled up.

He parked a few spaces down. A lightness came with his steps and his smile brightened when he saw me. "Hey, Elena—"

I pushed off from my back bumper. "I need you to tell me what happened with Cayden's accident."

His expression drained of joy. "What happened?"

"No, that's what I'm asking *you*. What happened that day at the park?"

Jonah slid his hands into his pockets, wearing cargo shorts streaked with grease, though his shirt looked fresh. "You were at the picnic with KJ today. Let me guess. He told you I caused the accident."

My breath hung by a string. "Is it true?"

Hurt flashed in his eyes. "No."

I wanted to believe him. So much. "Tell me what happened."

His eyes fell shut. "It will upset you."

"I'm already upset."

Music floated from the restaurant. A song from one of my running playlists that any other time I would sing along to.

Jonah stepped toward me but still kept some distance. "KJ and I used to run a ride together. A group of girls showed up to talk to him. KJ walked off with them and missed the next safety check. I'd seen the girls come over, but didn't notice he'd left with them until too late. I heard a scream. A kid fell in the water. I ran from my post and pulled him out. I radioed for staff to call medical. KJ came back when he saw the crowd gathering."

A chill ran across my skin. "He said it was you who didn't do the safety check."

"I know."

I rubbed the side of my face. "I don't understand. This means KJ left his post. The number one rule not to break. Why would he say you caused the accident?"

Jonah stared past me. "Seeing Cayden screaming and hurt—he freaked out. I don't think he could deal with it."

I swallowed any surfacing comments and waited for Jonah to tell me more.

"He told Terry and Uncle Frankie the ride had malfunctioned. The safety logs showed nothing had gone wrong. The safety check is a manual one. It requires a person paying attention so park guests aren't crossing the line into the ride when it's resetting."

Like the wave pool, a real human person needed to look out for swimmers, for anyone pulled under or hurt. The wave pool KJ was trusted to oversee.

"Cayden's family wanted a full investigation," Jonah continued. "KJ panicked. He came to me and begged me not to say anything about him leaving."

My head spun. "Weren't there witnesses? People would have seen that KJ was gone and you were the one who saved Cayden."

"That's why me saving Cayden stayed part of the story. Everyone saw that. Park guests don't pay attention to who's doing safety checks and monitoring beyond the line. KJ had a lot going for him. He—and his family—wouldn't let him go down."

A sinking feeling crept over me. "Were KJ's parents involved?"

"They had to be. KJ was only seventeen. They threatened to sue Wild Adventure. Cayden's parents threatened to sue the park and KJ's family for negligence." He sighed the sigh of someone who'd seen too much. "The family came to a settlement agreement. A bunch of closed-door lawyer stuff. KJ's name was removed entirely from the case. Mine was not."

"Jonah, no. Did you get blamed?"

"The settlement determined an electrical malfunction caused the accident. KJ moved to the wave pool and I moved to the Go Zone. I would have lost my job if it wasn't for the Moore family who knew the truth."

"But why didn't they fight for you? It sounds like this became your fault. That's so unfair."

"They fought for their son. That's what mattered to them. They didn't owe me anything. KJ's family hired top lawyers while the Moores had limited funds. They wanted their medical bills paid for and assurance this wouldn't happen again. The reason I don't talk about this is because I'm legally not supposed to. They were conditions of the court case."

Jonah wasn't to blame. He hadn't caused the accident. He *had* saved Cayden.

I let out a whoosh of air and nearly doubled over. "I was so worried. I'm so sorry I doubted you."

Jonah's voice came quiet. "You believe me?"

I looked at him. "Yes. I do."

He nodded, seeming to say something to himself. "I know you have a history with KJ. I didn't want to ruin what you thought about him. Or if you would even believe me. I was kind of freaking out the other day...being at Summerfest with you. Taking pictures in the photo booth. I kept thinking if you found out more, you'd never want to talk to me."

I stomped off a few paces and circled back. The way people wrote Jonah off as some scary weird dude sourced from KJ and his family saving face. The same family who wanted to do business with my stepdad.

"Does this mean I'm not allowed to say anything?" I asked Jonah.

He seemed to connect what I asked to what I hadn't said. "You can't say anything about the court case. I've already violated the agreement by talking to you about it."

Whoa, that sounded serious. "Then why did you tell me?"

He paused before speaking. "The way you looked at me when you asked—if I didn't tell you the truth, you'd never trust me. I'm kind of blown away you even do now."

I walked to him. "Jonah. I do. I may have known KJ longer, but I don't know him well. I watched him from a distance. It's not like how I've gotten to know you from sweating to death beside you on the daily at work." I laid my palms against his arms below his shoulders. "I know you don't lie. You keep things to yourself for a reason and it's usually to protect someone."

"I try to."

"I'd never want you to get in trouble. I hate that anyone believes you ignored safety checks." It turned my stomach thinking how the accident affected everyone so differently. "And Cayden...his life is permanently changed."

"I'll never forget that day and seeing him hurt."

"You *saved* him."

His jaw tightened. "The same could have happened to me. I could get distracted and a kid bypasses a barrier. I was lucky."

"No. It's not luck. You didn't walk away from your post. You don't let girls distract you."

"One girl, maybe."

"I don't want to be a distraction."

"I don't think of you as one. But we need to keep distractions in mind when we're working. The safety checks matter."

"This is why I don't think it was luck. You pay attention. You don't look for the easy way out."

He slid a strand of hair from my face. "I think KJ feels bad, but he had the money and power to make that feeling go away. I didn't."

"You learned from it." I wasn't sure KJ had.

Jonah nodded toward the patio and the voices beyond us. "Are you hungry?"

"Starving."

"I know this isn't the best start to a date, but I'd love to treat you. The open shell tacos are fantastic."

"Tostadas? Love 'em. I'll take the full meal with beans and rice on the side."

"Do I look like an order window?"

I grinned, still a little shocked from the day's revelations. "No, but I like the idea of ordering you around."

He kissed me lightly on my forehead. "I'd like to see you try."

We ate our delicious food and ended up back in the parking lot, loitering by my car.

"We spend a lot of time in parking lots," I commented to Jonah.

"My house is an option. It's just my mom and me and she's cool. I mean, for a mom."

I smiled at that. "My mom would probably make us do yoga to decompress. What's your mom like?"

"She's into her knitting club and her book club. Those make her sound old, but a lot of her club friends are younger than she is. Her nightlife is far more active than mine."

I didn't know anything about his family. "Has it been just the two of you for a long time?"

He leaned against my car. "Yeah. My dad passed away. Weird rare disease."

"That's terrible. I'm so sorry."

"I was young when it happened, so I'm used to it. But thanks." He removed his keys. "If you want a place to hang out, my house is safe."

Safe seemed an odd choice of wording. "Sure, okay."

We each got into our cars. I followed Jonah to a part of Ginsburg that wasn't that far from where I lived, but it crossed into the other school district. Weird how those invisible lines defined our lives.

I pulled in behind him to a ranch style house with bright blooming flowers lining the front walk. A cheerful yellow door faced out beside a bench swing under a covered porch. I followed him to the door but couldn't resist testing out the swing. Besides, his quiet street offered a good view of a clear night sky.

"This is real, right? Not just for looks?" I asked with my bum hovering above the bench seat.

"It's safe. Oh, and I texted my mom we're here. In case she peeps out the curtains and freaks you out."

"L-O-L—*Moms*," I said. I sat at one end of the swing. It struck me he'd used the word safe again. "You said this was a safe place to hang out. What's up with that?"

Jonah sat beside me. A cozy space for the two of us. "I asked about your stepdad when we were changing the tire. I just wanted to let you know things are safe here in case maybe it's not where you live."

"I meant it when I said my stepdad is great. He treats my mom well—all of us well. Way better than my dad ever did." I swung us back and forth. "My own dad started another family without telling us. While he was still with my mom."

Jonah sucked in air. "That's rough. It must be hard knowing that."

"You shouldn't feel that bad for me. It was my fault."

The swing stopped and I jerked forward.

"Elena, that's not true." Jonah stared at me with an intensity that at one time would have freaked me out. "That's impossible."

"Except it is true. I blabbed to my mom what I over-heard my dad say on the phone. I had no idea what I was getting us into. Things ended fast after that."

Jonah shook his head. "That's so not your fault. How old were you?"

I started to answer when he interrupted. "No—it doesn't matter. You were a kid."

"I know I was a kid, but my big mouth gets me in trouble. You've seen it in action. My first day at work—bam!—reprimanded by Terry. It's why Chelsea can't stand me. I am a ruiner of things, Jonah. I've made my peace with that. What I won't let happen is to ruin things with John. I know he wouldn't hurt us. I'm afraid...I'm afraid he'll leave. And that's on me."

Jonah didn't speak for probably thirty whole seconds. Finally, he did. "I don't say this often, but, Elena, you're being stupid. *You* aren't stupid but what you're saying and thinking is stupid. Just...stop. Stop it. Don't think it, okay?"

I twisted in the seat to face him better. "My thoughts and beliefs aren't stupid."

"Okay then, they're wrong."

I let out an exasperated huff. "They're my *feelings*. I can't just turn them off."

Jonah flung his hands outward in a rare burst of physical reaction. "You didn't cause your dad to leave you and you can't cause your stepdad to leave either. You're trying to fix something that doesn't sound broken."

I stood from the swing. "I shouldn't have even told you any of this. It's why I don't tell people things this personal."

None of my cross-country team friends knew about my fear of John leaving us. Or about my secret shame for causing my parents' divorce. Christina, Holli, and several of my other teammates had been invited to my mom's wedding. They all assumed I had a happy life. They just didn't know how I needed to maintain that happy.

"I'm glad you told me," Jonah said. "I don't tell many people about my dad. For a long time, the only things kids at school knew about me was my dad died and I was taller than them. I found it easier to go off by myself or play video games." He swung back and forward once in a controlled motion. "I'm not judging you. I'm judging your dumb, wrong thoughts."

I couldn't help it, I laughed. "You. Shut up, you."

Jonah cracked a smile. He stood from the swing and met me where I leaned against the outer porch railing. "I don't like knowing you hurt like this." He pressed a hand to his own chest. "That's deep hurt. And it's wrong and it's stupid."

"Tell me what you really think."

"You have to believe me, Elena. Just try."

I refrained from rolling my eyes. I turned to face the other direction, looking across the well-kept lawn and the little yellow mailbox at the street that matched their front door. Such a cheerful looking home for someone who at first glance appeared anything but. And his family had experienced loss. Hard loss. But they'd moved on.

I'd moved on. Our whole family had. But that nagging sense I'd caused our family to break apart couldn't be shaken loose. I'd tried.

"I've seen a lot of dirtbag guys try to take advantage of my mom," Jonah said. "I get protective, I guess."

"Did you fend them off?"

Jonah leaned a shoulder against the post connecting to the porch roof. "Didn't have to. Mom's book club took care of 'em."

My brows raised on their own. "That's a powerful book club."

"They're loyal, and they watch out for each other. The knitters were ready too. You haven't lived until you see a lady with a Master's Degree in library sciences threaten to purl stitch a dude's eyes out."

"Yikes." The visual alone freaked me out, and I knew zilch about knitting except it involved long pointy needles.

"She can fend for herself, but it doesn't hurt having a big guy like me as backup. You know, in case the book club and the knitters aren't around."

I found myself leaning into Jonah's solid body. "I promise I'll think about what you said. It's not possible to suddenly stop thinking what I've believed for so long."

Jonah let me ease back into him. He ran a soft touch across my shoulders. "You're not a problem. You solve them. Pretty well, I'd say."

"Ha. Nice try."

"You do. I want to see my friends more—that's because of you. I feel like sharing stuff that's important to me. You're changing things at Wild Adventure. You don't even have to do what you're doing."

"I guess I'm trying to prove myself." To who, everybody? How long could I keep this up?

I turned to face Jonah and sank into his hug. "Thanks for listening."

We stayed close for what felt like a moment and like it could last forever.

"Don't freak," Jonah said calmly. "But my mom is absolutely peeping through the curtains at us."

Chapter Nineteen

♥

Life returned to semi-normal at work with thicker crowds coming through the Go Zone. I liked when our side of the park buzzed with eager park guests. Even more, I liked working shifts with Jonah. We had moments to catch up and sometimes moments for more.

Quick kisses. A graze of our hands.

But only after safety checks.

I stepped back from Jonah having sneaked a kiss in the break room. For a moment, everything had fallen away. The crowds outside the door, the incessant humidity, the terrible wood paneling.

Back outside, we covered for Nando taking his break. A group walked over from Final Lap and handed us priority lap passes. I had this down now. When we shuffled the guests to the front of the line, I handed food promotion coupons to the people who'd been waiting already. I explained the promo.

A guy took the coupon with skepticism. "If we go and eat, they'll give us priority lap passes and we can come back and cut the line?"

"Yup."

He elbowed his buddy. "Good deal. The water park is a rip-off. We should come here next time with the cheaper park pass."

The kind of chatter I liked to hear. "Tell your friends!"

"You are way too into this," Jonah told me.

At this point, the satisfaction felt less about sticking it to the new parkies and more about carving out the recognition everyone here deserved for working hard every day.

Blender delivered a newly repaired kart beneath the overhang. He hopped out of the kart and strode to me and Jonah. He looked back and forth between us, noting our hands clasped together. He grinned. "Cute. Hey, so I have an idea. It could work for your zone domination thing."

Blender recognizing that Jonah and I were together and then sharing an idea for my initiative? It was almost too much. "I'm flattered." I pressed a hand at my heart. "Please, go on."

His eyes narrowed. "Don't be corny. I have a crew looking for a new venue for their muscle car show. Don't" —he pointed me— "sass about the muscle cars. They bring in a good crowd. We can use our side's employee parking lot. A little turbo weed killer on the old parking lot—I know a guy who can handle it."

My mind raced. "Jonah said Uncle Frankie lost money on the concerts, but a car show could work. Our parking lot is huge."

Blender's face lit with excitement. "We do a tie-in with park passes. Use the wristbands for our side and we get the Lap to do food specials. I already mentioned it to their manager."

"Good idea," Jonah said. He and Blender talked details for a few minutes as Nando and I schemed about the food.

The plan was coming together. "I'll ask Terry—"

"No!" all three guys said at once.

Okay. "You'll ask Terry?"

Blender made a motion with his hand like patting down the air. "Keep this to our level for now. Let's get some plans together."

"But we need permission to plan an event on park grounds," I said. "There's no point in planning if Terry or Uncle Frankie say no."

Blender gave me a steady look. "Asking gives them a chance to say no."

I looked at Jonah who shrugged. I struggled to wrap my mind around this concept. "We're going to sell tickets on our own for an event on Wild Adventure property? How are we advertising? How are we collecting money?"

Blender swatted my arm. "You're making this harder than it needs to be."

I couldn't shake the uneasy feeling.

"Here's how it works," Blender said. "You say, 'Sorry, Boss,' if you're caught. Once they see the sales numbers, they let you do it for real. This will be more of an informal gathering. Under the radar."

The Blender way sounded messy, but I appreciated the effort. Whether it would work was another matter altogether.

"The Keenes invited us for dinner," Mom said as I walked into the kitchen.

I paused in the doorway, still tired from a long shift the day before. It felt like days since I'd had an actual conversation with her. "I'm sorry, what?"

She operated in full meal prep mode with containers and fresh ingredients commanding all the space on the island counter. "We're having dinner with the Keene family at their house this weekend. I forgot to tell you. Make sure you have the night off."

I slid onto a barstool at the island. "I need more notice than a couple days to change my shift."

"You work with teenagers. What else do they have going on?"

I didn't have the energy to glare. "Rude. Lots of us have lives besides work."

I'd told her about the pit crew from time to time. It wasn't as if she thought I worked with nameless, faceless drones. Sure, my own social life involved hanging out with people *from* work outside of work, like Jonah. Nando and Mariela had officially gone out together beyond Wild Adventure gates. Mark had a family reunion this weekend and Audio apparently DJed events as a second job. Which I'd found out from Nando, of course.

Mom sighed as she poured a tall glass of water and handed it to me. "You look dehydrated."

Great. I took the water and drank half of it. I set the glass down.

"You switched your shift no problem for John's picnic," Mom went on.

And I'd had to lay groundwork for Nando's future relationship. No biggie. Speaking of John, though. "Why didn't you tell John I've been working at the go-karts? He thinks I work in the water park."

She blinked. "I didn't tell him? I could have sworn I had."

This was not good. "Remember you said no secrets?"

"He's been so busy." She opened the refrigerator and pulled out a plastic bin of spinach leaves. "I'm sure I told him at some point."

"This looks bad if we're keeping something from him. Now it's too late to tell him unless I say I just switched. But I'll need a reason."

Mom looked at me. "Elena, you're overthinking. John will be fine. He's impressed you've stuck with the job this long."

"I don't want to keep things from him." My mind raced to my conversation with Jonah. How he told me to stop thinking stupid thoughts about causing my step-dad to leave us. But now the possibility presented itself again. John could get upset being left out of family details. John could get upset with Mom for not trusting him.

Those thoughts led to the inevitable. John could leave us.

I didn't care what Jonah said. I couldn't be responsible for more destruction to my family. Not again.

Mom noticed me spacing out. "Honey. We'll talk to him tonight at dinner. It will be fine."

Eli wandered in and poked me on the bum. I swatted him before he could jump out of the way.

I kept it zipped about the park stuff because Eli would only make things worse.

"It will be nice to sit down with the Keene family for dinner," Mom went on. "Won't it, Eli?"

His cheeks reddened. "I guess. Can I invite a friend?"

Mom paused from her spinach rinsing. "I don't think so. This is still a business dinner. Maybe next time if this goes well."

I guess I had no chance of inviting a friend either. Like Jonah. Wouldn't that be a disaster.

Chapter Twenty

♥

The weekend arrived and so did my family on the doorstep of KJ Keene's house.

The Keenes lived in a neighborhood a few miles from us in homes built in recent years. Mom, Eli and I used to live in an apartment building up the street from the subdivision and watched the gigantic houses go up one by one. The three-car garages were probably bigger than where we'd lived at the time.

Mrs. Keene answered the door wearing a gauzy shawl over linen clothes that amazingly weren't wrinkled. I had a linen skirt that Mom bragged came from some classy brand she and her friends wore. It was always creased down the middle and looked terrible on me. Mrs. Keene did not look terrible.

Inside, a large foyer greeted us with a wide staircase leading to the second floor. Massive vases clustered in one corner by the door with decorative stuff spraying out of them. I didn't know what they were called except expensive.

The twins rumbled down the stairs. "Hi, Eli," Katharine said. "Want to see our video games?"

"Sure." Eli followed them past us deeper into the house.

"Lovely to see you all." Mrs. Keene led Mom, John, and I through a hall to an open area with a kitchen on one side and a large living room with a fireplace that stretched up two stories.

"Elena," came a voice behind me. KJ.

"Hey." I smiled. Things would definitely skew awkward between us now that he'd told me Jonah caused the accident and I knew he hadn't.

This would probably be more than awkward.

We let the parents do their thing as they migrated to the kitchen. I followed KJ to the living room with the fireplace. The interior wall I hadn't seen from the kitchen had a built-in entertainment center stretched across it. A massive TV showed a colorful animated kids show with the volume up super loud.

KJ took the remote and lowered the volume, then switched to a sports channel. "How have you been?"

I sat two cushions away from him on the long sectional couch. "Good."

He slung an arm across the top of the cushion with his fingers pointed toward me. "I haven't seen you at the wave pool this week."

"Business is picking up by us. In the *reject* zone." I don't know why I added that extra bit, but the salt was there ready to be sprinkled.

KJ shifted toward me. "Elena, I'm sorry. I knew it would be hard to hear about Jonah. I didn't want to be the one to tell you."

I sat on my hands and willed myself not to say anything to make this worse. "I just...see things differently."

KJ blinked. "I was there. I know what happened. I wouldn't lie to you."

I studied his face. How could he lie so easily? So carefree?

I knew Jonah wouldn't lie to me. I believed Jonah. I knew what it took for him to admit what happened and tell me sensitive information.

KJ went on. "I'm sorry if I hurt you. You know, I talked to Chelsea after I saw how upset you still were. I asked her to apologize. She's taking the mean girl thing too far."

As if someone could act like a mean girl in a positive way. I sat back against the cushions. "Turns out, I was the one who needed to apologize. I embarrassed her during the theater production. I didn't even remember."

KJ groaned. "She's a drama queen. Don't let her push you around."

I couldn't believe I felt defensive toward Chelsea, but that exact sentiment shot forward. "I did owe her an apology. I don't think before I speak sometimes."

KJ's attention drifted to the TV. "Well, I'm sure she appreciated your apology."

I laughed. "She did not."

He laughed too. "Chelsea is Chelsea. She'll come around."

I doubted she would, but Chelsea in general was a problem for another day.

The sports news on TV filled in our silence until the moms called to us. On the other side of the kitchen, a formal dining room offered long plates of finger foods and appetizers.

Mrs. Keene placed a hand at KJ's back and a light touch to my shoulder. "Look at you two. So beautiful together."

"Mom, come on." KJ shrugged her off.

I glanced at KJ. He was pretty dang beautiful. I waited for the rest to follow. The familiar warm sensation when I thought of him, the daydreams, the memories. Only nothing materialized. I saw a good-looking guy who I wasn't sure I trusted.

My own mom mouthed "Cute," and pointed to KJ when he wasn't looking.

It didn't matter whether I trusted KJ. My role tonight was to act as the good daughter who played nice with others. Maybe play a good mean girl, like what KJ assumed existed.

After tedious small talk about school and colleges, the dads came into the dining room and switched out the appetizers for the main courses. My brother and the twins were corralled and we all sat around the table together.

Mr. and Mrs. Keene talked about their travels and which ski resorts they liked best. Then about the girls' private school and how Mom and John should consider switching Eli there after the merger went through.

Mom looked a little nervous and laughed to cover it. My grandma, her mom, was a public school teacher and our family felt something fierce for public education. I didn't get the fuss, but at least I dodged wearing an outfit that looked like a Target employee.

"What I think we need is to get Elena working with KJ," John said as he caught my eye across the table. "I'm not crazy she's working in a grease pit."

We'd had the necessary conversation the other night at dinner to inform him I was in fact working in the Go Zone with the scary go-karts. I assured him they weren't that scary. I cleaned helmets—helmets some go-kart courses across the country didn't even require, but Wild Adventure did. I'd told him all about my pit crew and how we worked hard to keep the karts safe and never skipped checks or cut corners.

I wasn't sure I'd convinced him, but like Mom said, he didn't get upset. He'd never blown up about anything with us before. Like I'd told Jonah, my brain just went to the place where I assumed the worst.

"Is the grease pit the restaurant or those go-karts?" Mr. Keene asked, laughing.

Everyone at the table laughed except me and Eli. My brother nudged my foot under the table and rolled his eyes.

"I'm shocked Elena isn't already working with KJ," Mrs. Keene said. "We need to make that happen and get these two *together*."

My face burned at her phrasing. I looked up and swore she envisioned me in a prom dress beside her son in formal wear. I didn't dare look at KJ.

"Come on, Mom," KJ added softly. "Give it a rest, alright?"

Mr. Keene looked at his son. "That boy isn't still working out there is he?"

That boy—Jonah.

KJ nodded once without taking his eyes from his plate. "You know he is."

Mr. Keene sat straighter. "Elena, you'll be at the water park with KJ by your next shift."

A mild panic rose inside me. "I'm fine where I am. We're already halfway through the summer. I don't want to leave."

Mr. Keene and John had a side conversation going. About me.

My mom cleared her throat. "I'm sure we can include Elena in this conversation later."

John reached for her hand. "You're right. I'm sorry."

Mr. Keene rested his elbows against the table. "I only mean the best intentions to look out for your daughter. You might not know, but we had a situation last summer involving the park. An incident where staff didn't do their job and tried to tangle up our KJ in their negligence. We had our lawyers set the record straight."

My parents both looked at me. I focused on my plate and summoned a portal to another planet. My potatoes offered no help.

"Why is KJ still working at Wild Adventure?" Mom asked.

"Because his *friends* are there," Mrs. Keene responded in an almost playful way. "He begged us to stay. We lean back on steady employment looks good on college applications."

John sat back in his seat. "Was that in the news last year? A boy fell out of a ride? Was that at Wild Adventure?"

The adult Keenes looked at each other. Mr. Keene responded first. "It was a freak accident. The family involved in the lawsuit got what they needed, and we did as well."

KJ, on the other side of me from my brother, gave me a pointed look.

At the head of the table, Mr. Keene's expression intensified. "The park should have fired the boy on watch when that child was hurt. Instead, they demoted him. The family allowed it. I'm afraid Elena is at risk."

Mom swung back to me. "Elena, is that true?"

"I'm not at *risk* from Jonah," I burst out. "He's not a monster. He *saved* Cayden Moore."

"This is about Jonah?" Mom edged nearer to horrified. "The accident involved Jonah?"

"Is he the boy that changed the tire?" John mused. "Jo-*nuh*."

"That boy shouldn't have needed saving," Mr. Keene said.

"Of course he shouldn't have," I fired back. "That's what an accident means."

"*Elena.*" Mom used her *we're with company, now stop it* tone.

"I'm tired of Jonah being made out to be some kind of freak," I announced to the table. "None of the pit crew are. They're hardworking. Management should be the ones held responsible for accidents with rides. They barely pay attention to us out in the sticks."

"I don't like the sounds of this," John said, looking at Mom. "I should have been paying better attention. I've been working too many hours."

Mr. Keene lifted his glass but spoke before drinking. "You've been carrying the weight of your department too long. That will change soon. I promise."

Mrs. Keene placed her cloth napkin beside her plate. "Like my husband said, we'll handle it."

My mom seemed to have additional thoughts but didn't speak. I wanted to scream but stuffed the urge down.

"I've been trying to get Elena out of karts for weeks," KJ said. "I didn't think things were that bad, but then..." He looked at me. "They're dating. And he's already lied to her."

I gasped. "KJ!"

"Elena? You're *dating* Jonah?" Mom nearly shouted across the table.

John turned to Mom. "You didn't know your daughter had a boyfriend?"

"Don't put this on me," she shot back, pointing her finger.

"How could you consider anyone else when my KJ is right here?" Mrs. Keene declared.

"*Mom*," KJ seethed.

"You guys are acting immature," my brother stated. The twin Keene girls giggled.

I pushed back from the table. "This is ridiculous. Jonah wasn't even the one who missed the safety check. It was KJ."

The room fell silent except for a fork clattering to the table.

"Elena," KJ warned. "He's *lying*."

"He wouldn't lie to me." I swallowed back the thick feeling in my throat.

Mr. Keene's face turned hard as steel. "Who told you that? That boy?"

"His name is Jonah." I held my chin high. "And yes, he's my boyfriend. I'm not ashamed to say it because I'm not ashamed of him."

"You may not be aware, Elena," Mr. Keene continued in a cold tone. "Your *boyfriend* is forbidden from discussing the court case. It's why it's called a settlement—the matter has been settled."

John held up a hand. "We're very sorry. This conversation is not appropriate for dinner and we'll speak with our daughter after this. I'm sorry I overlooked so much at home."

"Excuse me," Mom cut in. "I am her mother and I have oversight of my daughter. She's shown herself to be responsible this summer including patching a tire on her own. She even offered to pay for the tire, but we told her we'd cover it."

I shot a thankful look at Mom for at least attempting to have my back.

"As for discussing confidential court cases—" Mom leveled a look at me. "That we will absolutely discuss as a family."

Needless to say, dinner with the Keene family did not go as planned.

"No speaking until I've said what I have to say," flew out of my mother's mouth the second the car doors closed. We still sat parked in the Keenes' driveway. As my brother snickered, she lasered a look at him from the front seat. "You're grounded with no video games if you make a sound, Eli."

As John reversed out onto the street, she continued. "We are calling Wild Adventure tomorrow to move you to another area. I'd have you quit, but quitting is irresponsible and doesn't teach you how to work through problems. We will discuss this boyfriend of yours. Then you will handwrite an apology letter to the Keene family. John had to do a lot of damage control after dinner to save this deal."

Out the window, the landscape blurred as my eyes brimmed with tears. I'd ruined everything. Again. I just couldn't help blurting out the truth even if it hurt my family.

John might not get his business deal, which, if I was being honest, I didn't care since the Keenes seemed worse and worse in my mind.

But I'd hurt him in front of people he thought were important. The looks between him and Mom. Secrets. Distrust. That was my fault.

At home, I shut myself in my room. Faceplanting against my pillow, I wished for a do-over, courtesy of an enchanted artifact. I'd always wondered if my ballerina music box my grandmother gave me had secret wish powers. I peeked up at the box across the room on my desk. I was too drained to even try.

Elevated voices carried up from downstairs. I finally cracked. They were fighting. I'd never heard Mom and John raise their voices at each other.

They were fighting because of me. I buried my face in my pillow and let the tears come.

I rolled over and grasped for my phone. Squinting, I deciphered the time. Yowza, nearly noon. Apparently, I'd cried myself to sleep and slept through the night in my clothes. At some point, I'd pulled the blankets over me and kicked off my socks.

With sunlight filtering in through my curtains, I rolled back to face the wall with my phone in my hand. I had a text. Scratch that, many texts.

Jonah: *Call me.*

I wasn't in the mood for chit chat.

Jonah: *Call me now.*

Jonah: *The Keenes called my mother.*

I shot up to sitting. I tapped the call icon but couldn't bring myself to press it.

Jonah. I'd betrayed him. I'd said what I wasn't supposed to say. Like always.

Laying back on my bed, I squeezed my eyes shut. I needed to face this. I tapped the call button.

Jonah answered on the second ring. "Why did you do it?"

"I defended you," I said in a rush. "They were practically bragging about paying a lawyer to make their little problem go away."

"That's what they do. I told you this." He paused, seeming to collect his words. "It wasn't your place to say anything."

"It just came up. They were all talking about moving me to the water park and—"

"You told him KJ was at fault for the accident."

"He was!"

"It wasn't your place, Elena."

I bit back any defensive comments. He was right. "I know. I'm sorry."

"They've already contacted their attorney's offices. They told them I violated the terms of the settlement."

"No!" My heart nearly shot out of my body. "Let me fix this, Jonah. Let me—I'll talk to the Keenes. I'll tell them—"

"Stop," Jonah said calmly. Almost too calm. "You can't fix this. You've done enough already."

My tears found their way out again. I gathered my strength. "I'm sorry, Jonah. I owe the Keenes an apology letter. I'll tell them to hold off."

"You don't get it." Jonah's voice came cold. "An apology note doesn't fix this. My family doesn't have the money to fight them. It's going to take my savings."

My breath left me. His money toward a career in game development—his dream. "I'm so sorry, Jonah. It doesn't have to be this way. I'm sure they're overreacting. Please, let me fix this."

"*I* fix this. Me. Like always," he grumbled.

I took a steadying breath. "I didn't mean for this to happen."

"Yeah, but it did. And it means a whole lot."

His words edged sharp and needled my skin. "If I can do something, Jonah, anything, I will." I couldn't express any more how bad I felt. I had to *do* something. I could drive there now and tell them to call off the lawyers.

The line stayed quiet. "I...I just had to hear it from you," he said finally. "That you think so little of me you'd risk telling them this."

"Little? No, that's not it. No." I rubbed my hands against my comforter, trying to wipe off the sweat and panic. "It was a mistake." I'd hurt him and I hated every second of it.

"I can't believe I fell for it."

My ability to speak left at the exact wrong time. Finally, I found words. "Fell for...what?"

His voice shifted from cold to glacial. "Fell for you."

Chapter Twenty-one

One time I'd spent an entire afternoon baking a pie from scratch. I'd never made a pie before, but the baking show I'd been watching made it seem almost easy. I read the recipe through, gathered the ingredients, and followed every step. Chilled the dough, rolled it out, and filled the pie with apples and sugar and seasonings. I set the pie on the counter to cool. I'd gotten excited and burst into a happy pie dance. Only I bumped the pie dish with my elbow and knocked it to the tile floor.

I'd placed the dish at the edge of the counter. The glass dish, which had also broken. Even the two-second rule couldn't save a pie with glass shards in it.

That's how it felt hearing Jonah say falling for me was a mistake. Except the pie dish was my heart. My shattered heart.

Worse, I'd shattered Jonah's heart. Or, maybe I hadn't, but I sure would be responsible for draining his bank account.

I had to fix this. I had to. The Keenes calling in the lawyers just because I said something out of turn? Ridiculous. I started a text to KJ. No, I should call.

The call rang to voice mail with an automated robot message—it wasn't even KJ's voice. I hung up and returned to the text.

KJ please tell your parents not to freak out and get Jonah in trouble—

I stopped and erased Jonah's name.

I retyped *get the lawyers involved.*

What was the point of a settled case if they were going to poke at it until it unsettled?

To my dismay, a response from KJ did not instantly appear. I needed another angle. I settled on my bed with my back against the wall and swiped through my phone contacts until I found Nando.

Nando! Hey it's Elena. Do you have Cayden Moore's number?

I waited.

Nando: *You're a little old for him. Awkwarrrrd...*

I gasped.

Not like to call him *call him. I mean like his parents' number. The Keenes are siccing their lawyers on Jonah again. I can't let them!*

My phone rang in my hand. I answered.

Nando didn't bother to say hello. "Elena—whatever you're trying to do, don't."

"It's KJ's family. They're like, obsessed with protecting this lawsuit. They blame Jonah for all of it. It's not fair."

Nando sighed. "KJ's family gets trigger-happy with the legal eagles. It's useless to try and stop them."

"Legal eagles?"

"It's a thing," he said quickly. "Look, talk to Jonah. He'll understand."

"He told me he feels stupid for falling for me."

The line went quiet. Finally, Nando spoke again, his voice edged with steel. "What did you do, Elena?"

"What did *I* do? Nothing!" Okay, so I'd done a few things. Of which I was very sorry. "I may have defended Jonah to the Keenes. In their own home. In front of KJ. It didn't go well and now they've stirred up the lawyers. Jonah was contacted. He told me he'll have to use his savings for the fees."

Nando made a sucking sound through his teeth. "Girl, you messed up."

I let out a defeated breath. "I *know*."

"Look, Jonah feels really strong about protecting his family and protecting Cayden. I think it's why he's still at Wild Adventure. He wants to prove he can do right by them."

"But the accident wasn't his fault. He *saved* Cayden."

"Yeah, but the court case cost his family a lot. His mom raised him on her own. The lawsuit really stressed her out."

That made sense. My mom had stressed constantly when she'd been on her own with us. She tried the brave face, but I could sense the cracks when she thought I hadn't been looking.

I rubbed my palm against my forehead to dull the throbs. "I wish I had a time machine."

"No, you don't. You'd end up stuck in the future or cause an apocalyptic event."

"I want to go *back* in time, not forward. And I'd be super careful. I'd only undo the part where I told the Keenes it was KJ's fault. Even though it was his fault."

"See? This is why you can't go back. Not only would you miscalculate and send yourself forward, you'd tell the Keenes the same thing because you don't actually believe their lie."

"Okay, I don't know why you're so insistent I'd mess up time travel, but point taken. I probably wouldn't be able to go along with them about this."

Ugh. I was going nowhere fast.

"Thanks for listening, Nando. I should probably go. I have an apology letter to write and it's going to take some creative wording."

"Stay sweet, girl."

I cracked up despite the heavy mood. "What?"

He ended the call. I shook my head. Any momentary lightness dried up and crusted over. I'd hurt Jonah. That hurt would continue so long as this issue with KJ dragged on. Timeline manipulation aside, I'd have to start somewhere more basic.

I dug out the stationery set my grandparents bought me and found a working pen.

I wrote seven versions of an apology letter to the Keene family. The first five drifted into angry accusations. They had no idea how much they were hurting Jonah.

Okay, *I'd* hurt Jonah, but they had a hand in it too. It wasn't like I'd blabbed their settlement business to a bunch of people at a party or at work where other people could hear. How dare they get their lawyer involved so fast without trying to understand?

Finally, version six of the letter came across less angry. Sort of. My handwriting had slashes for commas reminding me of knife marks. Maybe another try.

Only the words wouldn't come. I just...couldn't.

The Keene family owed Jonah an apology. How could I get them to understand?

Version seven, I convinced myself I was a girl named Helena who lived in Switzerland, where I'd read they were politically neutral. I channeled Helena's homeland virtues and stayed as middle of the neutral road as could be. None of my sass, none of my emotion. Three clear sentences. Signed my name and done.

I took the note to Mom who sat at a corner of the couch reading.

She took the note and scanned it. She slid her glasses down her nose to look over the frames at me. "This sounds like a third grader wrote it."

I flopped on the opposite end of the couch. "I was Helena. I was the Swiss."

She shook her head, her features scrunched. "You need to try again. Take this seriously."

"I a-*am!*" I stretched out the word like the mature seventeen-year-old I was. "I don't know how to apologize to them for something I'm not sorry for."

"*Elena.*" She tossed the note to the cushion between us. "This is not a game. There are real people's lives involved. Not to mention their business. I don't care if you're not sorry. Write the note like you are."

UGH times infinity. I needed to make her understand. "Mom, look. What I feel bad about is hurting you and John and hurting Jonah. I blabbed something I shouldn't have. But the Keenes, they aren't taking responsibility for what happened. KJ is the one who abandoned his post. He left Jonah alone and Cayden was severely injured. He uses a wheelchair because of the accident. *Jonah* was the one who ran to save him."

"I'm sorry to hear that happened. I didn't know the whole story." She sighed. "The theme park is responsible for their ride. Not a couple of teenagers. And your friend Jonah wants you to believe his version of the story. How well do you know this boy? I've barely heard you mention him and now he's your boyfriend?"

"*Was*." I picked at my fingernail. "The Keenes already called him and threatened eagles." I shook my head. "Legal eagles. The eagles who attack with legal action—whatever."

Mom flattened her lips.

"He wouldn't lie to me." Maybe it sounded lame, but I still believed it. "Jonah is friends with the boy he saved. It's like an older brother type relationship. Their family knows what happened. They can't talk about it either."

"These are other people's issues. *Legal* issues. It's no place for a teenage girl to butt in with her opinions."

Didn't I know it. I'd already lost anything I'd built up with Jonah, but I didn't have to let the Keenes get away with their refusal to take responsibility without a fight.

She'd given me her End of Discussion look and returned to reading a digital magazine on her tablet.

Silence would be the smart choice at the moment. Only sometimes speaking up was the smart choice. Like right now. Using words carefully and with good intent, that had to be smarter than sitting here playing at polite.

"Are you and John okay?" I asked, my voice barely audible.

She didn't look up as she spoke. "Are we okay? Of course we are."

"You were fighting."

"We were discussing."

"I heard you from upstairs. You raised your voice. So did John. You've never talked to each other that way before."

She lowered the tablet and looked across the room, straight ahead. "It was an emotional day and we had words. It's not your concern."

My blood chilled. Obviously, it was my concern. This was *my family*. What was I supposed to concern myself with if it wasn't my own family and my own friends?

I needed a different tactic. A helpful one. "Mom, I'm sorry I messed up. What can I do to make things better?"

"Write the letter. More than a few lines. I want you to sound like a mature high school senior who feels remorse for what she did."

I picked my nail until the edge ran ragged. "I mean for you and John. What can I do? I don't want... I mean, if we end up having to move..."

Her eyes sharpened. "What are you talking about?"

"Like, if things don't work out and we need to bounce. I need to mentally prepare."

She set the tablet aside. "No one is going anywhere. Why would you think we'd move?" Understanding dawned. "You mean us moving. Without John." Her eyes fell closed. "This isn't that kind of problem. We are *okay*. Circumstances are not."

I shifted to the cushion edge. "You don't know that. Things were okay with Dad too until I..." I bit back the words. Was it worth bringing up? Jonah had told me my parents' divorce hadn't been my fault. I wanted to believe him.

Except deep down, I knew I was the problem. I was always the problem.

Mom straightened her dark-framed glasses. "Elena, tell me what you mean about your dad. What do you think happened?"

I swallowed. "I told you he was with that other lady. And then he left."

She stilled. "Is this what you've thought all this time? That he left because of what you said?"

My muscles tightened. I pulled my knees up and hugged them to me, squeezing myself smaller and tighter. "If I hadn't blurted out how I'd heard him on the phone with her, telling her he loved her, then—"

"Then I would have found out another way," she finished for me. "And things were not okay between us. They hadn't been for a long time. You were so young. We kept it from you."

This wasn't new information, but we'd never talked about the divorce like this. It had always been Mom and Dad filling in details for me and Eli, a toddler at the time.

We'd lived with my Aunt Sam before finding our own apartment. I'd only seen Dad a few times since he'd left us, and the money stopped coming too. I only knew about the money stuff from hearing Mom talk to her sister.

And yeah, all that time I'd believed it was my fault. Because I'd been the one who told.

"Elena," Mom's voice grew soft. "Please know that no part of our divorce was your fault. Not even a little bit. I know we've talked about this. Remember Miss Carrie? The counselor? She told you the same thing."

It was hard to describe how I could hear what she said and understand the words, but not believe it. "I know she said that. I didn't think he left because of me, but I was the one who changed everything. It's why we had to share that room at Aunt Sam's and you had to get a job you didn't like because it paid more. Why you had to sell your special things to pay bills."

Mom used to have collectible figurines and glassware and cool shoes, all sold off when we'd moved to the apartment. Jewelry and her bedroom set, gone and sold. We'd kept our kid beds while her mattress laid on the floor until she bought a cheap frame from a garage sale. I remembered the day we'd loaded it in my mom's friend's truck.

"Honey, those things would have happened anyway. You telling me what you did only moved our separation along."

That was where I got stuck. I'd been the one who'd sped up the destruction of my family. Eli barely re-membered Dad. His memories were from pictures or stories we reminded him about, not his own memories. That was *my* fault.

She looked me over. "I think I understand. You saw what you said as causing what happened." She sucked in a breath and fanned her face. "I'm sorry." Her voice cracked. "Come here." She motioned for me to scoot closer, into her arms.

I untangled from my own tight hold and accepted her hug.

Footsteps sounded behind us. "A rare sighting—a mother and teen daughter hug."

Pulling back, I wiped my eye as John walked into the room.

He stopped at the sight of us. "Did I interrupt?"

Honestly, I was embarrassed to have him see me like this, but it was kind of nice to see him at the same time.

"It's nothing," Mom said. "We're fine."

I re-positioned myself. "Actually, we're not fine. I mean, we are, but sort of not." I cringed. "Sorry, I'm bad at this."

John sat in the chair across from us, leaning his elbows on his knees. "Anything I can help with?"

Mom looked to me. "Are you comfortable sharing what we just talked about?"

I nodded. As John listened, I filled him in on how I'd tried to be extra responsible to prove to him I wasn't a total screw-up. And then the harder things to admit about feeling like I'd caused my parents to split. "I'm afraid you'll think we're too much to deal with. I afraid I'm going to push you away and then...you'll leave."

There. I'd said it.

John's shoulders sank. "That's a big load to carry all by yourself. I'm so sorry you've been feeling that way." He looked at my mom and they did some kind of husband-and-wife telepathy. "I hope you know that no one expects you to have life figured out. And I'm not going anywhere."

Mom ran a hand across my back. "I'm sorry you thought you were at fault for the divorce. You weren't."

The truth sank in through the warmth in her hand. I knew she was right, but I couldn't convince my inside feeling to agree. *I'd been the one who told.* I'd blabbed what I heard and our family fell apart. Like how I'd blabbed the truth to the Keene family and things fell apart. Again.

The common factor was me.

"I think Miss Carrie would still see you if you wanted to talk," Mom said. "Or we could find a therapist who works with teenagers."

"I don't know."

"We could go as a family," John suggested. He put up a hand at my horrified face. "Or not."

Mom looked me over, seeming to see me in some new light. "I should have realized this transition would bring out old feelings. It hasn't even been a year since the wedding. I shouldn't have assumed everything was okay because nothing catastrophic happened."

Until now, I mentally filled in for her.

"I threatened John's business deal," I said.

"Well, you definitely brought up a few factors that need to be discussed," John pointed out. "And the way it came out was less than ideal. I want you to know, I love you just the same."

Mom pointed to the note card. "The letter is important, Elena. Please write it."

I took a breath. It started to stick that they weren't on the brink of filming *Divorce Part Two: Mean Streets*.

I had work to do. On myself for one. Maybe with an age-appropriate counselor.

And starting with version eight of this dang apology letter.

Chapter Twenty-two

♥

A full day passed since my conversation with Jonah. No texts or calls. No response from KJ either. Not that I wanted to talk to KJ, but I would if it made things right for Jonah.

I drove to work for my next park shift after having begged my parents to let me finish the summer at the Go Zone. I needed to talk to Jonah in person. I knew Jonah was on the schedule.

On the way in, Terry called.

"Stop by the main office," he said through my car's Bluetooth.

I cringed hearing Terry speak through my car. It felt so invasive.

Plus, now I had to park on the way far side of the park and then either move my car when I was done at the office or tram it to the Go Zone. Already this day started out complicated.

Already *I'd* made it complicated.

Okay, harsh inner voice. Enough of the shaming.

Mom already made an upcoming appointment for me with a counselor to talk about life changes or whatever, which I appreciated. To get a jump on things, I looked up the free resources on the counseling center website and found guided audio meditation. I'd fallen asleep to verbal affirmations assuring me I was the only *me* in this universe. The universe needed what I had to offer. The app did not fill in what that offer was. Or if it had, I'd already dozed off.

I pushed through into the Wild Adventure office.

At the sight of me, Terry sighed with the energy of a worn-down walrus. "*Elena.*" He dragged out my name. "My, my, what have you gotten yourself into."

It wasn't a question apparently. He faced out a handwritten note on his clipboard. "Our office staff took this phone message from KJ Keene's folks. They're moving you to the water parks. Uncle Frankie already signed off."

"My parents said I could stay in the Go Zone."

"Ah, ah." He wagged a finger at me. Literally, he *wagged* it. "When Uncle Frankie signs off, it's a done deal."

My shoulders slumped. The Keenes weren't even my parents and they were calling the shots? "I'm fine to work the karts. I *told* them."

Terry did the finger wag. Just that, no words.

I blew out a huff of frustration. "Who's taking my place?"

He gave me a practiced look of indifference. "Not your concern."

"Um, yes, it is. I need to let the guys know what's going on."

"They'll be fine without you." He folded his arms. "I'm honestly surprised you lasted this long. Usually sending someone to the old park is a sign they've hit bottom. They just leave."

"I'm special, I guess." So special, only one of me existed in the whole universe. Take that, Terry.

"You must be to get the Keene family involved. They love to get messy, if you know what I mean." He mouthed the word *lawsuit*.

"I got that impression."

Terry's walkie squawked and he spun on his heel to go elsewhere. Which left me to report to my new post. No need to move my car or hitch a tram ride.

Working at the water park felt like day one all over again. I was the new girl getting the odd looks and feeling out of place. Worse, no one seemed to need me. I folded rental towels that rubbed stiff and rough against my hands.

On my lunch break, I hoofed it to the Go Zone. Turned out, the tram was down for repairs.

As the track came into view, so did a pleasant sight. Crowds. One of the longest lines I'd seen for the karts at this time of day. OZW for the win!

A pang of loss hit me. The same pang that hit the first time I'd seen the cross-country team gathering for a run together without me. Until I'd realized I no longer had to deal with blistered feet, shin splits, and pains in my side. I could hang out with my former teammates at a coffee place or the movies and not even have to run.

I could hang out with the guys. We'd still be friends. Only a paved walkway or a tram ride separated us.

I jogged the rest of the way and slowed when I saw Nando positioned at the Paul Bunyan sign. A boy with spiky hair stood on the balls of his feet aiming to reach Paul Bunyan's beefy bicep holding an axe his shoulder. "Hair doesn't count, buddy. Give it another summer. Sorry."

The kid muttered and scampered off with his friends.

Nando turned to me. "You really blew it, girl."

The chill coming off Nando would have been welcome in this heat if it didn't also dredge up a hefty dose of guilt. My throat shrank but I pushed the words out. "I want to be back here with you guys." I belonged here, with Jonah.

Audio approached after sending off the latest batch of kart riders. He moved his headphones off an ear. "You're not working here either?"

"Either?" I looked at him, then to Nando.

"She's at the water park," Nando filled in. "With KJ."

"Friggin' KJ." Audio slid his headphones back and returned to the pit.

"Nando, what did he mean when he said I'm not working here either?"

"Jonah's gone."

I couldn't have heard him right. "I don't—"

"He was fired. Too much of a liability. Uncle Frankie." He mimed a signature motion in the air. "Done deal."

No. This couldn't be happening. Not Jonah, not this! "It's my fault. It's all my fault."

Nando didn't correct me. He didn't yell at me either. He just looked tired.

"I'm so sorry," I told him. "I'll fix this. I swear, I'll fix it." The same thing I'd said to Jonah on the phone. Only I hadn't fixed it and now look what happened.

Another group drifted toward the karts. "We've got a priority lap pass," a woman said, holding up a laminated card.

Nando's shoulders sagged. "Right this way." He looked his shoulder at me. "Now we're busier than ever and short two people."

Just when we'd gained ground growing business on our side of the park. No, not our side. I no longer belonged.

But my place in a theme park zone didn't matter right now. Jonah—he'd lost his job. Not only did he have to pay for legal fees, but he'd lost his income to make back that money. I could barely breathe.

"I'll ask to get transferred back," I called to Nando as he walked off with the park guests. "I'm going right now!"

Nando switched to walking backward. "Elena, please. Just leave us alone. You've done enough damage."

Chapter Twenty-three

♥

Damage. I'd damaged my friendships, my relationships—everywhere I went, a path of destruction.

Apparently, saying sorry didn't magically fix everything. Jonah wouldn't take my calls or respond to my text apologies. Hearing he'd been fired from Wild Adventure after all he'd been through sent waves of shock through me. Nando asking me to leave the pit crew alone drove the shock deeper.

I was an outcast from the outcasts.

Given I was due back to the water park to finish my shift, I had to leave anyway. This didn't feel like when I'd left the cross-country team. That, I'd left by choice. This exit from the Go Zone signaled I'd failed epically. I was no longer wanted. And worse now than in the beginning because I knew what it felt like to be part of the team.

Screw finishing my shift. Jonah didn't have a shift to finish, period. I needed to take this to the top. To the Big Cheese himself: Uncle Frankie.

I contemplated taking the golf cart, but then Nando and what remained of the pit crew wouldn't have the cart if they needed it. Instead, I ran.

Once I made it to the main building, I burst through the door and landed at the front desk with its high counter striped in wood paneling.

"Jennifer?" I looked at the woman beyond the counter sitting at a desk positioned in front of filing cabinets.

A white woman with tightly curled honey brown hair and a little flower poof for bangs continued typing at a desktop computer. "Yeah?"

I caught my breath. "I need to see Uncle Frankie. It's urgent."

"He's out," Jennifer responded.

"When will he be back?"

"Noon. Next Tuesday."

I blinked. "That's—no, I need to talk to him now."

Keystrokes maintained steady clacking. "He's not here."

"But he just signed off on moving me to the water park. He just fired Jonah!"

The typing stopped and Jennifer looked up. Aqua-colored eyeshadow lined her eyes with shades of yellow reaching her brow. Harsh pink blush striped her cheeks. I'd never seen those colors on anyone outside of *RuPaul's Drag Race*. "He signs off remotely."

"Well, can I talk to him remotely?"

Jennifer stood and approached the counter. Her outfit screamed retro from a past generation. A puffed-sleeved blouse featuring pastel polka dots cinched at the waist with a wide neon yellow belt. It must be 1980s theme day at the office.

"You seem like a good kid," Jennifer said in between loud chews of gum. "Some advice? A lot of kids revolve through this park. You can't get too attached. Maybe find them on the Facebooks or something."

"He shouldn't have been fired. He didn't do anything to lose his job."

Jennifer strummed pointy aqua nails along the counter. "Losing a job, that's tough. I know I couldn't fire a kid. To look in their eyes and tell them no more paycheck? No dice. I'm not taking that bet. That's why I stick to behind the desk. YouknowwhatImean?"

A desperate sense of hopelessness set in. This conversation was getting me nowhere. Down the hall, the Big Cheese's office door stood open with a vacant desk beyond it.

"Thanks, Jennifer. I'll have to try something else."

"Take care kid. Gum?" She slid a wrapped flat stick across the counter.

I took the gum and headed for the door. "Nice costume."

She smiled. "What costume?"

Outside, I scanned the area for Terry who usually moved between zones on this side of the park to monitor whatever he was supposed to monitor.

KJ appeared at the gate to the water park. "Elena, we've been looking for you. You're on shift, right?"

"I...yes, but I need to talk to Terry."

"Stand with me and check wristbands." KJ made space beside him, flashing me his easygoing grin. As if nothing had happened between us at his very own house.

"Things are not okay, KJ."

He rubbed the back of his neck, looking everywhere but me. "I feel bad about how things went down. My parents, they freak about anything to do with that lawsuit. I hate how you got sucked into it."

I believed he felt pressure from his parents. The pristine house and the nagging about private school. His parents talked about his college choice like they were enrolling for themselves. I wondered if KJ even wanted to go. His mom's weird insistence that he spend time with me... I mean, he didn't exactly have it *rough*, but I could see where he might feel worn down.

"Did you know it would happen?" I asked him.

"That they'd move you here? I figured. My parents said as much at dinner. Uncle Frankie listens to them. But it's all good. Bygones and all that. We'll be okay."

I tried to push back my irritation and failed. "I mean about Jonah."

His eyes darted past me. "Look, I warned you. I told you they'd get the lawyers involved."

"He was fired, KJ. He's gone from the park."

KJ blinked. "He is?"

I stared at him hard. I was fairly certain a noisy bunch of kids without water park wristbands passed through. I didn't care.

KJ shuffled his weight from one foot to the other. "I didn't know."

"I found out from Nando. And Uncle Frankie is out until next Tuesday, but somehow he still had time to fire Jonah. You know this isn't fair, KJ."

KJ seemed to register my distress. "How about I buy you a lemonade."

I almost laughed at the lemonade offer. "Jonah *lost his job*. That's on us." Now that KJ stood in front of me, his part in this couldn't be overlooked. KJ had doused that fire at the dinner table with just as much fuel as I had. "I'm standing here checking wrists while Jonah is figuring how to pay for a lawyer again."

KJ waved at another staff member and had her stand in our place. He took me aside. "Elena, I don't know what to say. Jonah—it's complicated."

"It's not." I focused on KJ, looking him right in the eye. "You know the truth. Maybe you can't change the settlement, but what's happening now, you can do something. You can fix this for Jonah."

His back stiffened. "You don't know my parents. They won't give in."

"They're ruining someone's life and for what? To protect their name? To protect you? Do you need their protection?"

KJ stumbled for words. He genuinely seemed to not know what to say.

"Look, I should get back to the wave pool," he said. "I'll talk to my parents. I can't promise anything, but I'll try." He eased back. "Then we can move past everything." He gave me the smile that once gave me pudding knees.

Move past everything. Just like that, as if I could forget the first half of my summer ever happened.

The next hours passed in a haze. I operated on autopilot.

I ran through my options. If I quit Wild Adventure, I'd further disappoint my parents, who I'd already disappointed by inserting myself in the Keene family's business. Mom said I needed to work through the problems I'd caused the way I was working through my daddy issues with a new therapist. Okay, she didn't say daddy issues, but truth.

Quitting also cut me off from access to the people who could get Jonah's job back. I needed to keep trying.

"Ooh—Terry!" I waved as Terry walked purposefully away from the glittering lemonade and frozen treats stand.

He made eye contact and muttered. Waving, he held up his clipboard with the other hand. "Busy! Catch you later."

"*Terry*," I bellowed. I would not let him go and I would not leave this post.

Finally, he marched toward me. "I'm very busy."

"Jonah was fired and—"

"Ah, ah." He wagged his finger at me.

"Don't—"

Wag

"Do—"

Wag

"That!"

Wag wag.

I clenched my fists.

"I don't have the authority to bring Jonah back." He lowered his voice. "You'd best move on. Just enjoy the view and collect your paycheck." He looked past me to the wave pool where surely KJ flexed shirtless or just looked hot in general. I refused to take the bait.

"The Go Zone is short staffed now," I told him instead of falling for the distraction. "I saw the numbers in the office. The Go Zone is in fourth place with park traffic."

The words *park traffic* won Terry's attention, though staffing should have already been on his radar. "I'll send Craig. He's worked the pit before."

At least the filler would be Craig.

"Elena," Terry said with a touch more kindness. "I mean it when I say it's best to move on. The Jonah-KJ incident was messy."

And it continued to mess up more people's lives.

Terry now gone, I remained in my spot of shade checking wrist bands when Chelsea approached me. "Hi, Elena. You doing okay?"

The unlikeliest of check-ins. "I'm fine." I wasn't.

"I see you're working here now and noticed you and KJ have some tension. But you don't seem sad about that. It's the other guy, isn't it?"

So, we were besties now? "I don't—" I almost said I didn't want to talk about it because I very much didn't, but I also strangely didn't mind this bridge forged with Chelsea. "Yeah. I involved myself with things I shouldn't have. I hurt Jonah."

"Craig told me more about the Jonah and KJ thing," she said, keeping her outward attention on park guests as they moved through our checkpoint. "I like KJ, but I know things about his family. They sued a friend of my parents. My folks can't stand the Keenes."

I didn't say anything. Chelsea kept going.

"I guess I liked going after the guy my parents couldn't stand. It felt kind of rebellious, you know?" She laughed with a bitter note. "It feels stupid now, knowing a kid got hurt because KJ was too busy flirting to do his job. I mean, everybody makes mistakes, but you only learn when you own up to it. Not run to your parents to make everything go away."

Chelsea fanned the back of her neck. "The people KJ's parents sued, they went out of business. My parents said things were rough for their company already, but that lawsuit did them in. My dad said the Keenes treat lawsuits like a game. They do whatever they can get away with."

This new information made my skin feel tight. "My stepdad is planning to do business with them. I tried to warn him, but I get in trouble when I meddle. You know better than anyone."

"Speaking of that." Chelsea turned to me. "I wanted to say thanks for talking to me even when I didn't want you to. I've been thinking about stuff and...I'm sorry for the way I treated you. I'm sorry for being a turbo witch."

"Turbo...witch." I had no idea what to say to that. I decided to focus on the sorry part. "Thanks. Why the change of heart?"

"When you see people every day at this job, some of the magic wears off." Her gaze followed KJ as he crossed from one end of the wave pool area to the other. "Also, Craig and I started hanging out and I see things kind of different now."

"Hanging out like..."

She grinned. "He's a really good kisser."

I couldn't help my own smile. "I'm happy for you."

And happy we could move beyond liking the same guy and the rivalry pitting us against each other. I fully intended to move on to new territory with Chelsea. Besides, I needed all the friends I could manage right now.

"Jonah was fired." At Chelsea's shocked gasp, I filled her in on what I knew and everything I'd tried so far to repair the damage.

"The more I hear, the angrier it makes me," Chelsea said. "Did you know KJ gets paid more than the other lifeguards? And he was paid even when he left for vacation? Not even Terry gets paid vacation."

"What?" That was all kinds of shady.

"Craig knows a lot of dirt. He talks to Jennifer—the gal in the office. She doesn't have much of a filter."

"Huh. I talked with her today. She's definitely...unique."

Chelsea looked thoughtful. "You said Uncle Frankie is gone?"

I nodded.

She looked past me, her eyes unfocused. "I have an idea. Are you up for a little adventure?"

If you'd told me two months ago I'd be breaking into the Midwest Wild Adventure offices with my frenemy/friend-again Chelsea, I might have believed it but for totally different reasons.

We'd gotten up to trouble before—strategically locating KJ's whereabouts to position ourselves at just the right time. Chelsea was a lurker. A lookie-loo. And the perfect accomplice.

Chelsea and I slipped into the main office building. She caught the door before it banged closed. The desk beyond the counter sat empty.

"Jennifer takes an extra-long break every afternoon according to Craig," Chelsea said. "She visits the guy running the Scrambler."

"A dry ride guy?"

She nodded. "Remember when you asked me if I put sugar in the go-kart gas tanks? I did some sniffing around. I'd heard rumors that Tilt-N-Turn and Thunderspeed were conspiring to win the prize money no matter who they took down. They've been sabotaging rides. Turns out they double-crossed the Scrambler. It got ugly." She gave me a solemn look. "Anyway, Uncle Frankie's door is wide open."

I'd noticed the open door earlier but hadn't thought to actually do anything about it.

"I'm thinking the kind of files we're looking for are in there." She pointed to the open door of The Big Cheese.

"He wouldn't leave incriminating files unsecured," I said, channeling the entirely of my sleuthing knowledge from the crime scene investigation shows my stepdad let run in the background on weekends.

"I kinda feel like he would. You've met him, right?"

Fair point. We headed to his office. I stood lookout in the doorway as Chelsea poked around.

"I'm thinking payroll would be Jennifer's territory," I told her. "Maybe we should check her files. What about the offices down that other hall?"

Chelsea looked up. "They're all overseas contracts. I've never seen as single person walk out of that hallway. Jennifer complains all the time she's bored because she works by herself."

At least our chances of being caught were fairly low. "How about cameras?" I scanned the walls and ceiling for signs of hidden security.

"Only on the outside of the building." Chelsea's voice came muffled from the far side of the desk. "These cabinets are locked, but I already found a key in this drawer." She opened the top cabinet.

My heartbeats came fast and hard. To me, B&E meant bacon and eggs, not breaking & entering. I wanted to keep it that way.

Chelsea let out a low, dramatic gasp. "Elena. I found something."

Since the hall showed no signs of life, I dashed into the office and slowly closed the door behind us. "What?"

She turned papers toward me. Court documents noting the Keene family. Freehand comments filled the margins. Sticky notes were affixed in a haphazard pattern at the top page. "The Keenes are still getting payouts from Uncle Frankie. According to these stickies, these payments go beyond the settlement."

According to these stickies would likely not hold up in a court of law. "He's paying them under the table."

"Cash to KJ...here, here, and here." She ran her finger along a column of dates.

"Why would he make it so obvious?"

"He wrote *for school* next to a figure. Maybe he thought it looked like he's investing in KJ's education. This one says *overtimes*. He probably just meant overtime. Which we both know we don't get paid for."

The creak and bang of the main building door opening and closing sounded from the hall. Chelsea and I ducked behind the desk.

"What are we going to do?" I looked at the papers.

"We should get these to Jonah. It might help his case."

"Somebody's in the hall," I whisper-shouted. "And we can't take his papers."

"There's a color copier by Jennifer's desk."

Still a risk. "Maybe it's enough to tell someone what we suspect without admitting how we found it. There has to be other ways to track shady payments, right?"

"Yeah, like an audit. My parents are obsessed about their business ledgers. Something like this wouldn't fly." She tapped the colorful notes.

"My guess is he's paying in cash. That's how it goes on TV."

Footsteps sounded in the hall followed by the main door opening and closing. We needed to make a break for it.

I slipped my phone out of my back pocket. One, two, snap, and I snapped a pic of the first page.

Chelsea looked up. "Quick thinking. My phone is in my locker."

Where our personal cell phones were supposed to be. I wasn't exactly in rule-following mode today.

I grabbed the file and stuffed it back into the cabinet. Chelsea locked the drawer and placed the key back in the desk.

I peeked into the empty hall. "Alright, let's get out of here."

Chapter Twenty-four

Once outside the Wild Adventure gates in the safety of my car, I pulled up the photo I'd taken of Uncle Frankie's sticky note-covered paper. Thanks to my recent phone upgrade, the writing on the papers showed clear and crisp.

I pulled up a new text with Jonah's name and attached the photo. The pic was saved to my phone's internal drive and not cloud storage. I planned to delete it immediately.

Only Jonah might have blocked my number. I decided to send it to one more person, hoping it would be enough.

That Friday, I showed up at the water park for my scheduled shift. Nothing had changed. No return texts. No breaking news or bombshell revelations. I'd been keeping tabs on the Wild Adventure fan account Nando ran, scouring for clues.

Chelsea joined me under the shade from the small canopy of the wristband checking station. My current lot in life. "Are you going to the muscle show tonight?"

"Huh?"

"The car show. Muscle cars. You know, the thing your friends are putting on?"

Chelsea dug out a folded flyer on an orange-colored half sheet of paper.

Show me your muscles

BYO Ride at 7 p.m.

Do a final lap for a wild adventure

My heart soared and sank simultaneously. I'd noted similar posts on the fan account and figured the car show would move forward. Good for them. I hoped it was a success.

"I'm going," Chelsea said. "You should come with me."

"They don't want me there."

In fact, I had a low-grade anxiety that Jonah sent the incriminating photo directly to the police. Any moment, cops could show up to the wave pool for my arrest. So far, only a group trip from Piney Acres Retirement Village gave me any trouble. A large-scale wristband mix-up.

I nodded to the flyer. "Terry knows?" Blender must have gotten permission after all.

"Heck, no." Chelsea laughed. "Look at the location. It's not even an address, just a super obvious code. I only found this because Craig had the flyer from working the pit. It's not being passed around on this side."

Chelsea continued to pester me about going to the muscle car show until our shift ended.

"How about this," she said as she closed her locker door. "We both go home, shower and change our clothes, and I'll come around to get you."

I swung my purse my shoulder. "Why do you want me to go so badly?"

A group of dry ride folks walked in and Chelsea zipped her lips. We continued our conversation outside. "The truth is, I feel horrible for harping on Jonah. I didn't know him or what he went through. I feel like I ruined your summer romance."

"My summer romance? You're probably making it more than it was." I tried to shrug off the hurt I felt over Jonah and having caused him more pain. "Nando told me to stay away. I don't think they'd like it if I showed up."

"Maybe they're waiting for just that. Sometimes a second chance takes nudging. I should know a thing or two about needing a nudge."

My gut told me she was right. I sighed, knowing my will had caved. "Okay. But I can't promise I'll like it."

After a much-needed shower, I obsessed over what to wear tonight to return to Wild Adventure. Finally, I decided on cropped jeans, a striped tank, and a light zip-up hoodie just in case.

Chelsea swung by my house to drive us back to the park. She'd made it all too easy to agree to going tonight by offering to drive. Almost like she wanted me to go.

Like she wanted me to be her friend again.

Back at Wild Adventure, Chelsea followed the road around the back end of the park. Potholes signaled we'd made it to old park territory.

Chelsea inched forward behind the cars in front of us. There was honest-to-goodness *traffic* out here.

Ahead of us, rows of colorful cars positioned at varying angles brightened up the usually desolate lot. Clusters of people gathered around and between the cars.

After Chelsea parked, we hopped out and made our way toward the cars. Music blasted from a sleek black Corvette with the hood and side doors open.

"Are you headed to go-karts or Final Lap?" a guy stationed in the parking lot directing guests asked. "Oh."

I did a double take. "Nando?"

The guy in front of us looked like Nando but with a Blender makeover. Spiky black hair, a plain white T-shirt paired with dark jeans cuffed at the bottom with black boots. A light gold chain at his neck.

"Oh, hey Elena. Chelsea." Nando's tone came out formal. "So, you came."

I hated the tension between us. Only I had to recognize he'd known Jonah longer than he'd known me. I'd hurt his friend. Lines had to be drawn.

"I know you're loyal to Jonah," I said. "I'm sorry for hurting you and I hope someday we can be friends again and—"

Nando gave me a light punch on the arm. "I still want to be your friend, Elena. Why haven't you come back around?"

"You told me to leave you alone."

"Yeah. I did. I was upset. Truth? Last time I saw you, I was heatstroking out by Paul Bunyan worried Mariela wanted to break up with me. Then the stuff with Jonah and losing two pit crew? It was too much. I may have overreacted."

"Oh." Obviously, Nando had a life outside of my own drama, and aside from Jonah too. "Thanks. I'd love to be your friend."

"Cool, cool. Just promise me you'll talk to Jonah so you two dummies can get back together."

"I know, right?" Chelsea said, as if she and Nando had been discussing this very thing.

"He won't talk to me," I told them both. "I got him *fired.*"

"Did you or did the Keenes and Uncle Frankie?" Nando handed me tickets he pulled from his back pocket. "Free soft drinks at Final Lap. Tell your friends. But tell them to buy food or we'll never be able to do this again. Now go on by those orange cars and tell Blender how cute they are."

As if I had a death wish. "I'm not sure Blender wants to see me either."

"Elena—we miss you. There's more going on if you look hard enough." Nando's attention moved past us to another group approaching.

"What's with Nando being cryptic?" I asked Chelsea, knowing she wouldn't have an answer.

"Who is Blender?" she asked. "I see the orange cars and—oh. *That* guy. I can't believe you've been holding out, Elena. You work with some hotties."

"Not grease monkeys?"

Her cheeks colored. "Never listen to me again unless I tell you to."

That sounded like something I would say. No wonder Chelsea and I got along.

She'd caught sight of Blender, given the hearts in her eyes. Blender wore almost identical clothes to Nando and was surrounded by tough-looking guys and pretty women. I hesitated.

"Elena!" Blender walked forward, his fist out for a bump. "And you brought a friend."

"I'm Chelsea." Her name nearly exploded out of her.

"Cool." Blender nodded. "You gotta show us your muscles to get in."

I gaped at him.

He laughed and flexed a bicep. "I'm kidding. I owe you for the inspiration, though. This is fun. We've got a bunch more who want to do this next time. I told everybody to go through and ride or get food. And did you see how clean this lot looks?"

Blender practically beamed with pride. True enough, the scrappy outer lot had been cleared of random trash and alarming chunks of dislodged pavement.

The music from the Corvette switched to a song with deep bass notes.

"Turn that up," Blender called to the owner. A group of college age women danced as the music blared.

"You call these cars classics?" An older man with sun-weathered skin and dark hair under an auto body shop cap strolled over. He pat Blender on the back. "I've got socks older than some of these cars, son."

"Is this your dad?" I asked Blender.

If Blender could blush, he almost did. "My uncle, actually. Dad is coming later. This guy here brought the old folks."

Blender's uncle laughed. "We drove our classics when they were new."

"This is about any era muscle car," Blender explained, probably more for our sake since his uncle obviously knew. "It's not a contest on who has the oldest set of wheels."

The two of them bantered about Mustang models and I found myself laughing along.

Blender edged toward me as his uncle showed Chelsea a closer look at a car. He clapped a hand at my shoulder. "Message received, by the way. Thank you."

My breath quickened. "You didn't write back. I didn't know if…"

"I got him the info and sent the photo to an encrypted hard drive. Already wiped my phone and change my number."

"Are you serious?" I wasn't sure how I'd explain to my parents I needed a new phone already. I'd only had mine four months.

Blender grinned. He was joking. At least I thought. "Thank you for passing that on. I wanted to make sure someone else had the evidence we…came across."

"Proud of you, Elena. You're welcome here anytime. I hope you know that."

It meant so much to hear, I nearly cried.

Other guests waited to speak with Blender and his uncle, so Chelsea and I made our way toward Final Lap. Only the waiting area didn't have a single square inch of space for us.

A hostess squeezed through the waiting bodies. "If you've got drink tickets, you can go directly to the bar.

Non-alcoholic, obviously. For food, I can put you on the waiting list. A one hour wait time."

An hour wait? At Final Lap? Wow. Business really boomed tonight.

We decided to skip the food and returned to the cars, drifting by a hot pink ride reminding me of a Matchbox toy car.

"Elena, what are you doing here?" KJ Keene appeared in front of us looking like he'd discovered somebody replaced his hair gel with denture cream. Beside him, three guys I recognized from the water park.

"Hey, KJ!" Chelsea smiled and waved. "Putting in a paid appearance?"

He shot her a confused look while I kicked her in the shin.

KJ pointed his agitation at me. "Are you working with *them*? For this?"

"It's just people hanging out."

KJ scowled. "This is an organized event. I bet it's part of your little contest to get people to care about your loser friends and the loser park. But this? This goes too far."

Whoa—big attitude change from KJ coming in hot. Something must have happened. I hadn't seen him all day—he'd been off the schedule at the wave pool.

"What happened to putting the past behind us?" I demanded. "And don't call my friends losers. It's an ugly look on you." It was hard for KJ to look anything but extremely hot, but honestly? His shine had tarnished in my eyes. "Secondly—"

I didn't get to my second point because KJ and his water park crew pushed past us. "We're not alone, you know," KJ said. "We brought friends."

More Wild Adventure staff approached. Familiar faces from the meetings, but not faces I saw regularly.

"Dry rides," Chelsea said low beside me.

A guy with a buzz cut and a Snoopy tattoo on his arm pumped a fist in the air. "Dry ride or die!"

Two women and three other guys assembled behind their leader, facing KJ's group. The Snoopy guy shook KJ's hand.

"We won't stand for it," he said to KJ. "That prize money belongs to us."

"I think he's Tilt-N-Turn," Chelsea filled in for me.

"What is this, a carnival version of *West Side Story?*" I turned to Chelsea. "Sorry." That was the school musical planned for senior year so she probably already dreaded the auditions.

"No problem. I can't tell if KJ should be a Shark or a Jet."

What worried me more was the Adventure Zone turf war playing out in front of us.

The group turned as a unified entity and barreled toward Blender. At the same time, Terry bulleted in from another direction. KJ's crew, the dry riders, and Terry moved ahead.

Chelsea and I rushed to keep up.

"I'm glad you reported this, KJ," Terry said as he walked. "This is far worse than I thought."

"They've been planning for weeks," KJ spat out.

"What seems to be the problem?" Blender's voice carried to us as we angled for a better view. "Terry, you look stressed. Business is good. We've got a ton of customers tonight."

"This is private property." Terry pulled himself to his full height. His neck ringed red from a splotchy sunburn. "This event is in violation of park rules."

"Parking cars in a parking lot is against park rules?" Blender laughed and the guests around him echoed his laughter.

Eek. *Not good to poke the bear, Blender.*

"It's a restricted area," Terry sputtered.

"It's a parking lot."

Blender's uncle sauntered toward us with the confidence of someone who was rarely told no. Two men probably in their fifties with tattoos on their arms and necks flanked him. "A group of us decided we wanted to spend our Friday night at Wild Adventure. Go-karts and dinner at your restaurant. Just look at those lines."

Terry's attention followed where Blender's uncle looked. Sure enough, the line to Final Lap now stretched out the door. Beyond the high chain link fencing, karts raced around the track. I watched Terry mentally envision how many paying park guests might be waiting to ride next.

"What about the cars?" Terry snapped his focus to a green Dodge with gleaming chrome accents. "They're all fancy."

"Vintage car club," Blender's uncle answered. "These are what we drive on Friday nights."

"*Any* era muscle car," Blender added. "Some of us like our cars from a recent decade." He shook his head, as if to remind himself that wasn't the point right now. "Imagine if every Friday our car clubs took a trip here to spend our money at the park. And what if we told the Detroit clubs. And the clubs around the capitol." He leaned closer to Terry. "What if we told Uncle Frankie this was your idea. All this extra park revenue and the idea came from *you*."

Terry's expression morphed from disgruntled to confused to curious. "If it was my idea...yes..."

KJ grabbed Terry by the shoulder. "You can't let them get away with this. They're pocketing cash and profiting. They did this without permission."

"It's *illegal!*" Snoopy Tat shouted.

Chelsea huffed beside me. "I'll tell you who's pocketing cash," she muttered.

Blender made a show of flipping the insides of his jeans pockets open. "What cash? Feel free to show us which laws we broke. The muscle car community is tight. We told some friends and they told some friends. Now they're all here spending money at the park. Where is the problem?"

Terry shrugged away from KJ. "Where *is* the problem, KJ? I'm not seeing it upon closer inspection." His attention turned to the entrance where guests filtered toward the park entrance and Final Lap.

KJ angled toward Blender. "Wait until my dad hears of this. You'll be out of a job and banned from this park."

"Is that your answer to everything? Running to your dad?"

I held my breath. *Jonah has joined your party.*

KJ whipped around. "You're treading on thin ice. The last thing you need is another lawsuit. I can't believe you dared show up."

Jonah moved forward, his large frame casting long shadows across KJ in the late evening sun. "Trouble at work? Ask daddy to clean it up. Bored of working? Ask daddy to get you paid anyway. Girl doesn't like you back? Ask daddy—"

KJ swung his arm. Hard. At Jonah.

"No!" I yelled.

Jonah deftly stepped aside, sending KJ stumbling forward and into the green Dodge. His elbow knocked against the driver's side door below the window.

"Hey! Watch the car!" A white woman in a black tank and black jeans bolted toward him. "You dent it, you fix it."

KJ righted himself and went for round two with Jonah.

Jonah dodged and caught KJ by the shoulder in a firm grip. "I don't want to fight you, dude."

KJ's eyes lit with fire. "Stop lying about what happened!"

"I think this is about more than the cars," Blender's uncle said.

Blender stroked his chin in thought. "Mmhmm."

The older men moved forward. "Step away from the vehicles."

Jonah stepped back from KJ, giving him space. He said nothing. The older men worked to disperse the crowd and took Terry aside, leaving a smaller crowd of us park staff.

"Why don't we get a car show?" the Snoopy guy blurted out. "We want a car show."

"Let's work together," Blender told him. "Dry rides need love, too."

The guy nodded and looked past him. "Is that a Ford Torino racing edition?"

"You bet it is." Blender pat the guy on the back and steered him toward the vintage vehicle. The remaining dry riders talked among themselves and drifted off to look at cars.

KJ kept his glare on Jonah. "You can't change anything. You don't belong here. You never have and now it's final."

"That's not true," I spoke up. "You can change what's happening right now. Call off the legal eagles. Get him his job back. You said you'd talk to your parents, what happened to that? Jonah doesn't deserve to be dragged back into some skeezy court case just because you and your dad are mad."

KJ looked at me incredulously. "Why do you keep siding with him? He's beneath you."

My face grew hot as tears sprung loose. Seeing Jonah flinch from such a crappy insult—I couldn't take it. Jonah might not want to hear this but I would say it anyway. "I care about Jonah. I'm...well, we'd probably still be together if I hadn't wrecked things between us. That's on me. But he shouldn't suffer."

Jonah's attention landed fully on me. I couldn't read his expression. It wasn't angry or shut off. It was something, I just wasn't sure what.

The water park guys muttered to each other. "This is boring," one guy said. "I'm gonna go look at cars."

KJ waved them off, still focused on me. "It's not about him *suffering*. This is bigger, Elena. You don't need to slum it with these losers. Think of our families. Think of all the things at stake for us."

At stake for him. He must have known about the extra cash coming his family's way. Maybe KJ took the money himself. Clearly, he felt the threat and understood Jonah needed to be out of their lives.

As for my family, I'd gently advised John to pursue a financial audit of the Keene family before he made any business decisions. I told him I'd learned about audits from a podcast.

"Maybe your parents need hobbies besides suing people." Chelsea pointed her scorn at KJ. "It's gross how obsessed they are with taking legal action against people who can barely afford it. Can't they like, bungee jump in Australia or go nuts in Vegas or something?"

KJ looked past us as if in a daze.

"You don't have to fight your parents' battles," I said, gaining momentum. "No one here wants to fight. Physically or in a court room. Don't you want a fresh start when you leave for college? You need to separate yourself from what they expect of you or you'll always be under their thumb. I know deep down you're a good person." If auditors dipped into his family's financials—or into Uncle Frankie's—he'd need something to fall back on besides his parents.

KJ's fire dwindled to embers. "But you said I'm your longest running crush."

Really? A bruised ego? "You still get top billing there. But I had to move on. Just like you need to move on. From all of this."

KJ looked from me to Jonah. "Is it true? You two would still be together if my parents hadn't called their attorneys?"

Jonah took in a silent breath. A moment passed where he seemed to wrestle with what to say. Finally, he spoke. "Yes. It just got too complicated."

My body numbed. *I* was complicated. Too much to be worth putting up with. Even if the universe believed I was special.

KJ looked around. His parkie defense buddies had deserted him. Terry had his head under the hood of Blender's bumble bee car while Blender narrated the details he loved to share with anyone who'd listen.

"I'm gonna take off," KJ said and peeled away.

Jonah stood by as a solid unmoving presence.

My heart thrummed in my chest. I wanted to run to him. To hug him. To...any kind of contact. But I couldn't. He didn't want to talk to me and I'd embarrassed myself in front of him yet again.

"*Talk to him,*" Chelsea whispered like a little scheming angel at my shoulder.

Turned out, Jonah spoke first. "You didn't have to say those things."

"I know I can't fix what I did. I'm sorry."

He sighed. "I know. Look, I need to go."

Before I could process what happened, Jonah turned and lumbered off.

"Well, I don't like how that went," Chelsea said as Jonah headed to the Wild Adventure park entrance. She said it loud enough he could probably hear.

Seeing him retreat signaled that what we had was done and over with.

"What can I say? When I hurt people, I hurt 'em bad." I pulled my hair forward across my shoulder, wishing I could hide inside it.

"Oh, stop." She shoved me. "I think you're scared to go after him."

"Scared?"

"What. Is happening?" Nando marched from his parking lot post looking stern and mildly murderous. "Why aren't you and Jonah kissing? Where is my make-up scene?"

"I know, right?" Chelsea added.

"Come on," I said. "This isn't a theater production."

"The only theater happening is you and Jonah acting like you aren't wild to get back together." He crossed his arms. "And yes, I used wild to tie in Wild Adventure. It's clever."

"I can't make Jonah want me back." I untied the hoodie from my waist and slipped it on to erase the chill as the sun sank lower. "If I press too much, we get into stalker territory. I don't want that on my permanent record."

"Did he go back to the park?" Nando asked. "I missed what happened after KJ left. These ladies in jeans and black tops wouldn't let up with questions about mojitos when I gave them the drink tickets. I'm like, they're free drinks for *soda*."

"He did," Chelsea answered. "He's not banned from Wild Adventure, right? He just doesn't work there."

"Exactly." Nando checked behind him. "No more cars coming in. Let's go." He grabbed my hand.

I reluctantly let myself get pulled. "What am I supposed to say to Jonah? I've apologized already."

"Do what you do best," Chelsea said. "Don't give up."

Chapter Twenty-five

♥

Inside the Go Zone, the usual amount of park guests waited in line for a Friday night, but more guests hung on the outskirts of the pit and in clusters along the path to Final Lap. Piped in music coming from the pit added a lively atmosphere.

"Audio got the speakers working again," Nando said as we grew closer. "Seems obvious, huh?"

"Audio fixing audio?" Chelsea giggled. "I like all your nicknames."

I guess it proved I never belonged since I hadn't earned a nickname. But I was tired of feeling sorry for myself. We were here to... "So, what are we here to do again?"

Nando sighed. "Face Jonah. Do forgiveness stuff. Happily ever after."

"It's not that easy."

"Then make it easy. Speak Jonah's language. You already know how."

What did that even mean? "We basically jumped the fence to bother him when he's already made it clear he's done."

Jonah, talking to Craig in the pit, noticed the three of us. He shook his head and turned away.

Craig came toward us and handed the green Go flag to Chelsea. "Hey." His smile centered on her and the two looked at each other in a way that hurt my bones.

"I get to wave this?" Chelsea hopped up and down.

"Absolutely."

I could practically sense the growl pulsing from Jonah.

Craig circled back to Jonah. "Hey, man. Let's all talk."

I put up my hands. "It's okay. I don't..."

And then Jonah turned toward me and every excuse fell away. His face. Jonah wasn't angry. He wasn't growling. He was...it almost looked like he was crying.

"Are you crying, dude?" Craig asked.

Jonah cut him a look. "I got dust in my eyes. No. I'm not crying."

My shoulders sank. So much for an emotional reaction over me.

"Elena!" Nando shouted from behind the helmet counter. His next words he mouthed. *Race him.*

"What?" Then it hit me. Speak Jonah's language. Neither of us worked in the pit any longer, so when else would we get this shot?

"Heads up!" Nando yelled from the stand. A helmet sailed and I caught it.

I whipped around to Jonah. "I'll race you."

He stilled. "You. Want to race *me*."

I walked closer. "We've raced before."

"And you lost."

"Now I've practiced. I know you can't pass up a chance to race. Especially with what I'm offering."

He raised a brow. "And what's that?"

I swallowed. Here goes. "Me."

"You?"

"Yup."

"You're offering yourself as a prize? Isn't that like, super un-feminist?"

I may be crashing and burning before I hit the gas. Oh well, plowing ahead. "I challenge you to a race. If I win, I get a chance to woo you back. If I lose, I'll...walk away. For good."

I shut my eyes. I couldn't face his face. Maybe not ever after saying that.

An unexpected sound triggered my eyes to open. He was laughing. Jonah was *laughing*. *At me.*

But he smiled. "You're on."

Jonah and I dashed to the spare karts in the pit. We each hopped in. Revved the engines. Jonah pulled up to the white line and I drove up beside him. He stared straight ahead.

This felt stupid, but then I remembered Jonah's smile. I really liked that smile. I really wanted to see that smile again. Especially if I put it there.

As if sensing me staring, we made eye contact. Jonah winked.

My heart backflipped.

"This is so *exciting*," Chelsea gushed from the side of the pit. "And romantic."

"Counting down," Nando said. "Three, two, one, Go!"

Chelsea waved the green flag and we were off. I slammed on the gas and tore out in front of Jonah. Knowing this lead would be short-lived, I eased up as we entered the track, checking behind for any early lappers. With the road clear ahead, I hauled it.

Jonah sped past. *Dangit!*

He took the first turn like a pro because of course he did—he could drive this track in his sleep.

But I wasn't half bad either, having practiced. I matched his speed, knowing he'd turn early and cut close to the side. I'd watched Jonah more times than I'd raced, and that intel informed my moves.

My mind drifted to his smile and warmth pooled in my limbs.

I couldn't think of that now. Not with Jonah only one kart length ahead and my favorite turn coming up.

He'd know I'd try to take him at the turn. I didn't have many tricks up my Wild Adventure T-shirt sleeve, and besides, I wasn't even wearing that shirt.

Each turn Jonah blocked me from passing. This next one wouldn't be any different.

Just like this race wasn't any different from real life. He blocked me from reaching him. No different on the track than off it. Wasn't that enough of a sign for me to back off?

If I lost, I'd have to make good on what I said. If Jonah didn't want me around, I had to stop trying to convince him. I'd already pressed him enough. I needed to honor his request if he was done with me. With us.

I'd have to be done with us too. And not like how I'd been pretending this past week. For real.

My eyes blurred and not from road dust. My lip trembled and then I burst. A sob so harsh it hurt my cheeks. I tried to gulp it back. There was nowhere for it to go. It had to come out.

My sobs came harder. I hadn't cried like this in a long time. Stupid, big breath heaving I couldn't control.

Jonah gained more and more distance. I was done for. He crossed the line ahead of us and approached the pit.

I let off the gas to coast. The pit entrance neared where not only my coworkers watched but a line of park guests waited their turn. They'd all get a chance to gawk at the deranged crying girl.

I eased my way into the pit and parked as far back as possible for a quick escape. Ripping the helmet off, I ignored the calling of my name and ran.

The dumb part about escaping at work was the people you worked with knew all the hiding places. I couldn't escape to my car since Chelsea drove.

To the garage it was. Blender's safe haven, and Blender was busy with the car show. I zipped around the staff building and took the route least visible from the pit. I had mere seconds of a lead.

I found the farthest darkest corner of the garage and sat on a low plastic stepping stool. I needed to buy some time and collect myself.

All these feelings ran wild inside me and I couldn't slow them down. I didn't know how to fix anything. The more I tried, the worse it turned out. I'd broken into an office. I'd dug up dirt on somebody and photographed illicit payments. What had this summer turned into?

"Elena?"

Crud. Jonah already found me. I crouched lower. I held my breath and wished for a teleporter. The only thing close by was a socket wrench.

Footsteps drew nearer and a light switched on overhead.

"Elena." Jonah's voice came whisper-soft, so quiet I thought I'd imagined it.

Glancing up to his silhouette, he stood a good ten feet away. I hugged my knees to my chest. "Just go."

He did not go. "Why did you stop racing?"

"I didn't. You won. Of course you won."

"You slowed down. You didn't try your move at your favorite turn."

There was a time I would have marveled he knew my favorite track turn. "What was the use?"

He slid his hands into his pockets. "I liked how you thought you could win. I thought you might."

"The whole thing was stupid." I tugged at my hair, now a mess of tangles from the wind and the helmet. "I can't believe I offered myself as a prize. That was *so weird.* I'm sorry, and I promise I'll do what I said. I'll leave you alone. I swear." Now, I'd sit with this humiliation until I could face the public for a ride home.

Without looking up, I sensed he'd moved closer. "It was sweet, what you did. It was cool and kind of funny and...I liked that you challenged me."

"You told me to leave you alone and I've been badgering you. I'm like a stalker starter pack. I swear, I won't bother you again."

His shadow colored the concrete floor in front of me. "I don't think you're a bother. When I said things were complicated, I meant things—life—not you. You deserve someone who won't push you away. I push people out. I wish I deserved you."

My head snapped up. "Deserve me? I don't deserve you. You don't know what I've done."

"I have a hunch. And I'm thankful." Jonah lowered to a crouch. With a tentative hand, he gently moved my hair back from my face. "You've been crying. I'm so sorry I hurt you."

"I'm crying because I'm a mess. I feel all these emotions and they had nowhere to go. I can't put that on you."

He dropped his hand. "I'd like you to. I'm a big guy. I can take it."

I half laughed at that, but it kind of hurt my face. "You shouldn't have to take on my emotional drama. That's for me and my counselor to sort out."

"Caring about people means sharing some of that load. I...I wish I'd been better about telling you about my stuff. I didn't know how. I freaked when the attorney called again. I panicked. I should have taken more time to talk it out."

"You don't have to make excuses. I messed up."

"What you sent helped. I needed to thank you, but I didn't want to say it in a text. As for the legal threats, my attorney handled it. There's nothing else. No more court dates. It's done."

"But you had to use your money, didn't you?"

"It wasn't so much. I didn't know enough about how these things work, but I do now."

"And you're not scared they'll come after you? Chelsea said the Keenes play games with lawsuits."

"I found out a lot of the Keenes' threats are empty. The attorneys had a hunch the family was getting kickbacks from the park. Pressuring Uncle Frankie to pay up or they'd dish park secrets. The cash went directly to KJ's dad. From what we can tell, I don't think KJ even knew. Now we know their weakness. Cayden's folks reviewed everything with the attorneys and looped in Uncle Frankie. The Big Cheese—his legal team is...let's say, *creative*. Uncle Frankie's a proud guy. He hates anyone thinking he's being manipulated. No one wants this getting out, so they agreed to stop pursuing us."

A chunk of my tension eased out. "I think KJ will back off. I've seen what his family is like. I think he has a lot of figuring out to do. What about your job?"

"It's mine if I want it."

A total relief. "And do you?"

Jonah nodded. "Most of all, I wish I could get this week back."

"What do you mean?"

"One week without you felt like...gasping for air. Like a vise clamping on my heart. Like I'd been run over by a fleet of karts."

I laughed and burst into a sob at the same time. I slapped a hand to my mouth. "I don't know what that was. I am totally reckless with emotion right now."

Jonah looked at me. All of me, somehow, right in the eyes. "I miss you, Elena. I've been wanting to tell you so many things but didn't know how. Pushing people away is what I go back to. It's my fault I pushed you from me."

My breath caught up as Jonah moved forward. He held out a hand. He stood and helped me to standing.

"I'd like to kiss you," he said.

My feet puddled into the floor. I traced my fingers from his wrist up his arm, stepping in. I tilted my chin up and looked into his eyes.

Jonah pulled me to him, moving his hand up my back to the nape of my neck. His fingers curled into my hair as his lips found mine.

He tasted like mint and summer nights. I sank into his arms, my emotions settling into a steady hum of affection and gratefulness, topped with happy.

My toes curled and I pulled back. "I missed you too. I'm worried I'll wreck things again."

"I'm worried I'll push you away."

We stood, still holding each other.

"I think it's worth the risk," Jonah said. "Even if we mess up. What if we don't? Or, what if we do and it doesn't matter?"

"Kind of like bonus lives in a video game. We start the level and learn from where we went wrong."

He laughed. "I like that analogy."

I moved my hands up his hulking biceps. They really were impressive. "I like these guns."

A quiet laugh shook him. "Is this what it's going to be like?"

"Me admiring your strength? Probably." I squeezed his arm muscles. "Definitely."

Now that we'd determined neither of us was perfect, we could get back to more kissing.

"Elena? Jonah?" a voice called.

As we turned, Nando, Chelsea, and Craig stood in the spot where Jonah had only minutes ago. "Oh good," Nando said. "It's the happily ever after part."

Chapter Twenty-six

♥

"This seems like a trap."

"It's only a trap if you let it be a trap," Jonah said. "Nobody even knows we're here."

Both of us stood side by side, sweating, in the small supply building otherwise known as the Love Hut. We were legitimately gathering supplies, but the full circleness of the situation was not lost on me.

I eyed the door. "The meeting starts in ten minutes. Some staff might be early."

Jonah took the box I held and added it on top of his, transferring both to one arm. With his free hand, he pulled me toward him and slid his fingers through my hair. A kiss landed on my lips. Just enough to scramble my insides.

"Is it hot in here?" I fanned myself.

"It's ninety degrees out and there's no air conditioning."

"I meant you. You're making me hot."

He grinned, clearly loving he'd made me say this out loud.

Jonah opened the shack door and this time only parched grass and the employee gate greeted us. No prying eyes waiting to crown me a virginal whatever. That seemed ages ago.

We took our supplies inside the main staff building and taped a sign on it: *Go Zone*. We left the boxes by the door. After our staff meeting, we'd deliver them by golf cart. Then we'd work our shift together.

In the three days since the muscle car show, we'd had Uncle Frankie remotely sign-off on moving me back to the Go Zone. Well, my parents had convinced him after I'd convinced them.

The past few days there'd been a lot of convincing going on.

Chelsea convinced her parents to call my parents for a heart to heart on the Keene family. I'd invited Chelsea first as an introduction to get the ball rolling. Chelsea, it turned out, was great at schmoozing with parents. She'd almost made it seem like John and Mom's idea to call her folks.

John and Mom talked on speaker phone to Chelsea's parents in our downstairs home office. From what I'd heard listening at the door, John had a lot of thoughtful questions about lawsuits and betrayals and financial audits. It was like an honest-to-goodness soap opera in there with the topics they'd covered.

And to keep myself on the straight and narrow, I listened to a podcast about financial audits. I lasted ten minutes.

I had a hunch John would not go into business with the Keene family.

I took a quick trip to the employee restroom to get myself together, then returned out back where Jonah, Blender, and Nando stood. Craig and Chelsea held hands in the area between us. More staff trickled in from the employee entrance.

KJ entered and hinted at a chin nod. We'd talked once since the car show where he'd mumbled a half apology, saying his folks wanted him to quit so he might not show up again. Yet here he stood. Maybe he'd stood up to his parents about what he wanted.

"Gather up, Wild crew!" Terry announced as staff accumulated. It was early enough in the day the sun wasn't yet at high scorch. "Let's get started. Progress update on our competition—we're close! The old park picked up the pace this season."

A smattering of clapping came from our small collection of Go Zone staff, joined in by Chelsea, Craig and a few others. KJ added a few claps.

"I wanted to give credit where it's due," Terry went on. "Bartholomew Lando"

Nando sucked in air.

I turned to him. "What? Who's that?"

"It's me." Blender stepped forward, almost sheepish. "I don't use my full name much."

Nando leaned into toward me. "He *really* doesn't like people using his full name."

"Blender?" Terry seemed to have trouble getting the nickname out. "Thanks to you and your car club spreading the word about Wild Adventure, Uncle Frankie approved an official car show on park property with a promotional park pass. This will benefit every area of the park, not just the Go Zone."

A collective cheer went up from the dry riders.

"We look forward to working together with you on it," Terry said to Blender.

Blender had been right. Uncle Frankie saw the dollar signs, and dollars made up his bottom line.

"Next on my agenda," Terry went on. "The way we talk about our parks. Old and new. And the old-new versus the new-new. There are a multitude of zone factions and frankly, it needs to stop."

The dry riders stirred themselves up again.

Terry held up a hand. "Here to explain more on this is our very own family leader—Uncle Frankie."

On cue, Uncle Frankie emerged from the staff building deeply tanned in a white polo shirt tucked into white pants with an ironed crease down the middle and shoes possibly made of alligator skin.

Frankie held his arms out. "My Wild children! I've missed you. Barbados isn't the same as Midwestern Michigan. Alas, I'm back and ready to talk the future of this park." He scanned the crowd looking at each of us. His gaze paused on me—nope, probably Jonah beside me. The boy he'd remotely fired and hired again in the span of a week. He smiled and a gold tooth glinted. "First, the friendly competition I hear turned not so friendly. Uncle Frankie doesn't like that."

All chatter faded. A lone throat cleared.

"But what I do like is seeing these numbers go up. Go Zone—gotta hand it to you. You kids worked your tails off and I'm loving it."

I had to admit, it felt good to hear. It took a group effort, and we'd brought recognition to our side of the park. I could fully call it our side now that I was back where I belonged.

Uncle Frankie clapped for a few beats. "I'm happy to say Uncle Frankie has come upon a windfall—that's cashflow, kids. It's finally time to unite the two sides of the park. More rides will connect the old Midway to the Go Zone. I only needed the right city representative in office to approve those permits to drain the bog. Construction starts this fall. In the meantime, we need to stop with the old vs new. We're all Wild here. Am I right?"

Murmurs surfaced through the crowd.

"Pride in your zone is golden," Uncle Frankie said. "Never stop! But we need to work together to live in harmony. That's what my chiropractor told me. Her name is Janet and we're engaged."

I clapped along with the rest of the staff because it seemed like the right thing to do.

"As for the competition," he went on. "I declare it a success. Complaints are down, the nurse's station has an excess of band-aids, and our older rides are seeing new fans. I'm so proud." He pulled a folded sheet of paper from his back pocket. "But we said there would be a winner."

Voices buzzed with anticipation.

Uncle Frankie grinned, holding up the paper. He soaked up our attention like it was breakfast. "The winner is...Little Adventurer Zone!"

A chorus of cheers and screams went up from the small group I would have worked with had none of this summer ever happened.

"Weird, I never made a point to look at the kids' zone stats," Nando admitted. "It's like I looked right past them."

True underdogs. They were the least flashy, least drama-prone staff in the entire park. Several of them worked as school teachers in the park off-season.

A scuffle broke out among the dry riders.

"Don't hurt him!" Bursting from the office, Jennifer ran toward a guy with long dark hair tucked behind his ears who fended off Snoopy Tattoo.

"*The Scrambler*," Chelsea mouthed to me.

Jennifer, in a hot pink tube dress paired with the neon yellow belt, tugged the Scrambler away from the chaos. As Uncle Frankie ordered the guys to break it up, our Go Zone crew folded around each other.

"Well, that's that," I said. "We lost."

"But did we?" Nando asked with a glint in his braces.

Blender narrowed his eyes at him. "Don't be corny."

"My whole aesthetic is corny."

"What do you say, Bartholomew?" I elbowed Blender lightly.

"Don't start with me, Lane Change."

"Lane Change?" I burst out laughing.

Blender shrugged. "Elena. Lane Change. I thought it fit. That's always your move on the course—you make a last second change to win."

"Except it never works."

Blender looked between me and Jonah. "Seems like it might have."

Jonah grinned, which was to say, his mouth turned up a fraction at the corners.

Jonah and I filtered out behind the others. As we gathered our supply boxes and headed out the door to the park, KJ caught up to us.

"Hey, Elena. Jonah." He stopped when we turned. "I'm glad to hear you both got your jobs back. I'm the one who went to Uncle Frankie about the parks being so divided. It was getting out of control." He rocked back on his heels. "Anyway, just wanted to say thanks for showing me I'd been kind of a jerk."

I glanced to Jonah who kept his expression neutral. At least he wasn't emitting threat pheromones. Jonah nodded once in recognition.

KJ took off, leaving Jonah and me standing in the now blazing sun.

"That was a good development," I said.

Jonah took the box I carried and loaded it on the back of a nearby golf cart. "I thought we could take the scenic route this morning. Will you let me take you for a drive?"

I slid into the passenger seat of the golf cart which had a little canopy on it. "Thank you, sir. I'd love to."

He leaned across the seat and kissed me sweetly on the lips. "Lane Change. Now, that was funny."

Epilogue

♥

"This is definitely the coolest end-of-summer bash Wild Adventure has put on," Nando told me as he returned to the pit after sending off the latest batch of kart riders.

"You've only worked here one other summer," I pointed out.

He gave me an epic eyeroll. "I've *visited* here other summers. And don't sass back."

"Sass backs are my favorite kind of sass." I sprayed down my nearly sparkling helmet counter. "I'm going to miss our mutual sassing when school starts next week."

"Aw. Elena, you've become attached." He slung an arm around me. "We can still hang out even if summer's over."

Technically, summer didn't end for another month, and the park would remain open on weekends through Halloween. But the water park would close for the season and most of the summer staff would be cut. Including me. It was a seniority thing, where those who stayed on for weekends were those who worked here longest.

I was cool with it. I'd had my wild summer.

Jonah returned from the staff lot carrying a bouquet of churros from a food truck parked just outside our entrance. "There's got to be double the people here for the car show than last time."

I grabbed a churro from him and bit into the sweet cinnamon and sugar fried dough stick. "Awesome. Blender has to be super pumped."

"I'm pretty sure he just got a job offer from a guy out there." Jonah nodded toward the gate. "An auto body shop that does higher-end detailing."

I hoped Blender would take the job, even if he was oddly loyal to Wild Adventure. Maybe not so odd. I'd grown to like these Midfits quite a bit.

Music started up again from the stage in the lot. Uncle Frankie went all out for the last full weekend of the season. Live music, more muscle cars, and a limited assortment of food trucks to take care of what Final Lap couldn't handle with the added crowds.

Jonah, Nando, I moved deeper into the pit to keep an eye on the line and the track. Mark wandered over followed by Audio.

Audio pulled his headphones fully down to rest around his neck. "It's been real, folks. I'm headed out." He did his elaborate fist bumps with the guys, and then for me did a simple high-five. Last time we'd tried the fist bump with more movements I'd ended up caressing his hand like an out-of-touch grandma. Super awkward.

"You coming back next summer?" Jonah asked.

Audio, still free earin' without headphones, shook his head. "I'm headed west."

"California?" I asked.

"Kalamazoo. I'm not coming back here after college next summer."

Still in Michigan, but I suppose it counted as going west. "Good luck."

Nando burst forward and hugged Audio. I grinned and piled on behind him. Mark and Jonah joined for a group hug. I didn't care that we were sweaty and smelled like burnt rubber and worse. I wanted to remember us just the way we were right now.

As Audio headed out, dusk drew in. I glanced to Jonah who steadied his eyes on the track. Always watching and thinking ahead.

Since we didn't live that far from each other, despite attending different schools, the summer's end didn't feel as bittersweet. We had friends in common now. Plus, I knew where he lived.

And where he worked.

"I'm going to use my employee park pass every weekend," I told him after the current riders lapped the track.

"I'll put you on cleaning helmets." He slipped his hand in mine.

I grinned all over. "Okay."

He shot me a look. "No, that's terrible. I'm not making you work for free. Don't agree to that."

I shrugged. "I would probably end up doing it anyway. I'll still come here to see you."

Jonah smiled in a very Jonah way—barely, but still noticeable, at least to me. "I'd like to take you out on a real date away from the park."

I squeezed his hand. "I'd like that. And maybe to my school's fall dance?"

He didn't visibly react. "Do I look like a guy who likes to dance?"

Nando appeared in front of us, moving his shoulders in time with the music from the parking lot. "Anything can be dancing if you want it to." He mimed putting on a helmet and steering an imaginary kart, still grooving to the beat.

Jonah laughed. "Only you can get away with a dance like that." He turned a fraction toward me. "Of course I'll go with you to a dance."

My delight burst out in a squeal.

"Elena!" a voice called out.

I turned. Familiar faces collected in line behind the waiting guests. Holli Hayes, her friend Tala, Holli's boyfriend Will, and a few of Will's friends from his small town on the coast.

Nando shooed me off. "You, go. You and Jonah both. Mark and I will move the next group in."

I led Jonah to my waiting friends. A round of introductions followed.

"Cool shirt," Jonah said to Will. It was a black T-shirt with a band name and a logo featuring a haunted pirate ship. "My cousin is the drummer for that band."

Will blinked. "What? They are the *coolest*. They're not local. Do you have family in Seattle?"

"Yeah, my mom's originally from there." Jonah went on, seeming to fully engage Will with stories about the band.

Holli leaned over the guardrail to half hug me. "This is cool to see you in your element. You look happier here than when you were doing training runs with us."

I couldn't deny it. "Yeah. Running is just not my thing."

Her friends Antonio and Piper chimed in about a charity race they all did, except for Will who had sworn off running after giving it a go himself last summer.

We kept chatting as the line progressed.

Nando came over. "You both should ride next." He looked at me and Jonah. "Go with your friends."

Holli clapped excitedly. "Yes! Drive with us."

Our group's turn came up and Jonah and I headed for our staff karts set back from the others. We piled in and donned our helmets. An engine revved beside me. Jonah caught my eye and winked. I revved my engine back and blew him an air kiss.

The timer counted down and Nando swung the flag.

We were off.

Driving the course was even more fun with friends. Maybe this could be our thing every summer. Meet up, ride the rides, and make new memories.

Jonah hung back so I could drive alongside Holli and Tala. Only Tala took a tight turn ahead of us and blew dust in our faces.

At the end of our ride, a familiar adrenaline-filled energy coursed through my limbs.

Ahead of us from the staff entrance, Chelsea and Craig arrived, waving.

"We're off shift," Chelsea announced. "Need any help?"

I introduced her to Will and his friends. She and Craig weren't holding hands and seemed to keep more distance between them. Since they'd walked in together, they must not be totally at odds, but something seemed up. Maybe her thing with Craig was only meant for the summer. Kind of like how I'd originally thought of this summer as my chance with KJ before he left for college. Weirdly enough, I never expected it to last. I'd only seen as far ahead as this summer, and nothing beyond.

Instead, I found something else. I glanced to Jonah, still talking with Will. He moved his hands around as he spoke. Will tipped his head back and laughed.

Jonah looked up and caught me watching him. He gave me a smile that shook my insides. I loved seeing him happy and making friends. I loved that we had more than a summer to look forward to.

After one more round of karts, it was time to shut down the park.

My friends drifted out the gate to where the live music wrapped up. The rest of us closed the Go Zone.

As the helmet gate locked into place, a smattering of fireworks lit the sky.

Jonah clasped my hand. "You ready to go?"

I hung back as Nando and Mark left through the gate. "Just a minute."

I whirled to face him, moving my hands up his chest and around his neck. He rested a hand lightly at my back, just enough to give me that safe and secure feeling.

He kissed me, and I nearly floated away. I laughed against his lips and kissed him back. Shivers danced across my skin and down to my toes.

We stayed like that, one perfect moment to end the season.

He pulled back. "Want to do this again next summer?"

I kissed him again. "Absolutely."

What's Next

Thank you for reading! Reviews help readers find books. Please consider leaving a review on your favorite retailer.

Next in series: Free Wheeling Summer
Read on for Chapter 1 of Chelsea's story!

Free Wheeling Summer

♥

The first day of the rest of my life, and I'd already screwed up everything.

Our class valedictorian, Holli Hayes, looked across the sea of faces from her position at the podium. "Our futures are wide open."

Yeah, that's the problem.

She went on about hope, change, achievement. Words meant to be inspiring, but they lulled me into a funk.

My life, my future felt as uncertain as ever.

Plus, listening to someone awarded a legit title for over-achieving only solidified my uncertainty. I'd never been an over-achiever. More like a medium-achiever.

Clapping filled the auditorium. I followed along—Holli was my friend, after all. I had nothing against her or her full-ride scholarship to University of Michigan. I just couldn't relate.

I fit nicely on the edges of a bell curve. I did average in my classes and liked every class about the same. I kicked butt as Townsperson #4 whose sole purpose was to stand to the side and let the star actors shine.

As the ceremony droned on, dread filled me at my future plans. Or lack of. I had my whole life in front of me, and I couldn't escape the thought I'd already been left behind.

An elbow pierced my side.

"Chelsea. *That's you.*" Beside me, my friend, Elena DeWilde, nearly shoved me into the aisle. We happened to have last names sorting us next to each other for the commencement ceremony.

Looking to my left, sure enough, the seat was vacant. Tyler Decker had already crossed the stage, high school diploma in hand.

"Chelsea Devlin," West Ginsburg's principal announced with a tight smile. It was apparently her second time saying my name.

I scrambled forward, cringing at the synthetic swish my graduation robe made as I headed toward the stage. *Don't trip.*

I made it up the steps, crossed the stage, and shook hands with important people. Grabbing the diploma was the easy part. Every step after this? Uncharted territory.

Off stage, my classmates with last names earlier in the alphabet stood in clusters chatting and high-fiving.

"Took you a second, huh?" Tyler laughed and patted me on the back.

We weren't exactly friends, but we'd known each other since kindergarten and ended up in classes together ever since I could remember.

My responding laugh came a little too loud. "Just excited I guess, so I missed my name." Which made no sense, but Tyler wasn't exactly a sharpshooter.

"Where are you headed this fall?" he asked.

Fall. When everyone else would move into dorms or commute to classes. A select few would travel abroad or join a non-profit service organization. All great ideas for someone else.

"Oh, you know," I told Tyler. "Figuring things out. I'm taking a gap year."

His face scrunched. "Gap year?"

I inwardly sighed. Mom said the term was totally mainstream. She'd suggested it earlier this year after what we now referred to as *that time*.

That time when I maybe sort of told my parents I was applying for colleges but didn't. *That time* where I melted down in sobs because nothing felt right about moving out and rooming with a stranger. Or signing up for classes I had no interest in.

"Nice move, Devil." Elena, now beside me, clutched her own diploma to her chest.

The play off my last name Devlin had become a regular occurrence with Elena, but today it made me feel more like an outsider. Like I'd devilishly worked a scheme to stay exactly the same, only now everyone else would move on without me.

Elena steered me away from Tyler. "Chels, are you okay?"

I tugged at the collar of my robe. "I feel lame."

"The robe isn't doing you any favors." She slung an arm over my shoulders. "Kidding. You're not lame. Not everyone is Holli Hayes with straight As and colleges salivating over her. Don't sweat it. Besides, we've got the summer together."

True enough. Another summer at Midwest Wild Adventure theme park where we'd grown closer as friends. After I'd stupidly spent half of last summer being mad at her.

Her boyfriend, Jonah, slipped into the increasingly crowded backstage area as more graduates exited the stage.

Elena threw her arms around his large, tall frame. "How'd you get back here? It's forbidden."

"I guess we'll live on the edge," he said before leaning in to kiss her.

I tamped down a wave of jealousy. They were so stinking cute together. I doubted anyone really cared if someone from our rival school East Ginsburg lingered backstage. But seeing Jonah here reminded me Elena had more going on this summer than hanging out with me.

Teachers funneled us out from backstage into the lobby, shushing us to keep our voices down along the way.

Soon, the lobby filled with parents and the rest of West Ginsburg's current crop of graduates. My parents, along with my aunt and uncle and three cousins, found me immediately and descended with hugs. My grandparents weren't far behind.

The whole dang Devlin family showed up. They were great at showing up and providing support. I smiled despite today's frustration. They loved and cared about me which felt great.

"Our very own graduate," Mom gushed. "How do you feel?"

I edged out of her embrace, her wispy sheer scarf sticking to my robe from static. "I'm fine."

Dad leaned in. "I hope you're celebrating today. This is a big deal. You have plenty of time to figure the rest out."

"You'll be enrolling to college before we know it," Grandpa added, which he surely thought was encouraging.

"Dad," Mom said to Grandpa. "Young people are pushed into a capitalist working culture as soon as the diapers come off. It's ridiculous. Chelsea needs time to discover herself and her passions."

"Back in my day, passion didn't put food on the table," Grandpa grumbled.

Mom looked at me with a reassuring smile. "Maybe you'll become an artist."

Never mind I was terrible at anything artistic. She should have known by now with all the crummy art projects I'd brought home over the years. Though I enjoyed gel pens and doodling, I wouldn't get into art school with my spiral notebook as my portfolio.

Elena and her family joined us then, sparing me from another session of Mom's outlook on discovering life, love, and—cringe—passion. I shuddered just thinking about it.

"Did you say Chelsea is doing art?" Elena's mom asked. "I thought she hadn't enrolled anywhere."

"Chelsea is planning to take a couple classes," Elena pointed out.

Her mom, lean and toned from regular yoga, smiled brightly. "Oh, great. Which ones?"

"Um, pottery?"

It wasn't a question. I really had signed up for pottery like Mom suggested. Only it wasn't for-credit coursework, but one of those life education courses retirees signed up for. I knew that last part because my own grandma had taken the same class. She'd been the one to recommend it.

"Pottery sounds cool," Jonah said from beside Elena.

I nodded. I had zero opinions on pottery. Vases and earthenware bowls existed, but I didn't really care how they came to be.

"I've got an internship at my office if you're interested," Elena's stepdad chimed in. "It doesn't pay anything, but I promise it will be more than making copies."

Dad raised a gentle hand in the air. "It's a kind offer, but Chelsea needs a year to breathe. To find herself."

Never mind I had no idea what I'd be doing this year in order to find myself. I found it hard enough to put into words what I was feeling about my future, so to have it explained out loud by my parents made it even more awkward.

Sometimes I wondered if it would be easier if they'd insisted I go to college. Like if they'd given me an ultimatum. *Go to college or else!* But imagining my parents delivering on any or else was pure fantasy. With my parents, groundings were empty threats. They were extremely supportive but not the hovering type. They loved to tell me to explore and decide my own fate.

As corny as it sounded, I liked living with my parents. Sure, they were dorks, but I had my own social life. I had a lot of time to myself since their friends and social commitments often kept them busier than me.

My cousins, all boys and old enough to know better, laughed loudly and shoved each other. Capital-L Looks came our way from families better trained to behave in public.

More friends and families stopped by to offer congratulations, to remind us of upcoming open houses, to pass along their well wishes. I lost myself to distractions and tried my best to enjoy the moment and celebrate, like Dad said.

The thing was, I'd grown to like high school. I'd found a comfortable rhythm with friends and afterschool clubs. I'd even dealt with past hurts and jealousies, a sure sign of maturity.

But right when I'd felt like I could make sense of my life, everything shifted again. Everything I knew was about to end. I had to change now and fast.

I wanted Time to freeze, to let me catch up. For things to stop moving so quickly.

Elena's family and ours headed our separate ways. We had dinner plans at a restaurant with my grandparents who had already left to, as Grandpa was fond of saying, beat the crowds.

Elena snagged my slippery robe sleeve. "Hang in there. Remember. We have the whole summer."

I hugged her back. That was the part hitting so bittersweet.

We had all summer but all we had was this summer. Then everything would change all over again.

Also by Stephanie J. Scott

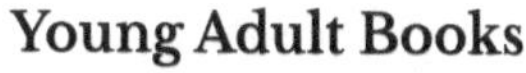

Young Adult Books
All Last Summer
Sunset Summer
Big Wild Summer
Free Wheeling Summer
All-Star Love
Alterations
Adult Romance
Falling Into Place
OMG Christmas Tree

www.stephaniejscott.com/books

About the Author

Stephanie J. Scott writes young adult and romance about characters who put their passions first. Her debut Alterations about a fashion-obsessed loner who reinvents herself was a Romance Writers of America RITA® award finalist. She enjoys dance fitness, everything cats, and has a slight obsession with Instagram. A Midwest girl at heart, she resides outside of Chicago with her tech-of-all-trades husband and fuzzy furbabies.

Photo: Leah Lewis Photography